The House on Seventh Street

Joan McGlone

THE HOUSE ON SEVENTH STREET

Joan McGlone

Joan McGlone

Dedication

For Nansy with love, without whom,
this story would never have been told.
This was the life she seldom spoke about but led.
The depth of her love and the number of difficult sacrifices
she made for her family was immense. I always thought
her story should be told; I pray I did it justice.

For Mom and Dad, who always believed in me
and taught me how to love through their example.
For my sister, Sandy, who tirelessly helped me
in this endeavor as my proofreader and editor.
Your help and guidance were immeasurable.

And for my loving husband, Mark, and my family,
who loved and supported me through this entire project.
I love you all.

Joan McGlone

Table of Contents

Prologue

Nina couldn't believe how pale and lifeless her beautiful, loving daughter looked as she rushed into the room. Theresa, with the same piercing blue eyes as her father, who was always so vibrant and quick to laugh, now lay unconscious under a hospital bed's crisp white sheets.

Theresa's arms and legs were covered in thick white casts. Several tubes were attached to her body and connected to a couple of ugly, noisy machines. She had fallen down a long flight of narrow stairs in her home, landing on the cold concrete basement floor.

Was her fall an accident or just made to look like one? How long had she lain unconscious at the bottom of the steps before Eric found her? Was Nina the reason her daughter was in this bed? Nina couldn't wait for Theresa to regain consciousness. She desperately needed to know what had happened.

As she looked at Theresa, Nina's thoughts flashed to the sweet baby she had held tenderly in her arms, the precious girl who made her father's eyes twinkle. She thought about the brave teen who put herself through beauty school and then married her best friend's brother.

Theresa was all those things and more. The whooshing sound, made by the massive hospital door opening, shook her out of her thoughts.

"Is Theresa going to be okay? What did the doctor say?" she asked Eric as he entered the room. "Does she have internal injuries?" "Does he know why she's still unconscious?"

Eric wiped tears away from his eyes and looked at Nina. "Doctor Barducci thinks she'll be fine. The shock of the fall caused her to lose consciousness. He thinks she'll come to once her body recovers from that. The ex-rays indicate a lot of bruising and several broken bones, but no apparent internal injuries."

"Thank goodness. Let's pray that the doctor is correct. I wonder what caused her to fall. I wish she'd wake up and tell us exactly what happened."

"The doctor said she'll be here for several weeks while her body heals. Then, after that, she'll have lots of physical therapy."

Nina sighed. "I wish I could help you out with the girls, but I'm sure Bruno won't allow it. You know what happens if I disobey him," she said hopelessly.

She felt hopeless and scared. Those were two emotions Nina knew well. She prayed to God Theresa would be fine. Her whole life, she had tried to protect her daughter from harm. Now, Theresa lay lifeless in a hospital bed, quite possibly because of her actions.

No mother should see her child in this condition. Theresa was young and healthy; she would recover and return to her husband's loving arms. She would bounce back quickly. Nina prayed to God Theresa would make a full recovery.

Nina thought about the note hidden deep in the pocket of her old coat. She had found it just this morning on the closet floor. She had been planning to run away again.

The note was a threat that someone would get hurt. Who wrote it? Was it meant for her or Bruno? Was Theresa's fall somehow connected to the note? Nina wasn't sure.

She spent the morning on a park bench, thinking about her life and wondering what to do. It was there that Domenica found her and told her that Theresa had been in an accident, and everyone was looking for her.

Nina needed to think about her next move, but the hospital machines' noise made a horrible buzzing sound in her head. She lifted her hand to her head to clear the noise.

Nina realized she was still wearing her wedding ring. Oh, how she hated it. Bruno had chosen the ring because of its' gaudiness. He wanted everyone to see his wealth. She wanted to take it off and throw it away.

She wished many things, but mostly she wished she could take away her daughter's pain. She needed to figure out if Theresa's fall was an accident or if Bruno had caused it as a warning to her. Was he the reason Theresa was in this hospital bed?

She had to find out, but as much as she loved her children, she wasn't quite sure her spirit could survive going back again. But what choice did she have?

Eric believed Theresa's fall was an accident, but Nina wasn't sure. Bruno was very good at making things look accidental.

If Bruno had caused Theresa's accident, it was done as a warning to Nina. How much farther would he go if she didn't go back home? Would he harm someone else? Nina didn't know, but she couldn't take that chance. Bruno, her husband, was evil.

Nina was used to living in constant fear. She knew what she had to do. She had to go home. It was the only way to find out what had happened. It was the only way to keep her family safe.

Part One

Nina

Scranton, Pennsylvania

E ver since Annina could remember, she loved the smell of baking bread. She learned to bake at a very young age because Mary, her Mama, worked long hours as a local factory seamstress.

Ross, her Papa, worked hard as a laborer in the Pennsylvania coal mines and came home with black dust all over his clothes each day. Each night Annina, or Nina, as she was called, would scrub and wash his clothes and hang them to dry by the crackling fire.

Papa had a chronic cough from working in the coal mines, and since Mama had her youngest child Mollie, she was always sick, so Nina took it upon herself to take charge of her siblings.

Mary had a challenging time with this pregnancy and had almost died in childbirth. As a result, she spent her days resting, taking care of the baby, and working as a seamstress, mending clothes for other people as best as she could.

Nina knew they were poor, but that didn't seem very important. None of the families that lived on their street had very much. Many were immigrants from Italy, just like them.

Mama and Papa were born in Pescara, Italy, and came to America right after their wedding. They had settled in Scranton, along with several other Italian families. Their parish priest at St. Lucy's Church was from Pescara as well.

On Sundays after Mass, everyone assembled in front of the church and shared news about relatives from the old country.

As the years passed, the Macciocco family did the best they could, but it always seemed like they could never get ahead. That didn't seem to matter, though, because they were happy. Nina and her siblings had many Italian friends up and down their street. They were close-knit, and the other Italian families in town looked after and helped each other.

Nina's family lived in a small nondescript clapboard house at the edge of town. The house had three bedrooms, a tiny bathroom, a small kitchen, and a large living room with a wood-burning fireplace. Her parents and baby Mollie slept in one room, her brothers slept in bunk beds in their room, and Nina and her sisters slept in two large beds in the third bedroom. The house was small and cramped but filled with love.

The house's best feature was the panoramic view of the rolling hills from their windows. The hills of Pennsylvania were stately and beautiful to Nina, and the spring flowers that grew wild at the foot of those hills took her breath away.

Nina had been born in that house in September 1905, and the small town she lived in was all that she knew.

Nina considered herself ordinary. She was petite in stature, with light brown hair and big brown eyes with green flecks. No other family member had such unusual eyes.

Even though she had an older brother, as the eldest daughter, she oversaw her siblings, especially after the incident from a few years before.

Her older brother, Frankie, had broken her parents' hearts by running away. He was supposed to marry a girl from the old country but had run away to marry an American girl instead. Heartbroken, the girl had joined the local convent.

Nina's parents were mortified. No one heard from Frankie in three years, and no one knew where he was. Her parents never spoke about him from the day he left, as if he didn't exist. Nina often wondered where he was and how he was doing.

By 1923, when Nina was seventeen, she did all the household chores and helped raise her younger brothers and sisters. She cooked, cleaned, and helped her siblings with their school work as best as possible, even though she didn't have much formal schooling.

At sixteen and fifteen years old, brothers Patsy and Larry quit school. They went to work in the coal mines, leaving Nina to care for Louis, Lena, Joseph, Gus, Mary, Nora, and Mollie.

It was a hot, sticky evening in late July when Papa and Mama called a family meeting. Everyone gathered around the kitchen table.

"Several months ago, Papa received a letter from his old friend Giuseppe Taglieri. They were neighbors in Pescara and grew up together," began Mama. "Ross, tell Nina."

"Well, my friend Giuseppe has a nephew who wants to come to America to get a fresh start and wants a wife. Giuseppe asked if I had any daughters of marrying age. I told him all about you, Nina. We both agreed you would make the perfect wife for his nephew."

"Giuseppe's nephew has offered to marry you, and everything is arranged. He's leaving Italy this month to come to America."

"Nina, isn't that exciting," exclaimed Mama. "I'm going to make you a beautiful wedding dress with some fabric and lovely lace I've been saving. I bartered for it a long time ago and have been saving it for a special event."

Nina could not believe her ears. How could her parents do this to her? What had she ever done wrong in her life that would make them want to marry her off? And marry her to someone they didn't even know?

"But Papa, Mama, I can't; I don't want to get married. I don't even know the man!"

Nina begged her parents to change their minds. Married; she didn't even want to think about it, but Papa and Mama were so excited.

"He's already on his way to America. Giuseppe told him all about you, and he's looking forward to meeting you." "Don't worry," said Papa, "all will be well."

Then Mama got out her sewing kit and began taking Nina's measurements.

That night Nina tossed and turned and cried herself to sleep. She couldn't imagine leaving her home and family. She couldn't imagine marrying a man she didn't know or love.

As each passing day dawned, Nina hoped and prayed her parents would change their minds. She wanted to show them she was needed and

3

couldn't possibly leave them. She worked a little harder each day, hoping they would notice everything she did for her family.

Her efforts, however, went unnoticed.

Patsy came home one day and told her that the *SS Canada*, a ship from Italy, was due to dock at Staten Island, New York, in a week. It was the ship carrying her fiancé to America.

Once he reached New York, it wouldn't take long to travel to northeastern Pennsylvania. Her time was running out.

Her efforts to change her parents' minds fell on deaf ears. She thought about running away, but those thoughts quickly left her mind. She couldn't hurt her parents as her brother Frankie did before her.

Her mother continued to sew and talked about how lucky she was to be marrying an honorable man who wanted to settle in America. She said he had served in the military in the Great War. He had been an officer.

She told Nina they were doing what was best for her. Her fiancé had promised to take good care of her and give her a better life.

Nina didn't want to hear any of it, and Mama didn't want to listen to her protests or see her tears.

The following week, Papa said he received word the ship had docked, and Angelo, her future husband, was on board. He spent a few days making arrangements for their future home in Ohio.

It was the first time Nina realized that she would be moving away from her home and family once she married Angelo. She couldn't bear to think about leaving home. Who would take care of her siblings? Who would do the myriad of chores she did each day?

Nina's heart felt so heavy; she spent the next few days crying whenever she had a few minutes. On the other hand, her parents made her clean the house like never before.

Mama had finished her wedding dress and was now busy making a bridesmaid's dress for her younger sister, Lena. It was all Lena would talk about; she was so excited.

Nina wished she could make it all go away. Papa smiled each time she looked at him. He promised her all would be well, and she would be happy. Nina highly doubted that.

Her parents spoke to Father Grisette, and the wedding was scheduled for the Sixth of September, right after her birthday. Their neighbors, Pietro and Fannie Cologne agreed to witness the ceremony.

The day she dreaded finally arrived. Angelo Taglieri, her fiancé, arrived in Scranton on August 20. It was a lazy hot, and humid summer day, and she had spent the morning taking care of Mollie, who was cranky because she was teething.

Mollie had slobbered all over the lovely dress Mama made for her to wear today. Thanks to Mollie, it was wrinkled beyond repair, and Nina didn't care. She and Angelo were going to have their engagement picture taken.

At this point, she hoped if she was unpresentable to Angelo, he might change his mind.

Papa and Patsy went into town to meet the train from New York and pick up Angelo. Meanwhile, Mama and the rest of her siblings fussed about the house preparing for her engagement party.

Her younger sister Lena was busy arranging wildflowers she had cut from the backyard into a vase. She kept talking excitedly about the upcoming wedding. She didn't think it was terrible their parents were making Nina do something she didn't want to do.

At thirteen, Lena thought it was romantic and exciting. She believed in fairy tales. Nina, on the other hand, did not.

Just then, Mama came into the kitchen and saw Nina's dress. "Nina, what happened to your beautiful dress? It's all soiled and wrinkled!"

"Mollie slobbered on me as I was trying to soothe her. I can either change it or put an apron over it. Unless you think I have time to take it off and iron it before Mr. Taglieri gets here."

Exasperated, Mama replied, "Just go put a sweater on over it," and she took Mollie from Nina's arms. Nina went to the bedroom for a sweater.

Noise from the living room indicated that Papa was back. Nina felt sick to her stomach. She closed her eyes and prayed everything would all go away.

Unfortunately, she heard a knock on the door, and Papa entered the room she shared with her sisters. "Papa, please tell me I don't have to do this," she pleaded. "I promise to get a job in town and earn money for our family. I'll do whatever work I need to do. Please don't make me get married."

"Oh, Nina, I love you, and I only want what's best for you. Angelo's a decent man. He's anxious to meet you and make you happy. He'll be able to give you a better life, I promise."

"You're only moving to a small town in Ohio, several hours away from here. You'll be able to visit us from time to time." He pulled her into his arms and hugged her. "Come and meet Angelo. I think you'll like him."

And with that, Papa led her out of the room. In the living room stood her family speaking Italian to a tall slim man with brownish red hair and a soft voice. Papa led her to where they were standing, and he turned.

Angelo had olive skin and striking blue eyes. Papa introduced her, and she watched Angelo smile. He had perfect white teeth, and his smile reached all the way to his eyes. "Nina, it's a pleasure to meet you finally," said Angelo. When he spoke her name, she felt strange.

"Why don't you show Angelo the gardens in the back yard before we eat dinner," said Papa. And with that, he gave her a quick squeeze before he put her hand in Angelo's large one.

"Papa, I'm sure Angelo is tired from his travels and isn't interested in seeing our vegetable garden or flower beds."

"Nina, Cara, I would love to see them with you," Angelo said. His eyes never left hers as he said it, and his voice was like a caress. "Please show them to me." All eyes were on them as she led him to the garden. He never let go of her hand. She felt breathless as she turned to look at him.

He was very handsome, and his look made her blush. She tried to look away from him, but he brought his left hand to her chin and held it there as he smiled at her. "The gardens are beautiful, and so are you. I believe you have flecks of gold in your brown eyes. A man can get lost in them."

"I want to tell you about myself," he said. "I'm an honorable man and served in the Italian army. My rank was colonel, and I had many men under my command."

"My men and I were in combat several times and saw things no man or woman should see. Even though the war ended, I could not bear to see how badly it ravaged Italy. I have come to America seeking a fresh start."

"My sister Domenica wed last year and came to America. She and her husband Tony live in Ohio. He's helping me get a job at the steel mill where he works."

"I want to share my life with a wife and family. Cara Mia, I promise to give you and our future children a good life."

Before Nina could respond to his declaration, Lena and Nora ran out to the garden to announce the photographer had arrived and was ready to take their engagement picture. They went in and sat for the photograph.

Nina was quite aware of how closely Angelo sat next to her on the chair for the picture. She sat very still as her mind raced to process the information she had just learned about her future husband.

Pietro and Fannie joined them for dinner. Pietro and Angelo got along quite well. They knew some of the same people back in the old country. Nina tried to follow the conversation but found it difficult to concentrate.

Nina wasn't sure, but her stomach felt funny, and all during dinner, she noticed Angelo watching her intently. She could barely eat what was on her plate.

The rest of the evening went by quickly. Angelo decided to stay with Pietro and Fannie instead of the local hotel. Before he left, he gave Nina a big smile and a quick hug.

Over the next two weeks, he spent time with Nina in the backyard garden, church, or other public settings. Each time he talked to her in his calm, soothing voice.

He told her about his family back in Italy. Nicolette and Charlotte, two of his sisters, still lived with his parents. They were still young but already talking about their dreams of coming to America.

His sister Domenica was a year older than him, and he was looking forward to introducing Nina to her. She was the married sister living in Ohio with her husband and daughter. Her husband could not get time off from work, so they could not travel to Scranton for the wedding.

His baby sister, Elizabeth, had died at the age of two, and his mother had never really gotten over her death. It had left her in a semi-fragile state.

His parents weren't happy when he told them he was leaving Italy, but they understood his reasons for beginning a fresh start. They were glad he was going to Ohio to be near Domenica.

On September 1, Nina's eighteenth birthday, Angelo gave her a pair of solid gold earrings. They were lovely little gold balls, and she shook as she opened the present. Mary and Lena excitedly chattered as Nina took them out of the box. She had never received anything so pretty.

The earrings were for pierced ears, and Nina's ears were not. So, Mama pierced her ears with her new earrings on her birthday. It only hurt a little, but it was well worth it to see the look on Angelo's face once completed. As he left her that night, he gave her a quick kiss on her cheek, and she felt a little shiver down her spine as he did.

They would go to St. Lucy's and rehearse their wedding vows tomorrow afternoon. Nina was overwhelmed by the past few weeks' events. She was confused by the feelings she was starting to have for Angelo that she couldn't sleep.

Angelo seemed nice, but she didn't really know him. How could she be expected to spend the rest of her life with someone she hardly knew? In a matter of days, she would marry him and leave everything and everyone she loved to go to Ohio, a place she had never been.

The rehearsal went well, and the next couple of days flew by quickly. Mama and Papa had given Nina a cloth suitcase for her birthday, and Nina packed her meager belongings in it. Besides her engagement and wedding dress, Mama had sewn her a few more dresses to travel and go out. It seemed Nina had a whole new wardrobe.

Mama was an excellent seamstress, and Nina did appreciate all she had done for her. However, she was still confused by everything that had happened in the past few weeks.

Her brain and heart didn't know what to make out of these recent events. She just wished she had more time to sort everything out. She thought she didn't want to get married, but after meeting and getting to know Angelo a bit, she started to have feelings for him.

Unfortunately, time was the one thing she didn't have.

The Pagano Brothers

Calabria, Italy

Rosa Pagano gathered her rosary beads from her nightstand, made the sign of the cross, and began to say her morning prayers. She was worried about her sons, in particular, Enzo and Bruno. They had chosen to follow in their father's footsteps a few years ago and become a part of "la Famiglia."

All she could do for them now was pray for their safety. She had hoped they would not join the mob, but times were tough, and decent jobs were hard to come by since the end of the great war. So, they had each joined the family. Luckily, the mob had not gotten their hooks into her youngest son Guido; he was in the seminary. She figured it was in their blood.

An hour later, as she sat in the morning sun in the backyard of her spacious villa, sipping her espresso, she wondered if her life would have been any different had she not married Nunzio.

Nunzio, her husband, had seemed like a knight in shining armor to her all those years ago. He brought her to his villa in Calabria, where he treated her like a queen. He saved her from a life on the streets.

Nunzio had given her fancy clothes, jewelry, and a lovely villa. She, in turn, gave him her heart along with three healthy sons.

Oh, she knew that he wasn't faithful to her, but she took what he gave and kept quiet about what she knew. Being faithful to your wife was hard for a member of the family.

Her sons thought their parents had a perfect marriage, and she did nothing to dispel those thoughts. They knew nothing about their father's little puttana in the next village. Nunzio didn't even realize that Rosa knew about her.

He loved Rosa, but there were certain things his puttana did for him that Rosa did not. So, Rosa gladly feigned ignorance when he said he had to go on a secret mission for the famiglia. She knew where he was going and didn't care.

Nunzio worked for the Santucci family as a collector. He had gone to collect the gambling debt her father owed. Rosa's parents had died when she was just fourteen years old, and she had no one to turn to for help.

Frail slender Rosa knew nothing about her father's debt when she opened the door of the small tenement apartment she lived in with her parents. They had been innocent victims of a bloody attack in her village by the mob the previous week. Rosa was still in a state of shock and disbelief that she was now an orphan.

The large bulky man bullied his way into her home that day. He encountered a slim, dark-haired beauty with big blue eyes full of unshed tears. He didn't know that her father had just died.

When Nunzio demanded payment of the debt, she offered him the family silver. As she handed him the silver to repay her father's debt, she began to cry. It was all she had. Her large silent tears unnerved Nunzio.

He gathered the girl into his arms and told her that he would repay the debt if she would come home with him. He said he would take care of her. She had no family and no one to turn to, so she said yes.

She had been with him from then until the day he got shot by a member of the Pettina family, sworn enemies of the Santucci family. Each wanted control of Calabria.

Rosa spent her whole married life praying for her husband's safety, and once her sons entered the family business, she prayed for their safety as well.

Their oldest son Enzo took after his mother in the looks department. He was tall and slender with thick black hair and large blue eyes. Popular and a natural-born leader, Enzo was adored by all who knew him. His friends envied his good looks, easy laughter, and happy-go-lucky attitude.

He quit school at the ripe age of fifteen and went to work as a runner for the family. He had a pretty face that everyone trusted, and he could run very fast. Thus, he could always elude the police in a tight situation.

Now, at twenty-two, he was quickly the most trusted runner of the Santucci family.

Son Bruno, on the other hand, took after his father. He was bulky but not as tall as his brother. Bruno had his father's brown hair and eyes and always seemed mad at the world like he had a chip on his shoulder. He had street smarts, a fierce temper, and a very short fuse. While Enzo was loved, trusted, and envied by all, nasty Bruno was feared.

While Enzo smiled and easily charmed his way out of trouble, Bruno used his fists to do his talking. He spent many days fighting in the village streets and would come home with a bloody lip or a black eye most days. Bruno would tell his parents, don't worry, the other guy looks worse than me. Nunzio would smile and clap him on the back; he loved that Bruno was a scrappy fighter. Rosa would just shake her head. Bruno was as stubborn as his father.

Even though different, the two brothers were fiercely loyal to each other. Bruno joined la famiglia two years before the death of his father. At twenty years old, he was one of the family's youngest but most effective collectors.

Seventeen-year-old Guido was the apple of his mother's eye. Slim with wavy brown hair and green eyes, his brothers called him a mama's boy and sissy growing up. He had studied hard in school and brought home good grades. His peers usually teased him until they found out who his brothers were, and then the teasing stopped.

He didn't smoke, drink, or go to parties like his contemporaries, but he could be found most weekends at the library or church. He attended Mass daily in the summer with his mother and had served as an altar boy in his youth.

Now that his studies were complete, he was studying to become a priest in the seminary. Rosa was thrilled and told anyone who would listen how her youngest son was in seminary.

Enzo's girlfriend was Jesse Salvatore. She was the prettiest girl in the village and had staked her claim on Enzo from an early age. When they played on the playground in the fifth grade, she had gone over and punched him in the arm.

He didn't know what to do because his mother had taught him never to harm a girl, so he just laughed when she punched him. She told him to carry her books while he walked her home from school, and he did. He did that every day since that first day until he quit school to work for the family.

Even after he quit school, Enzo always tried to walk her home if he was not taking care of business for the family.

Jesse's father was Luca Salvatore, second in command of the Santucci family. Jesse's mother, Elizabeth, was Vito Santucci's younger sister. Vito was the head of the family.

Vito's daughter, Maria, was younger than Jesse, but the two girls were best friends and cousins. Maria loved bad boys and had a significant crush on Bruno.

Over the years, the brothers often double-dated; Enzo and Jesse, Bruno and Maria, siblings dating cousins. Where you found one couple, you invariably saw the other; it was the way things were.

Olive skinned, dark-haired, Jesse only had eyes for Enzo, and she had already picked out her wedding dress even though she and Enzo were not engaged yet. She knew that they would eventually get married just as she knew the sun would rise in the morning. She had a slim athletic build, was soft-spoken and kind, and was always ready for an adventure.

On the other hand, Maria had fair skin and reddish auburn hair. She also had a curvaceous body that men loved, and she knew it. She used it to her advantage whenever she wanted something.

However, Maria always got her way since her father was the head of la famiglia, and she had her sights set on Bruno. She liked his rough edges, hot temper, and bad boy image.

She loved to watch him fight, and she knew just how to set him off. She loved to set him off sometimes just to watch him beat up some poor helpless sap. The sex they had after a fight was always rough and tumble. In bed, they were like animals, and she loved it.

That part of their relationship had to remain a secret because her father would kill Bruno if he found out that his daughter was not a virgin. Because of her constant bodyguards, their sexual encounters were few and far between, much to her dismay.

Vito idolized his daughter. He was a bit disappointed they never had more children, but he was very protective of the one he had.

Their home was like a fortress, and Anna and Maria often complained there was too much security around them. Because of that, Maria always tried to give her bodyguard the slip to have some time to herself. She tried to elude her assigned protector, and over the years, many had complained to Vito about her foul mouth and rough ways.

He never believed them; all he had to do was look at his precious daughter and know she was pure in all things.

He knew the Pagano brothers, Enzo and Bruno because Nunzio had been his best collector and best friend growing up. Vito had relied on Nunzio and now trusted his sons.

They were part of the young recruits to la famiglia and had proven themselves worthy in his eyes. He told Nunzio one of his sons would marry his only child, his daughter Maria.

Unbeknownst to either Rosa or Anna, the two men had decided that one of Nunzio's sons would marry Maria and become the Santucci family's head. At first, Vito thought Enzo would be best because he seemed a natural-born leader.

However, as the years passed, he changed his mind and now favored Bruno because he was such a scrappy fighter and trusted only himself.

Nunzio and Vito spent many late nights discussing how they would enjoy seeing their two families connected. They looked forward to becoming Tatones and imagined many little grandsons in their future.

After Nunzio's death, Vito and his brother-in-law Luca spent many hours discussing each of the brothers' merits while deciding which one should marry Maria and lead the family.

As time went by, it became apparent Maria liked Bruno better than Enzo, so things were going according to Vito's plan. It would be a shame to make Maria marry one brother if she preferred the other.

In his eyes, his daughter didn't even have a say in whom she married. In Italy, especially among la Famiglia, the father made those decisions.

An Arranged Marriage

Nina woke up on the morning of her wedding to the sounds of her sisters quarreling. They each wanted to sleep in her bed after she was gone. Mama quickly came in and stopped it by telling them to get cleaned up and dressed for the wedding.

Nina was so confused she didn't know what to think or feel anymore. She did know she would miss her home and family terribly. She would miss washing Papa's coal-covered clothes, helping her siblings with their school lessons, and picking the wildflowers in the backyard.

She would miss baking bread for her family and comforting a cranky Mollie. Who, she wondered, would do all those things once she was married and gone to Ohio?

Too soon, it was time to put on her wedding dress. Mama had done an excellent job on it, even if Nina didn't want to admit it. Mama gave her a special lace handkerchief that had once belonged to her Nonna, who still lived in Italy.

Nonna and Tatone were her Mama's parents. Papa's parents also lived in Italy. Nina had never met her but had heard so many stories about her and Tatone that she felt she knew them.

Nonna and Tatone had arranged her parents' marriage, and they were happy. Maybe things will be okay after all, she thought. At least she wasn't moving to another country like her parents before her.

Nina, Papa, Lena, and Fannie went to the choir room at the Church. It was almost time to begin. Angelo, Pietro, and her brother Larry were near the altar with Father Grisette. Everyone else was seated, and the music started. Lena and then Fannie walked down the aisle, and then Papa gave her a quick kiss and escorted Nina down the aisle. He put her hand in Angelo's and then sat with Mama.

Father made the sign of the cross and began the ceremony. Angelo placed a slim solid gold band on her finger ten minutes later. It felt strange and heavy there. Nina and Angelo both said I do at the appropriate time, and then Father proclaimed them husband and wife. Angelo gave her a quick kiss on her lips, and Nina was married.

After the ceremony, everyone went back to the house where Mama had prepared wedding soup and homemade spaghetti. Father Grisette gave the blessing, and everyone ate. Nina was aware of Angelo glancing her way several times during the dinner.

After dinner, Mama brought in a small white cake and a knife. She placed the cake in front of Angelo and Nina and told them to cut it together. Nina took the knife, and Angelo placed his hand on hers. He guided their hands, and together they cut a slice of the cake. He took part of the piece and fed it to her, then had her do the same.

Lena thought Angelo was dreamy and asked if he had a younger brother she could wed. That made everyone laugh except Nina. Suddenly, she felt as if her whole world turned upside down.

After everyone had cake, Mama took Nina back into the bedroom to change her dress. Mama lovingly folded it and placed it into the small suitcase where Nina had placed her meager belongings.

"Mia dolce Bambina. My sweet girl, I'm going to miss you so much. Don't be nervous tonight. Angelo will teach you what you need to know about loving him. He seems to love you already, and in time you will learn to love him."

After she changed into traveling clothes, they went back into the living room, where Mama, Papa, and her siblings said goodbye. Nina was in tears. Angelo promised to take good care of Nina and write once they arrived in the Ohio Valley. He helped Nina put on her thin coat and scarf, and they left with Papa.

Papa drove them to the hotel where they would spend their first night as a married couple. Papa gave Nina one last hug and kiss, and she brushed away a couple of tears that threatened to fall on her face.

"Arrivederci, amore mia. I know you will have a good life with Angelo in Ohio. Be good to him and love him," Papa said before leaving her. His oldest daughter was now married.

Once registered, Angelo took their bags up the narrow stairs and down the hall to their room. There, he opened the door and carried her into the room. It was small but clean and without much furniture. It had a writing table and chair, a small dresser and mirror, a nightstand, and a bed. There was no bathroom.

Nina just stood in the center of the room where Angelo had set her down, unsure what to do. Angelo put their bags on the small dresser and then turned to help her out of her coat.

"Cara Mia, I want you to know how happy you have made me today. I'm excited to be in America and beginning this new life with you. I know you must be scared, but please don't be afraid of me; I will never hurt you," he said.

He led her to the chair, and she sat. He sat on the bed and gazed at her through those piercing blue eyes. She shivered, not from the cold but rather from his look. She was rendered speechless.

Angelo pulled her to her feet and embraced her. "You've had a difficult day with getting married and leaving your family. Come, let's get ready for bed. We need to get some rest because we leave early tomorrow morning for Ohio."

And with those words, he grabbed his nightclothes and left the room. While he was gone, Nina quickly put on her nightgown and got into bed. She was scared about what would happen next.

When he came back into the room, he got into the other side of the bed. He gently pulled Nina close and caressed her face, his blue eyes looking deep into her soul. She was nervous and confused by his look and touch. She had no idea what to say or do, so she didn't do anything.

He placed a gentle kiss upon her lips. "Pleasant dreams, Cara Mia," he whispered as he held her in his arms and fell asleep. She was scared to move for fear that he would wake up, so she didn't move at all.

Finally, exhaustion got the best of her, and she fell asleep thinking about this man who was now her husband.

When she woke up, she was surprised to be alone in bed the following day. She pulled her hands out from under the covers to look at the slim gold band on her left hand. It felt foreign on her finger.

She wondered where Angelo was and what her family was doing back home. Who was going to take care of her siblings?

Just then, Angelo came into the room carrying two steaming cups of coffee and a bag. "Buongiorno, Cara Mia. Come and have something to eat." He placed the cups of coffee on the writing table and a couple of sweet rolls and blueberry scones from the local bakery. They smelled delightful.

She threw off the covers and joined him at the table. The coffee was strong but hot and warmed her up, and the pastries were delicious. After they ate, she quickly got dressed, and they began their journey to Ohio.

Journey to Ohio

Angelo was full of surprises along their journey to the Ohio Valley, thought Nina. He was sweet and kind to her, calling her his "Cara Mia" each night when they went to bed. He kissed her gently on her lips and held her close, but that was all.

Nina knew there was more to being a wife, but Angelo had not tried to consummate their marriage, and Nina was silently relieved.

She remained aloof and tried not to think about it, but she couldn't help but notice the looks her husband received from many of the female passengers on the train with them. Angelo was always polite to them but reserved his smile and attention to his young bride.

After two days of traveling on the train, they finally reached their destination in the Ohio Valley. Angelo anxiously gathered their things and grabbed her by the hand. As they disembarked from the train, he held her close and kissed her. "We're finally here, Cara Mia," he said with a twinkle in his eyes.

Just then, a man yelled out his name, and Angelo turned to greet him.

"Ciao, Tony! It's so good to see you." Tony Stellano, Angelo's brother-in-law, was not as tall as Angelo but attractive. He had wavy brown hair and brown eyes and an easy way about him.

"Tony, I would like you to meet my wife, Cara Mia Nina," said Angelo.

Tony hugged her and said, "Nina, benvenuta to our famiglia and Steubenville, Ohio." To Angelo, he commented, "She's as bellissima as you said in your telegram."

"Let's go; Domenica is anxious to see you and introduce you to your niece."

"Grazie, Tony. I'm anxious to see them too."

The three of them started the short walk to the house on Eighth Street that Tony and Domenica rented, with Tony pointing out landmarks and telling stories along the way. By the time they got to the house, Tony had Nina and Angelo laughing.

Once there, Nina met her sister-in-law, Domenica, who looked just like Angelo and had the same piercing blue eyes as her brother. She gave Nina a big hug and told her how happy she was for them. Nina immediately liked her. She hoped they would become close.

Just then, they heard a small cry from the other room, and Domenica went to pick up their daughter Yolanda. "Yolanda has been cranky lately because she's teething."

Yolanda looked like her papa with brown hair and eyes and immediately responded to Nina's outstretched arms. Tony said, "Just wait, soon you two will start a family, and Yolanda will have a cousin to play with."

Angelo just chuckled and watched as Nina played with the toddler.

Angelo and Nina stayed with them for a few weeks until they found a house of their own to rent. The two-story house they found on Seventh Street was a few blocks away from Tony and Domenica's. It was a palace in Nina's eyes because it was so big.

It was red brick with a big covered front porch with an old comfortable bench perfect for sitting out in the evening. The living room contained a massive fireplace with a marble mantel, and the kitchen and dining rooms were spacious and airy.

The rent was more than Angelo wanted to pay, but once he saw the look on Nina's face when she walked through the door, he had to have it. Three large bedrooms were upstairs, along with a large bathroom. There was also a full basement and a flat backyard.

He was utterly smitten with his bride and wanted to please her. He also hoped to fill it soon with children.

The house owners were an older couple with no children. They were on an extended trip back to the old country, so the house was available to rent with all the furnishings. Two days after they saw it, they moved right in, and Nina immediately cleaned it from top to bottom until it sparkled.

19

Nina teared up when they left Tony and Domenica's as she had quickly become attached to baby Yolanda, but Angelo was anxious for them to have a place of their own.

Helping Domenica care for Yolanda made her think about her home and family. She missed her family terribly. But she learned to trust Angelo and responded to him whenever he kissed her.

Somehow, she had gone from not wanting to get married at all to having feelings for her husband.

The first night in their new home was the first time they made sweet love. Angelo had been very patient and gentle with Nina. He kissed away all her fears as he took her innocence. She was so flush with emotion that she began to cry. Angelo kissed her, wiped away her tears, and held her. He told her how happy she had made him and promised to always take care of her.

A couple of months after their wedding, their life soon settled into a comfortable routine. Each morning after Angelo went to work at the steel mill in Weirton, across the river from where they lived, Nina would clean the house and then walk over to help Domenica with Yolanda. Then, she would stop by the market on her way home and pick up something to make dinner.

Helping Domenica with the toddler made her think about and miss her home and siblings, but she knew Domenica appreciated the help. When she thought about it, Steubenville was a lot like Scranton. Many Italian families lived on Sixth, Seventh, and Eighth streets, and everyone seemed to look out for one another.

St. Anthony's Church was the parish that most Italians went to, so they joined there. Father Paul Victor, the pastor of St. Anthony's, was a tall slim man with kind eyes and a quick laugh. He made Angelo and Nina instantly feel welcome.

Everyone at St. Anthony's welcomed them to Steubenville. After Mass, Sundays was always a get-together with other families to share news about the old country, just like at St. Lucy's.

A Nasty Fighter

It was a chilly Thursday evening in November 1925, but Bruno was impervious to the fine mist of sleet falling. He had more important matters on his mind.

Bruno had a clear view of his intended target from his vantage point behind the building's pillars. His target was currently across the street in a corner bar. The punk laughed at something the bartender said, and Bruno's blood was at a slow boil.

The guy, some dark-haired punk, dared to approach his Maria a few weeks ago at the movie theater. Not only did he approach Maria and talk to her, but the poor sap had flirted with her. In Bruno's mind, that was utterly unacceptable.

Bruno couldn't believe his eyes and ears that day when he saw the dumb punk talking to his precious Maria when he came out of the theater restroom.

Oh, he was cordial enough as he approached them. He smiled and greeted the stranger pleasantly enough, but the vein near his temple started to twitch, and his hands began to clench, two sure signs that he was about to lose his temper.

The punk was oblivious to everything except his beautiful Maria; he kept chatting.

She knew Bruno well enough to know those signs very well. With a big smile on her face, she simply looped her arm through Bruno's, her ample breasts brushing against him as she did.

At her touch, he instantly changed. Through her actions, she showed the punk that she belonged to Bruno. Only her sense of breeding and class made her remain civil. The guy quickly got the message and moved on to join his friends. The situation was over.

Maria quickly forgot about it, but Bruno did not. He mentally noted every detail he could about the guy and his friends before they left the theater's lobby. He would make the guy pay for flirting with his Maria.

So now, two full weeks later, Bruno knew the punk's daily routine. After working at the fish market, he would go to the same corner bar and have two beers before walking home.

He lived in a small tenement in a poor section of Calabria with his elderly mother. She had a terrible cough and walked with a cane.

Bruno figured he could quickly attack the punk as he walked daily through one of the two narrow alleys on his way home. Bruno would be waiting for him in one of them.

Bruno quietly walked to the first alley and hid in the shadows as the punk paid the bartender for his daily beer. His temples were twitching, and his hands were pumping in anticipation of a fight.

He had brought a wooden timber with him to expedite things. He wanted to get this over quickly as he had to be home for dinner tonight. Mama Rosa was cooking dinner for her boys. Guido was home for a visit but had to leave tonight to return to the seminary.

The punk was whistling to himself as he entered the first alley. Bruno waited until the guy was ahead of him and attacked him from behind. He quickly whacked him over the head with the timber. The guy cried out in pain and stumbled around to see who had just attacked him.

Bruno sneered at him as he swung the timber again, hitting the punk in the legs. The guy buckled over, and Bruno dropped the wood. He began using his fists, punching him in the face, ribs, and chest. The punk tried to fight but was no match for Bruno as his eyes began to swell.

Bruno was smiling. His smile got more prominent as he heard the punk grunt with pain and double over. He pleaded for Bruno to stop as he crumpled to the ground, but Bruno only laughed. "Stay away from my girl, you loser," said Bruno.

He continued the onslaught of punches and threw in a couple of well-placed kicks to the ribs and groin. He was sure he had given the punk a broken nose as well as a few broken ribs. The guy continued to plead for Bruno to stop, but Bruno only continued the beating.

Finally, the punk stopped grunting and lost consciousness. Only then did Bruno stop. He spat on him, straightened his clothes, and left the alley. He felt so good that he whistled all the way home.

At home, he threw off his clothes and cleaned up. He didn't want to be late for dinner, and he didn't want Mama to see the punk's blood on his clothes or shoes. Enzo came into the room as he was shining his shoes.

"Who was the unlucky sucker tonight?" he asked Bruno when he saw what his brother was doing.

"Some punk who dared to flirt with Maria when I took her to the movies a few weeks ago. Why do you have such a silly grin on your face?"

"Man, I just had some mind-blowing great sex with Jesse. I'm gonna marry that girl. She's amazing in bed!"

Just then, their younger brother Guido came into the room. He saw the rumpled clothes on the floor and the shoe-shining kit on Bruno's bed. He knew what those signs meant.

"Bruno, why do you feel the need to hurt people? Don't you know that's wrong? The Bible says to turn the other cheek."

Bruno just chuckled at his younger brother. "Guido, what do you want me to say, huh? Do you want to hear my confession? I could tell you things that would make your face turn redder than Mama's favorite shade of lipstick."

At that, Guido just shook his head and answered, "At the seminary, I pray for you both. I just came in to say that dinner is ready. Mama wants all of us at the table."

Although grown-up, the three brothers filed out of the room to sit together and eat dinner with their Mama. She didn't ask for much.

A few months later, Bruno couldn't believe that Enzo and Jesse were married, let alone that they were leaving Calabria for some small town in America called Steubenville, Ohio.

He didn't want to admit it, but he would miss them terribly. Enzo, though, was thrilled. He was married to Jesse and soon would be a father.

Jesse's dad Luca Salvatore was being sent to Steubenville to help Vito's cousin, Vincenzo Santucci, run the family's operations there. He had asked Vito if he could also take Enzo because he knew that was the only way his wife, Elizabeth, and daughter would go. It was a great honor, and he was taking his family with him.

Nobody was happy if Elizabeth wasn't happy in his family, and his wife was not satisfied unless Jesse agreed to go with them. Jesse had confided in her mother the previous month that she was pregnant with Enzo's baby, so the two young lovers had a quick marriage.

Instead of killing Enzo, Luca forgave the boy and welcomed him as a son. Besides, he would be a Tatone, and Enzo could work for the family in Steubenville.

So, Rosa threw a simple farewell party at her villa for newlyweds Enzo, Jesse, and her parents. It was a bittersweet day for her.

Rosa, who had been having severe headaches for months, had just found out that she had a cancerous tumor in her brain right behind her eyes and that she was going blind. During the party, she held back tears as she realized she would never see Enzo, Jesse, or her as yet to be born grandchild ever again.

She did not tell any of her sons about the tumor. There was nothing they could do, so there was no point in worrying them.

Rosa and Nunzio frequently entertained in their lovely villa in their younger days. Then as the boys were born and grew, the estate was full of loud, boisterous voices and shouting matches between the brothers.

Enzo and Bruno were always bringing friends home with them. They loved their Mama's cooking and wanted her to cook for their friends. Her sons would coax her into making fresh sauce and homemade pasta for groups of hungry boys with poor table manners many nights. But she loved and cherished those memories now.

These days, the villa was pretty quiet. Bruno, although he technically still lived at home, was seldom there. She didn't know where he slept most nights and thought it better not to ask. Guido lived at the seminary and only came home for occasional visits, and Enzo and Jesse had a small flat near the center of town.

So, when the chance arose, she gladly hosted the small intimate gathering. Even the thought of having Vito and Anna Santucci in her home didn't scare her. She knew them but always stayed out of their way. She knew her place and the value of keeping her mouth closed.

Vito and Nunzio had been childhood friends, best friends, actually, but they never interacted socially, only professionally as adults.

The evening was beautiful, and she served nothing but the best. It was the least she could do for her eldest son.

During the evening, she noticed the furtive glances between Bruno and Maria Santucci. She hoped her son was smart enough to know his place and stay away from Maria. Sadly, she realized how wrong she was when she spied them hiding in the grove of fig trees in the backyard, kissing each other hungrily.

Oh my, what fire she saw between them. She wondered which one would get burned first. She knew they dated, but she hadn't realized how earnest they were.

The following day Rosa watched her eldest son and his pregnant wife board the ship that would take them to America. She bravely smiled as she waved goodbye to them.

As the ship left port, their silhouettes were merely a blur upon the deck of the enormous vessel. Luckily, Guido had been able to come and say goodbye as well, and she stayed right next to him for support. He had promised Enzo he would take care of her, and it was a promise he intended to keep.

Bruno, on the other hand, had not come to say goodbye. He had told his farewell to them the previous night, and he was busy this morning on a job for Vito. And besides, Bruno thought, he didn't need to say goodbye to Enzo since he was sure he would see him again someday.

Bruno planned to marry Maria and take over the Santucci family for Vito. Then, as head of the famiglia, he would ask Enzo and Jesse to return to Calabria.

He didn't need America at all; his bright future was here in Calabria.

Life In Ohio

Located on the state's eastern side, Steubenville, Ohio, was a bustling city on the Ohio River banks. The town was a melting pot where many Italian, Irish, and Polish immigrants settled because of various industries, including coal mining, paper mills, glass and nail factories, potteries, and steel mills.

At the start of the century, Steubenville was home to almost a hundred bars and breweries where anyone working in the different industries could find whatever they wanted. There was also an opera house, several theatres, numerous boarding houses, gambling houses, and brothels.

Many of those establishments were closed by 1920, with Prohibition in the United States. But many establishments still operated illegally in town, run by the Italian mafia, led by Vito's cousin, Vincenzo Santucci.

In the fall of 1923, when Nina arrived in Steubenville, she didn't know anything about prohibition. She was naïve. She never went into any bars or breweries as she didn't have any business or need to go into them.

She learned the Polish and Irish immigrants lived on the upper hills of town and the Italians lived mainly in the middle of town. The business district downtown was always busy. She hadn't ventured across the Ohio River to Weirton, West Virginia, either. Her whole world now centered on her husband.

All that concerned her was learning everything she could about Angelo, and so she spent hours asking Domenica all about him. As the only son, she knew his parents depended on him for many things and were not pleased when he enlisted in the military.

They worried about him the whole time he served during the war, even though he sent letters to them every week. He doted on his sisters and protected them fiercely while they were growing up, and even though Domenica was older, he protected her as well.

Domenica said many of the girls from their village had set their sights on marrying him, but he was never interested in any of them. He said he was waiting for the right girl to come along and hoped to have a large family someday. Nina thought about all this and felt she was learning more and more about her husband each day.

Several months after they were married, Nina woke up one morning feeling nauseous. She had tried a new recipe and wasn't too sure that Angelo had liked it, even though he said he did. She figured it was just the chicken she had cooked for dinner the night before.

She felt sick to her stomach as she got out of bed and ran to the bathroom, where she promptly threw up. As she went into the kitchen, Angelo took one look at her and told her to lay back down in bed. He brought her a small orange, a few soda crackers, and a glass of water before he left for work.

"I'll send word to Domenica that you aren't feeling well today. Maybe she can stop by and check on you." No sooner had Angelo left the house when Nina got sick again.

Nina began to worry; she was never sick. Nina was never the patient. She was the one who always took care of others when they got ill. She drank a bit of water but didn't eat anything.

A few hours later, she felt well enough to get out of bed. It must have been the chicken dinner. She felt silly when Domenica stopped by with Yolanda to check on her.

Domenica took one look at her and told her she was pregnant. Nina was shocked. She thought back to when her mother was pregnant with Mollie. Mama was sick each morning and couldn't eat certain foods because she couldn't stand the smell.

Nina put a hand on her belly and hoped that Domenica was right. She wanted to have a baby with Angelo and began to wonder what their child would look like. She hoped the baby would have Angelo's piercing blue eyes and smile.

Nina thought about what Domenica said and silently said a prayer of thanksgiving. Could she possibly be with child? Nina looked at the calendar on the wall and realized she must be. Domenica chuckled at her as she gave her some advice on doctors. She also promised to keep the news quiet until Nina was ready to announce it.

Nina couldn't wait to tell Angelo. She tried to imagine what his reaction would be. Would he be happy or not? All afternoon she caressed her belly and said prayers of thanksgiving for the baby growing inside her.

Domenica had told her Angelo's favorite meal was cheese ravioli and meatballs. That evening when Angelo got home from work, Nina had his favorites prepared for him. He was concerned about her health when he walked through the door and made her sit down. She told him she was well.

He was surprised to see that Nina had made his favorite meal. She had also baked fresh bread, and the aroma filled the house. After dinner, Nina asked him to take a walk with her. He wasn't too sure since she was sick that morning, but she just chuckled and said she had something she wanted to show him.

They walked a few blocks down the street to a park. At the park, she sat on a bench overlooking the deep blue water of the Ohio River. Several boats were meandering along the river, and there were other people in the park enjoying the crisp, late fall evening.

There was a swing set in the park, and children were happily playing while their parents relaxed on the grass. It was the perfect setting for Nina to share her news.

"I like coming here with Domenica and Yolanda in the afternoons. We put Yolanda on a swing, and she laughs as she flies through the air. Do you think our children would like to come here to swing?"

Angelo looked at the children having fun on the swings. "Yes, I think our children would like that. That is when we have children."

"Well, do you suppose that you would like to bring our child to this park?"

"Of course," answered Angelo. "Nina, why are you asking me such things?"

"Well, I believe next year this time, we can bring our child here," and she put her hands on her belly and smiled at Angelo. He looked at her hands and then her face. She was beaming.

"Do you mean to tell me that we are going to have a child?"

"Yes, we are," she answered. Angelo pulled her close and kissed her. Then he laughed and said, "We're going to have a child! Cara Mia, you have made me the happiest man in the world! I love you!"

On the way back home, Nina told him that Domenica had given her information about her doctor. Nina said she would call and make an appointment with him.

That night, Angelo held her so tenderly in his arms and told her he loved her dearly. She told him she was happy, and she loved him too. They fell asleep while making plans for the baby.

Domenica's doctor, Dr. Barducci, was a short husky man with kind brown eyes, wiry grey hair, and a mustache. He reminded Nina of her doctor back in Scranton, and she was instantly comfortable with him. The baby, he said, was due in mid-July. After the first few months, the morning sickness and tiredness subsided, and Nina was the picture of health.

Nina wrote to her family to give them the good news. Mary and Lena had taken over her chores at home, and everyone there was well. They wrote back that they were happy for Nina and Angelo. They made plans to send Lena to Ohio to help her once she had the baby. Lena was looking forward to visiting, and Nina was looking forward to seeing Lena.

Angelo and Nina spent Christmas with Domenica and Tony. They went to Mass and ate dinner together. Yolanda loved the cloth doll Nina had made for her. Nina had hand-sewn the doll and two outfits for it. Yolanda declared it was her favorite gift and kissed Nina.

The Stellano's shared the news that Domenica was also expecting. Her baby was due in September. The two women spent the rest of the day comparing pregnancies and commiserating together about their growing bellies while the men enjoyed a glass of Tony's homemade wine.

A week later, they celebrated New Year's together as well. Nina could not believe how her life had changed as they welcomed in 1924.

The next few months flew by quickly, and soon it was May. Seventh Street neighbors Mary DiFederico and Santina Farchione became dear friends to Nina. They spent many lazy summer afternoons sitting on the porch with glasses of iced lemonade, chatting about everything and anything while their husbands were at work. Both Mary and Santina had young children who were very well behaved. They played quietly in their backyards and were never loud. Nina wondered if her children would be that way.

Over those months, they transformed the bedroom next to theirs into a nursery. Angelo spent many evenings working on a cradle and rocking chair for the baby in the basement. He had inherited his woodworking skills from his grandfather back in Italy. The cradle and chair were labors of love and made him so happy to create. Nina cried tears of joy when she saw how beautiful they were.

Domenica planned a small baby shower for Nina with a few other Italian ladies on their street. The day of the shower arrived, and Nina didn't want to go because she felt fat. She told Angelo she couldn't even see her feet! He just shook his head and chuckled.

He told her she had never looked more beautiful to him as he helped her put on her sandals. It was the beginning of July, and very soon, they would be a little family.

They walked to the Stellano's, where Domenica had transformed the living room into a banquet room. Several ladies were seated at card tables, and one table held a cake decorated with tiny pink and blue flowers. He helped Nina sit in her seat and then searched for Tony. He found him in the backyard with a few of the other men. They were drinking wine and smoking cigars.

Angelo enjoyed a good glass of wine but had never found smoking enticing. Neither did Tony. He and Tony had grown very close since they had come to Steubenville. Angelo loved him like a brother.

A few hours later, the party ended, and Angelo and Nina had lots of presents to take home. Gino Penta, a friend of Tony's who worked as a taxi driver, offered to help drive them home. Gino and Angelo loaded the car with Nina and the presents.

Nina was grateful for the ride as she was feeling uncomfortable. She fretted about making dinner for Angelo, but he made her go to bed and rest as soon as they got home.

The following two weeks flew by, and Nina woke the morning of July 14 with a sudden gush between her legs; her water broke. She woke Angelo, and he jumped out of bed and called Gino. Gino came over right away and drove them to the hospital.

Once Nina was admitted to the hospital and settled into a bed, a nurse notified Dr. Barducci. Being the second oldest of eleven children, Nina had witnessed several of her siblings' births and knew what to expect. On the other hand, Angelo fretted about his sweet Nina when he saw the pained expression on her face from her labor pains.

Dr. Barducci promptly ordered him to the waiting room. After several hours of labor, Nina gave birth to a beautiful, healthy baby girl. Angelo beamed at Nina with such intense love as she held the baby.

She had blue eyes, dark hair, and olive skin, a perfect combination of mother and father. They named her Theresa Adeline after both of their grandmothers.

Two days later, Angelo brought Nina and Theresa home to Seventh Street. His heart was so full he thought it would burst. He had a family.

He helped Nina to bed and promised to be back as quickly as he could. He was going to the train station to pick up Lena. As promised, Lena was coming to help her sister.

When Angelo arrived at the train station, Lena was already waiting. Her train had pulled in ahead of schedule, and Lena had used her time chatting with the ticket sellers behind the counter. She was very charming and had several young men there hanging on her every word.

Angelo wasn't sure if she knew what effect she was having on them, but he knew he needed to get her out of the station and back to the house as swiftly as possible. He collected her quickly, much to the chagrin of several of the young male workers there. She gave them all a sweet smile as she left.

Once they reached the house, Nina and Lena hugged each other fiercely. Lena brought gifts from Mama and Papa for the baby. They were so happy for Nina and Angelo and anxious to meet their new granddaughter. Lena was full of news and shared that Patsy was getting married, a local farmer was courting Mary, and Joe hoped to enroll at the local college.

Their Papa had gotten a promotion at the mine, and people were asking Mama to design and sew their daughters' wedding dresses after seeing Nina's photos in her wedding dress. Nina just marveled at how life had changed.

She was happy for her family and no longer upset that her parents had made her marry Angelo. She realized she loved Angelo dearly.

Nina couldn't believe the love she felt each time she held her daughter Theresa. Her heart was complete, and she couldn't imagine her life any other way. Nina thanked God she had given birth to a healthy baby girl. She thanked God she had a loving, caring husband.

Lena stayed with them for several months and was a big help with the baby. She seemed a bit upset when Nina announced that Domenica and Tony were Theresa's godparents, but Nina told her she would be the godmother for their next child. Lena was thrilled when Nina told her Theresa's middle name was Adeline; that was Lena's given name.

Lena enjoyed Steubenville and wrote to her parents, begging them to stay there. Mama, though, declared Lena was needed at home. A day after Theresa's baptism at St. Anthony's and a week before Christmas, Nina, Angelo, and the baby walked Lena to the train station. As they said their goodbyes, Lena promised to come back again soon.

An Italian Wedding

In 1924, two years after Enzo and Jesse left for America, Bruno married Maria. It was a lavish, beautiful ceremony; Vito spared no expense for his only daughter's wedding. Maria looked like a princess in her wedding gown.

Rosa was completely blind by that time. She couldn't see how beautiful Maria looked as she walked down the aisle or how handsome Bruno looked in his tuxedo as he waited for Maria on the altar.

Guido had recently been ordained a priest and was on the altar. It was the first wedding ceremony he would officiate.

Guido prayed daily for both of his brothers, but most especially Bruno. Guido was thrilled for Bruno because Maria always brought out the good in him. He knew how ruthless Bruno could be. He prayed Maria could tame his coarse brother; as she softened all his rough edges.

Enzo and Jesse had been unable to travel home for the wedding because Jesse was about to give birth to their second child. Their first child was a boy; they promptly named Nunzio after his grandfather.

They had sent pictures, but Rosa could not see them. Bruno and Guido told her the baby looked just like his daddy.

Vito and Anna were thrilled with Bruno, their new son-in-law. Maria loved him very much, and they wanted their only child to be content. Anna had lost their only other child in pregnancy, so they had spoiled Maria profusely.

Anna simply wanted her daughter to be happy, and Vito wanted to mold Bruno into the Santucci family's next leader since he had no sons.

Bruno had grown ruthless in his quest for power within the family and had as many Pettina enemies as Vito. So, there was a heavy security presence at the wedding and reception. Even Rosa and Guido had to undergo a pat-down to enter the Santucci family compound for the wedding. Bruno and Vito were leaving nothing unchecked.

Rosa was just pleased knowing her son was happy and settling down. She hoped they would start a family soon. She hoped to at least be able to hold a grandchild in her arms before she died.

The medicine the doctor had given her for the headaches no longer worked, and sometimes she could not even get out of bed.

Bruno and Guido had finally found out about the tumor and were angry that Rosa had not told them about it sooner. As soon as he found out, Bruno strong-armed a specialist from Rome to come and examine her.

The specialist told Bruno the tumor was inoperable, and Rosa had only a year or less to live. Bruno shared that news with Guido, and the brothers tried to spend as much time as they could visiting the villa and their mother. Bruno even hired a nurse to live with and take care of her.

Rosa felt Nunzio's presence more and more each day. There were times she even heard his voice calling to her.

She mentioned it once to Guido during one of his weekly visits, but he sounded concerned when she said it, so she never mentioned it again. Maybe she only imagined him; Rosa wasn't sure.

She spent most of her days in her backyard near the grove of fig trees sipping espresso with her nurse and talking about her lonely childhood.

The turf war between the Santucci and Pettina families had grown rougher over the past few years. Things continued to escalate between the two families, who wanted to control Calabria. It was no longer safe for the ladies to go to the market without a bodyguard.

Each day brought some new affront or conflict, and the priests were kept busy either hearing confessions or saying a funeral Mass.

Bruno and Maria shortened their honeymoon in the French Riviera to return to Calabria. Bruno wanted to keep Maria safe, and he wanted to be part of the action. In the midst of all this, Maria found out she was pregnant. Everyone was thrilled; Rosa, most of all. She prayed daily for a healthy grandchild.

When Maria was in her sixth month, Rosa passed away quietly in her sleep. No one was with her at the time. The nurse was in the next room having sex with Bruno, and Guido was at Church saying Mass. Unbeknownst to Maria, Bruno was cheating on her with the nurse he had hired to care for his mother.

Fr. Guido concelebrated his mother's funeral Mass with Fr. Edmund at St. Gabriel's Church. She was buried next to her husband in Holy Spirit Cemetery.

The whole Santucci family attended the funeral, as well as the nurse who cared for Rosa in her last months. Bruno told Maria the nurse was distraught, and he had hired her to look after their baby once she gave birth.

Maria was thrilled since she wanted to have someone else look after their child. She wanted to be free to do whatever she chose to do. She was getting bored with being pregnant, and the thought of going through childbirth was beginning to scare her.

Having a nurse on hand would surely be helpful, thought Maria. She had no clue Bruno was having sex with her.

The last few months of Maria's pregnancy seemed like forever to Bruno. He loved Maria, but she had gotten so big during her pregnancy; the sight of her turned him off.

She was always complaining about something or other, and he couldn't stand her whining. Her voice sounded like the screech of a cat, and he hated cats.

They had moved into his parent's villa after his mother died. The nurse he was having an affair with had witnessed his foul temper once too often and had disappeared. Someone told him she jumped a ship last week bound for America.

He was in such a bad mood that he snapped at everyone around him. He had even gone so far as to take a trip two villages away to hire and beat a puttana to rid himself of his foul mood. It hadn't helped.

He found many reasons to stay away from the villa and kept only his most trusted men there.

One of those men was a new bodyguard named Marco. Marco had a broad chest, bulging muscles, and huge hands. He was from Rome and looked like an ancient god with curly black hair, bright green eyes, and a classic nose. He was sent by his Zio Matteo, a mafia don in Rome, to

Calabria to learn from Bruno. Bruno's fierce and ruthless reputation was well known throughout Italy.

Marco was also a ladies' man and envied Bruno with his beautiful wife. He found her perfect creamy skin, ample breasts, and round belly intoxicating, but he did his best to ignore her. She was off-limits, and to entertain any thoughts of bedding her would bring swift action not only from Bruno but, more importantly, from his Zio Matteo in Rome.

Marco had no problem finding a woman, any woman, to entertain in his bed. With his looks, women always threw themselves at him. So, while Maria's luscious body filled his thoughts, he found a willing partner to bed in the form of Liane, one of the kitchen maids. She was easy on the eyes and ready to lift her skirts for him at any time, day or night.

Liane was in love. She couldn't believe her good fortune to have someone as handsome as Marco interested in her. Liane treated him like a king, giving him the best cuts of meat instead of giving them to Bruno. She prayed Bruno never found out because he would surely beat her.

Marco was getting bored with Maria's bodyguard duties and missed his home in Rome. He missed all the sights and sounds of that great city along with his friends and family. Marco hoped his Zio would soon notify him that he could go home.

Liane had begged him to take her to Rome when he left, and he lied and said he would. She showed her gratitude to him daily in his bed.

After breakfast, Maria summoned Marco to her room. She specifically asked for him. Marco wondered what she wanted this time.

Maria sat in a chair by the window overlooking the backyard and the grove of fig trees that grew there. It was a pretty spot and somewhat secluded. Just last night, Marco had sex with Liane there. He tapped on the door, and she said to enter.

Maria had a pout upon her luscious full lips but smiled as he approached. She was dressed to go out.

"Buongiorno signora Pagano," said Marco. "Come stai?"

"Marco, I'm disappointed. Last night, I saw you and Liane having sex in the grove of fig trees. You know Bruno forbids the servants to entertain one another, especially while on duty."

Marco retreated a few steps. "Signora Pagano, I'm sorry if Liane and I have offended you. Perdonami; I will report to Bruno when he arrives home later. I'll tell him what happened and beg for forgiveness."

Maria just continued smiling and replied, "I could be persuaded to forget what I saw. I know Bruno doesn't want me to leave the villa, but I want to go shopping today. I'm so sick of staying in this villa and being cooped up here. I need to get out. I know Bruno won't mind if I go as long as you are with me. Capisci?"

"I need you to get me out of here today, just for a few hours. If you take me to town for a while, I promise not to say anything to Bruno about you and Liane. What do you say?"

Marco thought about it and nodded. What harm could come from taking Maria to town for a few hours?

He knew Bruno was visiting a puttana a few villages away and wouldn't be home until dinner. He could take Maria and keep her happy. She, in turn, wouldn't spill the beans about him and Liane.

"I'll take you to town for two hours, and then when we come back here, you must rest in bed until dinner, so Bruno doesn't see any fatigue on your face while dining."

Maria smiled, "You've got yourself a deal. Give me ten minutes to finish getting ready, and I'll meet you in the courtyard."

Ten minutes later, the two of them left the villa. Maria was thrilled to be going anywhere and felt completely safe with Marco by her side.

They took a shortcut to the market in the village square. Maria wanted to pick up a couple of new scarves. The shortcut was through a narrow alleyway that led out into the market. Several vendors dotted the square selling their wares.

Maria was so beautiful trying on the different scarves that Marco spent his time looking at her instead of looking at their surroundings. If he had done his job, he would have noticed the three Pettina goons that were watching them from the shadows.

The goons recognized Maria instantly and watched her intently. They couldn't believe their luck and quickly came up with a plan to kidnap Maria when she and Marco left the square to walk back home.

The goons hid near a car parked in the alleyway and figured they could overpower Marco and snatch Maria. They would put her in the car and drive her to a nearby villa where one of their bosses lived. There they would hold her for ransom.

They knew that Vito and Bruno would pay anything to get her back, especially in her condition.

After two hours of shopping in the square, Marco told her they needed to go. He was starting to feel uneasy in the pit of his stomach and wanted to get her back home.

Maria complained loudly but complied with his request because she was feeling exhausted. She wished they had driven there instead of walking, but she didn't complain because she was thrilled to be outside the villa walls and with people. They began their trek back home, and Maria happily chatted about her purchases. As they entered the alleyway, Marco wondered why women talked so much.

The smallest of noises made him pivot away from her for just an instant. One of the goons hit him over the head with a jack and knocked him out cold. At the same time, another grabbed Maria from behind, covering her head with a cloth and pinning her arms behind her, binding them together.

She tried to scream, but her voice was muffled from the cloth. She was quickly dragged to a waiting car, all the while kicking and trying to fight off her kidnappers. Her efforts were futile.

They just laughed at her and rudely shoved her into the back seat of a car. She landed roughly against the back seat with such an abrupt stop; it made her stomach twinge. She quickly stopped fighting with them because she didn't want to harm herself or her baby.

She heard a loud thud, and then the trunk slammed shut. She wondered what happened to Marco; he was supposed to protect her. He hadn't done a very good job. Stupido, she thought. She didn't know, was he still alive, or was he dead?

She guessed there were three kidnappers present in the car with her. She was trying to listen to their words for any clues as to where they were taking her. She stayed quiet and let them think she had passed out. Her hands hurt from being bound together so tightly.

Did they know who she was? Her father and her husband would make them pay dearly for hurting her, and she would enjoy watching them.

The car went very fast, and Maria quickly lost any sense of where she was. She tried to listen for sounds like the whistle of a train or the horn of a ship, but she couldn't distinguish anything but the sound of her own heart beating very fast.

She just tried to stay calm for her baby's sake and thought about what Bruno would do to these men once he found her. She figured the goons were from the Pettina family. She was confident she wouldn't be with them long, and they wouldn't dare hurt her.

The only problem was no one at the villa knew where she and Marco had gone.

The car came to a quick stop. She was thrown against the back of the front seat by its quickness and cried out in pain. Fanculo!

She had tried to show no weakness, but the force of the stop had made her slide off the seat. She hadn't known, so she could not brace herself.

Somehow, in the attack, she had twisted and hurt her ankle. It throbbed, but she tried not to show any pain as they pulled her from the car. They pushed her along a gravelly path, and she got rocks in her sandals, adding to her discomfort. She lost her footing and fell.

Someone grabbed her from behind and dragged her through some sort of brush. Finally, they stopped, and while still holding her, knocked on a door twice. She heard someone unlock the door and open it. A goon shoved her in, and again she lost her balance and fell, hitting her head on something hard. She cried out in pain as someone hit her in the head, and she crumpled to the floor.

She awoke sometime later, tied to a bed with a scarf still tied against her mouth. Someone had removed the cloth over her head; at least now she could see. Her head, arms, and legs all hurt, and her ankle, now an ugly shade of purple, was swollen. She couldn't move.

The room was dim and only lit by a single candle burning on a nightstand. Two ugly men were sitting at the foot of the bed, watching her.

One grinned at her when he saw she was awake. "Buonasera," he said as he smiled. He had rotten teeth, and his face was filthy.

39

The other man also had rotten teeth and a patch over his left eye. "Bellissima, you finally decided to wake up." He sneered. "We were just talking about you."

"My, my; you are belladonna up close and personal. No wonder your husband keeps you tucked away in that villa with so many guards."

She couldn't answer him, so she just glared.

"Man, I am gonna have fun with you," he said while he put his hand on her foot and moved it up her leg. She tried to kick it off but couldn't. Her eyes were like daggers.

He removed his hand but just for a moment. "You see this patch; your husband made me lose my eye in a back alley fight a few years ago. He fought dirty; now it's my turn."

He glared at her as he told the other man to leave them alone. Once he was gone, the man with the patch went to the door and locked it.

He turned around and looked at her. He took off his belt and began to beat her. She screamed as the first blows struck, and her tears flowed freely down her cheeks. He punched her in the face, and instantly her eye began to swell.

He ripped off her clothes and raped her several times as she prayed for her unborn baby. She prayed Bruno would find her soon and kill her captor. She lost consciousness as he continued his brutal assault upon her body.

A Difficult Delivery

Bruno arrived home to find Maria missing. Liane said Marco was missing too. Bruno sent out search parties after them. Word came back that they had been at the market in the village square earlier in the day.

One vendor told Bruno's men that he sold a couple of scarves to a pregnant woman matching Maria's description. Another vendor stated he saw three Pettina goons at the market as well.

Bruno was furious and strode about the villa in a rage. His servants had never seen him in such a state. He sent Santucci henchmen to all known Pettina hideouts, and they beat men until finally, one talked. Bruno's henchmen killed him after mentioning where he thought Maria and Marco were.

Several hours after their abduction, Bruno was on his way to the countryside hideaway of a Pettina family member. His temples twitched wildly, and his mood was as black as the moonless night. He would kill the men who took his precious Maria, and she better not be harmed.

His goons burst into the small dark cabin, guns blazing. The men inside were instantly shot and killed. A bloody unresponsive Marco was in a heap upon the floor. A stray bullet from the gunfight had hit him in the head; he was dead. Bruno would have to explain to Don Matteo what had happened to his precious Marco.

One of his men quickly located the locked door and shot the lock off. The man with the patch had heard the gunshots and quickly grabbed his gun. He shot the first man through the door and killed one of Bruno's best henchmen.

Bruno immediately entered the room after the henchmen and took in the scene. He saw his unconscious, naked wife tied to the bed, beaten and abused.

He was like an animal possessed as he went after the man with the patch. The man with the patch was no match for Bruno. Bruno beat him to a pulp and strangled him with his bare hands.

Once the man was dead, Bruno gathered his unconscious pregnant wife and carried her out of the cabin to his car. In the rearview mirror of his vehicle, Bruno could see the house burst into flames as he sped home. His henchmen poured gasoline all around the place and lit a match.

He needed to get Maria home and get her some medical attention. She hadn't regained consciousness, and he was worried about her. She was battered and bruised all over. He suspected she had been raped since her clothes were in tatters.

His palms itched, and his temples throbbed, but he was trying to calm himself down for her sake. He needed to focus on her.

They arrived at the villa, and he carried her into the house and straight up to their bed. Her parents and her doctor were on their way to the estate. Word of what had happened at the cabin quickly spread, and Bruno's men reported the rest of the Pettina family had gone into hiding.

The doctor examined Maria and determined the baby appeared fine. Maria awoke as the doctor examined her and recounted to them what had happened. She hurt all over and suffered a couple of cracked ribs, a sprained ankle, and two black eyes.

The doctor immediately wanted to take her to the hospital, but Bruno would have none of it. He could protect her best in his own home, and so they did the best they could to clean and comfort her. The doctor then gave her a mild sedative to rest before leaving the villa.

Vito and Anna arrived and immediately interrogated Bruno about how this could happen to their beloved daughter. He briefly told them what little he knew about the shopping excursion and abduction.

An all-out war on the Pettina family began that very night. Vito and Bruno vowed to show no mercy.

Maria awoke in the night to sharp pains in her lower belly. She let out a bloodcurdling scream. Something was definitely wrong.

Bruno, who was sleeping at the foot of the bed, knew at once something was wrong. He could tell by the sound of her scream. He turned on the small lamp by their bed and immediately sent for the doctor again.

Her pale skin had an unnatural gray color, and blood rushed down her legs. She looked to be very scared and in pain. Bruno had never seen her look that way before.

He climbed into bed and cradled his wife, his beloved Maria. He began to pray. He prayed the prayers that Rosa taught him as a young boy. Prayers he hadn't said in decades, much less thought about.

He screamed out for help. Finally, Anna came rushing into the room. She saw the look of pain on her daughter's face and immediately realized Maria was in labor. She prayed both mother and baby would be okay.

Maria cried out in pain and agony as each new contraction began. She tried to remain focused on Bruno, but the pain was too severe. She felt like her body was ripping in two.

Anna told Bruno to try and keep Maria focused on just breathing through each contraction. She ordered Liane to bring in clean sheets and warm water. Anna wiped Maria's brow and face between contractions. She was worried about the amount of blood she saw in her daughter's bed.

Anna hoped the doctor got there quickly. There was something wrong, and she prayed all would be well. It was going to be a long and challenging night.

The doctor arrived at the villa again. This time he brought Fr. Guido with him. The doctor was anxious about the amount of blood Maria had lost. The baby appeared to be breach, and he was trying to turn it as Maria labored in pain.

He wished he could get her to a hospital, but she had lost too much blood now and was too weak to be moved. The baby also appeared distressed, but he did not tell anyone.

Fr. Guido immediately began to pray with Anna. When Maria let out another scream, Anna demanded the doctor do something to help her daughter. The doctor remained calm and said he was doing all he could for Maria at the present time.

Bruno stayed by Maria's side, continually wiping her brow and trying to keep them both calm.

Maria had no energy and was very pale and fragile from her abuse at her kidnappers' hands. When another contraction hit, the doctor examined her again and said she was still not far along enough for him to try and help the baby come out of the birth canal.

The doctor showed Bruno how to massage Maria's belly during each contraction so the baby would move into the proper position. Bruno stayed focused and did as the doctor instructed. Both men were working in unison.

Anna stayed with Maria, but she had to leave the room to cry. It was hard to see your child in such agony.

Finally, after several long hours, the doctor examined Maria and said it was time to push. Maria, who had no energy left, couldn't push, so the doctor tried to pull the baby out. After three unsuccessful attempts, the baby finally exited the birth canal but had the umbilical cord wrapped around its head; and wasn't breathing.

The housekeeper took the baby from the doctor and cleaned it up. It was a boy. The doctor quickly examined the baby and tried to get him to breathe but was unsuccessful. The baby was stillborn.

Bruno got off the bed to see the baby upon his birth and howled in pain as the doctor looked at him and shook his head. The lifeless baby was blue, and Bruno could not contain his anger and grief.

Bruno was heartbroken. He grabbed the baby from the doctor and fell to the floor with it, cradling the baby in his arms. The baby looked just like his mama with fair skin and a shock of auburn hair.

The doctor went back to attending to Maria, but she had lost too much blood. She slipped into unconsciousness and died. Maria died without knowing anything about the baby.

Bruno, who was still on the floor, clutching the lifeless body of his infant son, could not comprehend what the doctor was telling him. He couldn't believe both Maria and the baby were gone. He became a man possessed with grief, and the doctor had to sedate him.

Anna called Vito and Fr. Guido into the room. Their grief was unbearable as well. Fr. Guido carried his brother into the next room and put him to bed. Then he went back and performed the last rites for Maria.

He baptized his nephew, giving him the name John, their grandfather's name. He prayed for Rosa, his mother, to watch over Maria and the baby.

Vito and Anna had to make the funeral arrangements for Maria and the baby as Bruno could not. He remained sedated in bed for two weeks; his brother never left his side.

As Guido tried to comfort his brother, Bruno simply turned away. He was mad at his brother, angry at God, and mad at the whole world. Bruno prayed to God to save his wife and child that night, but God did not. Bruno told Guido he no longer believed in God.

Two months after Maria and the baby's death, Anna, who could not bear losing her only child and grandchild, drowned herself in her bathtub. She was heartbroken by the loss. Vito understood her anguish too well; he felt it also.

The all-out war between the two families continued, and Vito worried he was fighting a losing battle. Bruno, his scrappy fighter, his son-in-law, and his chosen successor, was just a shell of a man. Bruno was still in mourning.

The long-standing battle for control of Calabria was coming to an end. Now that both Vito and Bruno had lost their wives and children, there was nothing left to fight for. Vito was tired and just getting too old to fight anymore; he knew what he had to do.

He contacted his cousin Vincenzo in America and made arrangements for Bruno there. Bruno would work alongside his brother, Enzo, for Vincenzo Santucci. Now all Vito had to do was to convince him to go.

Bruno agreed to go to Steubenville without hesitation when Vito brought up the subject. There was nothing left for him in Calabria.

The day Bruno left Calabria, Vito Santucci, head of the Santucci family, sat in the bedroom of his vast compound and shot himself. The war between the Santucci and Pettina families in Calabria had ended.

The Telegram

Theresa was a happy baby, and Nina was a natural at taking care of her. She had lots of practice since she had taken care of her younger siblings for so many years. As promised, Lena made several trips to Steubenville to visit them. She wanted to stay and work in Steubenville, but each time she asked, her parents said no.

Angelo was a doting father and spoiled Theresa any time Nina would let him. The three of them lived happily in the house on Seventh Street. The owners had decided to stay in Italy and were pleased to have such decent and dependable renters.

Angelo was very handy and fixed anything that broke. He was also a good provider and had gotten several promotions at the mill. They were saving to buy a house of their own.

Times were challenging, though, as the Great Depression began. The small family took in a couple of boarders to help the less fortunate. Angelo invited a couple of men, Benny Alonzo and Joe Parsons, who were coworkers from the mill, to move in. They were recent immigrants from Italy that he knew. They slept in the large back bedroom of the house and were very courteous to Nina and Theresa.

Nina was happy in Steubenville and loved her husband and daughter very much. Nina loved taking Theresa to the park to play on the swings. She met several other young mothers there, and many times they talked about their families as they shared advice.

In the blink of an eye, Theresa was four years old. She loved playing with cousins Yolanda and Dora. They were like three peas in a pod. Domenica and Tony's second child, Dora, was a few months younger than Theresa. She was just like Yolanda in looks and demeanor.

Nina and Angelo prayed to get pregnant again, but it had not happened. It had happened once and would happen again when God was ready for them to have another child. Nina fretted over this a lot and spoke to Dr. Barducci about it. He just chuckled and said not to worry. Nina still worried herself sick about it and prayed daily.

Nina and Domenica were at the park on a late summer day, and the girls were playing on the swings as their mothers sat chatting on the bench. It was the first outing for Domenica since she gave birth to her third daughter, Mary, born a bit premature just three weeks before.

"I'm worried I'll never get pregnant again, and I know Angelo wants a son so badly," Nina said as she held Mary in her arms. The baby was so tiny; she looked lost, swaddled in her blanket.

"Oh, Nina, don't worry, it will happen. Dr. Barducci said it would when you least expect it. You and Angelo just need to relax. I, on the other hand, have to tell Tony that we can't have any more babies."

"After the complications with Mary's delivery, the doctor said I shouldn't have any more children." Domenica had tears in her eyes as she looked at Nina holding her baby. All three of her girls looked like their daddy. She hoped Tony wasn't upset. Their third child was another girl, and she knew he wanted a son. Domenica knew how Nina felt.

Nina knew Angelo wanted a son, and she worried about her inability to get pregnant again. She and Angelo had an active sex life, but each time she thought she was pregnant, her hopes were soon disappointed by the start of her cycle.

Each time the disappointment showed on her face, Angelo would hold her close and brush away her tears. "Cara Mia, I love you, and I'm not disappointed. When the time is right, another little bundle to love and care for will come along from God. Until that time, we must be patient and trust in Him. And besides, we have our sweet Theresa to keep us busy."

Angelo always brought wildflowers or a little trinket, such as a small broach or a lace handkerchief, to try and cheer her up. Nina always thanked him for the gift and treasured each one. She prayed novenas to the Blessed Mother that someday she would have another child.

She became very protective of Theresa. She wouldn't allow her to do certain things because she didn't want any harm to come to her daughter, her only child. Sometimes her father would intervene on her behalf. Theresa was too young to understand her mother's worry and cried to her father when she couldn't do something.

Crime in Steubenville seemed to escalate recently, and Angelo was worried about his small family. The mafia was as rampant in Steubenville as it was in Italy.

Angelo told Nina to stay away from Vincenzo and Mary Santucci. Everyone knew Vincenzo Santucci ran the mob in town and had several policemen, lawyers, and judges on his payroll.

The Santucci's lived in an immense mansion on Eighth Street with a gardener, maids, and security guards. They were members of St. Anthony's Church and considered themselves pillars of the community.

The Santucci family always went to the ten o'clock Mass on Sundays. They sat on the right side in the front row of St. Anthony's Church. No one dared sit near them. Vincenzo and Mary both wore beautiful clothes, and their children did as well. Many other members of the famiglia attended that same Mass.

The parish priests always ensured that Vincenzo and Mary's children, Dominic, Maria, and Elizabeth, were chosen first for any honors in the parish or school. A Santucci child always did the May crowning or served at any special Mass.

Angelo and Tony, along with their families, went to the early morning Mass on Sundays. Both men wanted to steer clear of the Santucci family and any trouble.

They both had steady jobs at the steel mill and were happily married men who never once stepped foot into one of Judy Jordan's places of business.

They never went into any of Vincenzo's establishments, so they figured they would never have any problems with the mob. They were just Italians living everyday life in Steubenville.

In the late spring of 1931, Angelo received an urgent telegram from his mother, notifying him that his father was gravely ill and asked to see him. Angelo knew he had to travel to Italy.

He decided to take his family with him. Nina had just had another miscarriage and was very depressed. They had been hopeful with this pregnancy, but she had lost the baby in her third month. He hoped the trip would be suitable for her.

Theresa had just finished the first grade. She would get to meet her grandparents. She would be thrilled to go on a grand adventure with her parents.

Angelo asked his boss about taking time off from work when he walked into the mill that day. His boss said they could only allow him to take one month's absence. Angelo said it would take that long to get to Italy, so he sadly turned in his resignation. His boss was compassionate and gave him a good recommendation. He always liked Angelo.

Angelo left the mill armed with a letter of recommendation and his final paycheck. He went to the travel agency in Steubenville and purchased the tickets for their trip. He sent a telegram to his mother with their itinerary and then returned home to break the news to Nina.

Nina was apprehensive when Angelo said they should all go to Italy. She said it would cost a lot of money for the three of them to go. She told him he should go by himself. He refused and said that it was going to be a family trip. He wanted his parents to meet his wife and daughter.

Over the next few weeks, they prepared for their trip. They contacted the house owners on Seventh Street to let them know what was going on. Benny Alonzo and a couple of other mill workers would be staying there while they were gone, and the owners were okay with that.

Nina sent a telegram to Lena informing Lena the family planned to go to Italy. Lena planned to come to Steubenville for a summer visit to see Nina, Angelo, and Theresa and see Benny Alonzo. She and Benny had been courting for a while.

Lena and Benny had set the date to marry in November. Nina thought they would surely be back from Italy by then. Benny had recently asked her parent's permission to marry Lena, so there was a lot of excitement and planning ahead.

Nina was apprehensive about the whole trip, but Angelo and Theresa were looking forward to it. Domenica told her about different places to go and see while there and which stores had the best bargains. Angelo said they would be gone about six months at the most.

Nina's Italian was rusty, so she and Angelo practiced conversing in Italian around the house. It didn't take long for her to become good enough to have a conversation with him. She worried about what her in-laws would think of her and the fact that they had been married for almost eight years but only had one child. Angelo told her she worried too much. He said his parents would love her and Theresa.

Seven-year-old Theresa couldn't believe that she was going on a ship to Italy with her parents. They were going to visit Papa's parents, and she was so excited about it. She had never been on a ship and had never been to Italy.

Since Papa and Mama had told her about it last week, she kept talking about it with Yolanda and Dora. They had come for a visit, and their mothers were chatting in the kitchen.

Theresa couldn't remember a time when they weren't there. Theresa would miss them terribly while she was in Italy, but she promised to tell them all about her trip when she got back home.

Papa seemed anxious to go on the trip, but Mama was not. She had been pretty sad lately, and Theresa couldn't figure out why. Yolanda told her she had heard Mama and Zia Domenica talking about losing something, but they stopped when Yolanda entered the room.

Theresa wondered what Mama had lost. Maybe she could help her find it. She would ask her after Zia Domenica left to go back home.

Theresa, Yolanda, and Dora were in the living room playing with dolls because Mama didn't want her to play out in the backyard. Sometimes she wondered why Mama was so scared to let her play outside. Why was Mama so afraid she would get hurt?

Just then, Nina came into the room and said she had a plate of cookies and glasses of milk for them out in the kitchen. All three girls abandoned the dolls and ran to the kitchen.

After they had their cookies and milk, Zia Domenica said it was time for them to go. She had just had baby Mary but always seemed tired anymore. She liked to take an afternoon nap with the girls before Zio Tony got home from work. The girls cleaned up their dolls, and they left to go home.

Nina washed up the glasses and dishes from the milk and cookies while Theresa put her dolls away. Once she finished, Theresa went into the kitchen to help her Mama dry the dishes. "Mama, why are you so sad?" she asked.

Nina looked at her daughter and smiled gently. "Papa and I have been trying for a while to have another baby. We want you to have a little brother or sister. I thought I was finally going to be able to give you and Papa another baby, but I'm not, and that makes me sad."

"I did have a baby in my belly for a short time, but God wanted that baby up in heaven, so he came and got the baby and took it up to heaven. That's why I have been so sad lately." Nina's eyes filled with unshed tears as Theresa hugged her mother.

"Mama, the baby must have been pretty special for God to take it up to heaven. Is the baby an angel now?"

"Yes, Theresa, I guess the baby is an angel now."

"Then we should be happy that God loved the baby so much he made it an angel," answered Theresa as she hugged and kissed her mother.

Nina could not believe how loving and caring her young daughter was. She hoped she was always that way. Nina only wished she could give her siblings.

Growing up in a large family had given Nina many happy memories, and she wanted the same for Theresa. She also knew that Angelo wanted more children and had been so delighted when she told him she was pregnant just two months ago.

After losing the baby and with the strain of knowing his father was sick back in Italy, Angelo was distraught. Maybe this trip to Italy was just what the family needed.

The day of the big trip finally arrived. Nina was still apprehensive about the whole thing, but Angelo and Theresa treated it like a great adventure.

Theresa wore a new pink dress embroidered with little white flowers and tiny ruffles that Nina had made. It was Papa's favorite color on her. Papa had a special gift for her and Mama. He pulled out two long slim velvet boxes from his coat pocket and gave one to each of them. Inside each box was a string of beautiful pearls.

He said they were his special girls and belonged in pearls. Once he gave Theresa the necklace, they danced around the living room with Nina telling him to be careful with his precious cargo. The two of them just laughed and continued dancing. Theresa had her father's easy laugh and demeanor.

Now, he carried their luggage out to the taxi. Gino was taking them to the station where they would board the train to New York. From New York, they would board a ship, *MS Augustus*, to Naples, Italy. From there, they would travel to the province of Pescara, Angelo's home.

 Theresa could not believe that she would ride on a train and a ship for the first time. She was a little bit nervous but was trying not to show it. Mama had been on a train before but never on a ship. They would experience it together. Angelo told them not to worry.

The train was full of people. Theresa had never seen so many people before, and she was slightly intimidated by her surroundings. Nina sensed it and held onto her hand a little bit tighter than she usually did. Her daughter didn't object.

Angelo led the way through the crowd of people and found their seats. Once they were seated, Nina, who usually didn't let Theresa have any candy, handed her daughter a peppermint stick and told her to try and not get any on her new dress.

Theresa gladly accepted the candy and promised to eat it carefully. While she was eating her treat, the train whistle blew loudly, and then it lurched and took off. They were officially on their way to New York.

After a while, Nina took the candy, wrapped it up carefully, and put it back into her pocketbook. She told Theresa she should try to rest as the trip would be long. The train's steady movement lulled Theresa to sleep until Angelo shook her gently to say they had arrived.

Once their train pulled into the station in New York, Angelo gathered their luggage as Nina held on to Theresa. They walked the short distance to the hotel where they would spend the night.

At the hotel, they all slept in the same bed. When Theresa was younger, she sometimes slept with her parents, especially if she had a bad dream. Now that she was seven, she always stayed in her own bed. Sleeping with Mama and Papa made her feel safe.

Nina was tired from the day's traveling and fell right to sleep, but Theresa was wide awake, so Angelo stayed awake, telling her all about Italy and his parents. She was excited about getting on the ship tomorrow. She was excited about meeting her grandparents.

Angelo had been teaching her a little bit of Italian so she could speak to them. They didn't know any English. Papa said she was smart because she was learning Italian so quickly. Theresa finally fell asleep, and Angelo turned the light out and thought about what lay ahead.

A Year Abroad

Nina woke up with a headache and a large pit in her stomach. She had never been to Italy before and had a sense of impending doom. She woke up Angelo and Theresa; they didn't have much time to get dressed and get to the port.

Once there, Nina and Theresa could not believe their eyes; *MS Augustus* was a big ship. It was not just big; it was huge! Theresa wondered how a big boat could float on the water without sinking. Angelo just chuckled when she said that, and Nina looked distressed.

Angelo told them *MS Augustus* was an ocean liner and that more than 2,000 people would be on the trip. He said it was the largest diesel engine passenger ship ever made.

He said the crew was Italian, and it would be an excellent way to practice it. It would be a wonderful surprise for Nonna and Tatone Taglieri, Papa's parents.

A steward took their luggage onto the ship and to their room. They were traveling in something called first class. Theresa wasn't sure what that meant, but the steward was very friendly to them.

Nina suddenly looked like she didn't feel well, and Angelo put his arm around her to reassure her all would be fine. Their room was about the same size as the one at the hotel in New York. Besides the bed, it also held a small sofa and chair. Angelo gave the steward a couple of coins before he left the room.

He wanted to go on deck to watch as the ship departed from the port, but Nina wanted to rest, so Theresa went with Papa while Mama stayed in the room. There were so many people on the deck that they couldn't get a good view, so they decided to explore the ship a bit before going back to their room.

Theresa was in awe as they peeked into many fancy dining rooms, salons, and ballrooms. Papa said it was decorated in a Baroque style; Theresa just called it fancy. She wanted to explore more, but Papa said they would do so another day. He wanted to check on Mama, so they returned to the room.

The journey to Italy took several weeks, and Theresa found the ship and its crew very interesting. She practiced her Italian by asking the crew questions about everything and anything. They always smiled and answered her questions politely.

Nina told her not to bother them and let them do their job, but Angelo said the ship's Captain told him they enjoyed Theresa's curious nature. So, she continued questioning everyone she had contact with, from the maids and butlers to the ship's stewards.

The trip aboard the ship was difficult for Nina. She was seasick. The constant rocking of the vessel made her retch. It was worse than the morning sickness with this last pregnancy. That made her think about the miscarriage and compounded her feelings of depression, making things worse. It took her at least two weeks to find her sea legs, and even then, she always seemed queasy.

Thankfully Angelo entertained Theresa most days. Nina couldn't believe how much her daughter was like her husband. They had the same carefree, straightforward way and quickly made friends on board. On the other hand, Nina stayed mainly to herself and was quiet and reflective.

Nina was proud that Theresa was so grown up and poised for one so young in years, and Angelo was a great father. He was patient, kind, and loving to his daughter, never dismissing any of her questions but always answering them in a way she would understand. Theresa was like a sponge, learning to speak Italian, learning about the ship, and learning about life in general.

Nina continued to pray that someday they would have another child. Maybe she would get pregnant while they were in Italy. She prayed for a son for Angelo.

It was July by the time they reached Naples, and Theresa not only knew much about the ocean liner, but she was fluent in Italian. Angelo was thrilled that she learned it so quickly.

The crew all said goodbye to them as they went ashore. Theresa was captivated by the Piazza del Plebiscito and Mount Vesuvius sights. Angelo told her there would be time later to see the sights. Now that he was back in Italy, he wanted to get home as soon as possible.

Angelo expertly navigated his way through the traffic and tourists of Naples. They reached the train station in no time, and he quickly arranged their passage to Tocco da Casauria, the small town in Pescara, where he grew up. The province of Pescara was on the coast of the Adriatic Sea. The village in which he grew up was in the mountains above. It was where he was born and where his family still lived.

Once he had secured their train tickets, Angelo took them to the Villa Comunale, a beautiful public park. He sat them in a semi-shady spot and went to purchase some pizza. He returned with three slices of the most delicious pizza Theresa had ever eaten. After that, they had some gelato and enjoyed watching the tourists for a while.

They had a few hours before the train was scheduled to leave. Angelo took them to the Piazza del Plebiscito, the beautiful large square in Naples, bordered at one end by the Palazzo Reale or Royal Palace and the other by the Basilica of San Francesco di Paola.

Nina and Theresa were amazed by the beauty of the place. It was a crowded and busy space filled with tourists worldwide, and Nina held onto Theresa's hand tightly. Theresa wanted to explore the Piazza but knew Nina would worry about her, so she stayed by her mother's side.

Soon it was time to go back to the train station for their journey to Pescara. Theresa was excited but exhausted from their travels; she quickly fell asleep on the train. Nina and Angelo talked about his parents. He was apprehensive about his fathers' health. He hoped the doctors were wrong in their diagnosis.

Once they arrived in Pescara, Angelo's Zio Giuseppe picked them up at the station. Nina thought Giuseppe was an older version of her handsome husband. It was very late in the evening, and Theresa was still asleep, so Angelo carried her off the train, and she missed her first spectacular view of the Adriatic Sea and the town of Pescara.

Giuseppe delivered them to the family villa in Tocco de Casauria, and Nina found herself surrounded by Angelo's boisterous but loving family. Everyone made Nina and Theresa feel welcome.

Angelo's mother was thrilled to meet Nina and thankful her son had a loving wife and daughter. She was honored that Angelo and Nina had named their daughter Theresa and surprised Theresa spoke Italian.

Angelo was shocked to see Paolo, his father, in poor health but tried not to show it. Paolo had always been so strong, but cancer had riddled his body, making him very weak. The doctor answered Angelo's many questions about his father's treatment but did not provide much hope.

Paolo was dying and didn't have much time left. Angelo was sad to hear that but grateful he had made the trip with his family. Angelo vowed to stay with his parents for as long as he could. He gladly did whatever his mother and father asked of him. Nina also got to spend some time with Paolo. He reminded her of her father, Ross.

Once they settled in, Angelo took Nina and Theresa around Pescara, the province's spectacular port city. Nina was much more interested in learning about Angelo's childhood from his mother. She gladly told Nina stories about her only son.

Theresa loved meeting her Nonna Taglieri and her two Zias. They were all beautiful and spoke in Italian very fast. She had a hard time understanding what they said.

Tatone Paolo was very sick and made scary noises. Luckily, Papa was with her and held her hand whenever they were in his room. She didn't stay long in his presence.

The villa was so large and spacious that she sometimes got lost in it when she went exploring. She loved the vast gardens in the backyard and adored Zio Giuseppe. He could be found most afternoons tending to the garden.

Theresa thought it was delightful that her grandparents had vegetables in their backyard and didn't have to go to the store to buy them. Zio Giuseppe told her she could pick any of the tomatoes, beans, or grapes off the vine that she wanted, as long as she ate whatever she picked.

Summer quickly turned to Fall, and they were still in Italy. Nina worried about Theresa's schooling, so Angelo enrolled her in the village school. Theresa was upset when the officials said she had to go to first grade again since she didn't complete it there.

Theresa hated school in Italy since she didn't know anyone. She wanted to go home to America so she could go to school with Dora and Yolanda. Nina told her to do as she was told.

Angelo helped Giuseppe make wine from the grapes in their vineyard. It was something his father and Zio did annually. Paolo rarely left his bedroom now and spent most of his days sleeping. During one of their daily talks, he asked Angelo to care for his mother. Angelo promised to care for his mother and sisters.

One day, when Theresa came home from school, she found everyone crying. Nina told her God had come for Tatone Paolo to take him to heaven. Mama said everyone was sad because they would miss him.

Tatone Paolo died in October and was laid to rest in the Taglieri family plot behind the church. Theresa missed a few days of school because they were in mourning. She tried hard to cheer everyone up; she didn't like to see Papa or Mama sad.

Angelo's mother and younger sisters were grief-stricken, and he did his best to console them. Over the next few months, he put all his parents' affairs in order.

Angelo didn't want his mother to worry about anything. He told her the family villa was debt-free, and he had paid all of his father's medical bills.

He tried to persuade her to sell the family estate and move back to America with them. He promised to take care of her. She thanked him but refused; she wanted to stay in their villa. She had lived in it for almost forty years.

He said he understood but held out hope she would change her mind. She tried to persuade him to stay in Italy, but he said no. His future was in America.

After Paolo went to heaven, Angelo was so busy helping Nonna and Zio Giuseppe that he didn't have much time to spend with Nina or

Theresa. That made Theresa even more homesick. A few nights, she even cried herself to sleep. It seemed everyone in the villa cried at night.

Nina told her she should pray instead of shedding tears. She said prayers were more powerful. So, Theresa prayed nightly they would soon go home to America. Italy was beautiful, but it wasn't home. Theresa especially missed her cousins.

Nina was homesick as well. They had missed Lena and Benny's wedding in Scranton. Angelo felt terrible, but by the time he had tried to purchase tickets for their passage home, the ship was full. They would have to wait until Spring.

The holidays came and went; nobody felt like celebrating. After that, Angelo's mother became ill with pneumonia, and Nina spent several months nursing her back to health. Her mother-in-law was grateful.

Nina was more than ready to go home. She wanted to get back to her own family. Lena's last letter indicated that their father was ill. Nina was afraid he would die, and she would never see him again. Finally, in late Spring, Angelo booked passage for them back to America.

Angelo promised her they would go to Scranton as soon as they returned to America. They left in June 1932 to go back to America. They had spent almost a full year in Italy.

Angelo's father had passed away, and his mother and two sisters remained in Italy. Zio Giuseppe promised to look after them.

When they got back to America, they took a trip to Scranton. Nina's father, Ross, was feeling much better. He and Mary were doing well, and Nina's siblings were happy to see her. Several of her brothers and sisters were now married and living in their own homes. Nora and Mollie were the only two siblings still at home.

Nina was relieved to find her family was doing so well. They spent a month in Scranton and left for Steubenville in August. Angelo needed to get his mill job back, and Theresa would soon start back to school. She couldn't wait to see her cousins.

Brothers Reunited

In the summer of 1932, when his ship docked in Canada, Bruno went directly to the United States by train. He had an appointment scheduled with Vincenzo Santucci for the following week in Steubenville, Ohio. Enzo picked him up at the train station.

His brother was a sight for sore eyes. They hadn't seen each other in over five years. Enzo's hair had thinned out a bit, and he wore wire-rimmed spectacles. The two brothers embraced for quite a while until a small voice said, "Papa, is this Zio Bruno?"

Bruno turned and saw his nephew, Nunzio, the spitting image of Enzo. "Yes, I'm Zio Bruno, and you must be Nunzio."

"I am," replied the boy. "I want to see your hands; Papa says they are lethal weapons. They don't look lethal to me."

Enzo cuffed the boy on the ear. "They are and don't you forget it. Zio Bruno can kill a man with his bare hands, so don't you be getting on his bad side." The boy just nodded and walked along with his father.

Bruno grabbed his suitcase, and they started towards home. Enzo and Jesse rented a house on Seventh Street. Bruno was going to live with them until he got settled.

Enzo gave him the lay of the land and the Santucci operation while they walked.

Vincenzo Santucci, Vito's cousin, was the owner of Santucci's Hotel and Restaurant. There was also a gambling casino in the basement of the restaurant.

He was the undisputed mob boss and ran all the county's illegal gambling and bootlegging activities. Vincenzo, and his wife, Mary, had three children; Dominic, Maria, and Elizabeth.

Vincenzo also had a girlfriend, Judy Jordan. Judy was a madam and oversaw all the brothels in the area. Vincenzo and Judy personally picked and trained each girl who worked in any one of his establishments.

He had a large payroll that included several city cops, judges, lawyers, doctors, and politicians. Nothing happened in Steubenville unless he approved of it, and he always took thirty percent of the profit as his share.

Luca Salvatore, his second in command, ran the Diamond Cigar Store. It was the front for Vincenzo's gambling and numbers business, and he had a private office there.

Luca also oversaw the men who ran other business ventures for Vincenzo. A runner from each business would stop by the Diamond Cigar Store and drop off gambling receipts daily.

The men would all gather at Santucci's Restaurant on Monday afternoons for lunch. They each gave a weekly report on their business dealings and brought what they owed to Vincenzo. Enzo would collect and record everything into two different sets of books. One book for Vincenzo and the other for the feds.

Judy would bring over her best girls, and the men could retire to one of the hotel rooms with a girl or choose to gamble in his secret casino below the restaurant after paying their due to Vincenzo. The cops would make sure they were not bothered the whole afternoon.

Enzo explained that he spent long days working on the books for each account. It was meticulous work and often took a long time to ensure the correct numbers went into each book. He noted that because of this, he now wore glasses.

By the time they reached the house on Seventh Street, Bruno knew all about the illegal businesses in town owned by Vincenzo Santucci. He would meet Vincenzo and work for him. Bruno would make himself indispensable to Vincenzo. It was the only way of life that he knew.

At the house, a pregnant Jesse welcomed Bruno to town. Jesse's parents were there as well. He also met his niece, Rosemary, named after her two grandmothers. She was a beautiful, healthy toddler who looked like her Mama. As he looked at Jesse and his niece, he remembered all he had loved and lost in Calabria.

He told Enzo that he would quickly find a place to stay. He didn't want constant reminders of what he didn't have around him each day; it was just too painful.

His reserved manner made him seem even more menacing. Enzo and Jesse both noticed it during his short stay with them. A few weeks after his arrival in town, he found a room at a boarding house on Third Street near one of Judy's places and moved in there.

Neither Enzo nor Jesse said much when he moved. He had a brooding air about him that made the kids uneasy, so it was for the best that he lived elsewhere.

Vincenzo Santucci quickly noticed that brooding air and manner. Bruno met with him on a Monday afternoon at Santucci's Restaurant, where Vincenzo was conducting business. Jesse's father, Luca, brought Bruno there and made the introductions. Vincenzo wanted to meet the young man Vito had groomed to take over for him.

Of course, Vincenzo knew all about the turf war and everything that had happened in Calabria. News of the family business always traveled fast. It was Vincenzo who broke the news of Vito's death to Bruno. Bruno was not surprised.

Vincenzo decided that Bruno would run one of his newly acquired restaurants, The Roma Café, near the railroad tracks in the south end of town on Sixth Street. It was a small place but had bocce courts right next to it, and Vincenzo wanted to install gambling and runners there.

He figured the popularity of the bocce courts would be a good cover for runners coming and going. All they had to do was pretend to be at the courts to either play or watch the games and slip into the back room of the Café to turn in their daily receipts.

Running the Café would be a good test for Bruno because the south side of town was a bit rough, and Vincenzo thought he would fit right in there. Bruno would still be a collector, but the collections would come to him. He would only have to go out to collect if the person didn't go to the Roma Café.

One month after arriving in America, Bruno became the manager of The Roma Café and its staff of five employees. Filomena was the cook; Cassie, her assistant; sisters Caterina and Carmela, the two waitresses;

and Carlo, the dishwasher. All were females except for Carlo, the dishwasher. He was Vincenzo's wife's favorite nephew, who was not tough enough to enter the family business.

Bruno had never run a restaurant before, so he was a little apprehensive when Vincenzo gave him this assignment. He had promised himself, though, that he would do whatever Vincenzo asked of him and more. Bruno wanted to make himself indispensable to Vincenzo. He knew he had to work his way up, just like in the old country.

He soon realized the Roma Café pretty much ran itself as long as the assistant cook, Cassie, did what Filomena told her to do. If Cassie did that, then things ran smoothly. But she was lazy and liked to sit and chat with the customers instead of working, causing friction between herself and the other employees. Caterina and Carmela both resented her because she didn't do anything but flaunt her family connections.

Cassie complained to Vincenzo that Bruno was mean and nasty to her. She was Vincenzo's relative and thought it beneath her station to do actual work. Bruno found himself in the unenviable position as a manager, telling her she must do her job.

What Bruno wanted to do was to beat her and fire her lazy ass, but he didn't do either of those things. He found that the more time he spent at the Café and the more attention he gave her, the more uncomfortable she became until she finally quit.

He considered it a significant victory. He then hired a friend of Filomena's to fill the position. Her replacement, Elena, did the job well. After that, Bruno concentrated on opening up the back room of the café for illegal gambling.

Bruno was in Steubenville for almost a year before he felt himself starting to come back to life. He was the manager of a profitable Café and reunited with his older brother Enzo, and he was beginning to know a few people in town. Steubenville, Ohio, wasn't Calabria, but he felt at home here somehow.

Last week, he had to break up a couple of fights between gamblers in the back room of the Roma Café, and then he had to break up a fight between his cook and the waitresses. He had to be forceful and nasty with the people involved each time.

Each time he had to threaten someone with bodily harm, and each time his temples twitched, and his blood began to boil. He couldn't quite put his finger on when he felt like his old self, but it may have been either of those events.

Of course, the throbbing veins and itchy palms appeared when he beat up a drunk who was trying to leave the gambling room without paying his debt. Bruno followed the man out of the Café and beat him up in the alley before taking his money.

Bruno walked back into the Café with a smile on his face and a spring in his step. He was in the mood for some fun. He decided he'd visit Judy's place on Water Street later.

He had frequented Judy's a few times since he came to Steubenville, but tonight he felt different. The fight made him feel good. He felt alive when he walked into the house on Water Street.

"Ciao, Bruno. I haven't seen you in a while. How can I help you?" asked Judy.

"I need a woman," He answered.

"Who do you prefer?"

He walked through the salon, where the girls hung out waiting to entertain customers. A girl with creamy fair skin and red hair immediately caught his eyes. She wasn't as voluptuous as his Maria, but her skin tone and hair were close. Her name was Suzette, and he chose her.

He and Suzette retired to one of the rooms upstairs. He instantly grabbed her and shoved her down on the bed. She wasn't ready for his quick action and bumped her head on the headboard. She turned over and glared at him. She said she bruised easily, and if he wanted to be rough, it would cost extra.

He just laughed at her and shed his clothes. He told her to shut up as he shoved his cock towards her mouth. She took him into her mouth, closed her eyes, and started to pleasure him. She thought she heard him call her Maria.

He pushed her away a few minutes later and roughly ripped off her clothes. He ordered her onto her knees, and when she didn't comply fast enough, he smacked her hard across the face. He pushed her onto her knees and entered her from behind. She was a bit startled but didn't say so.

He called her Maria as he rode her, and she said her name was Suzette. At that point, he slapped her again a couple more times and said her name was Maria. Dazed by his rough treatment, Suzette let him continue until he was done. Afterward, Bruno said he hoped he hadn't been too rough on her, but that was just for her benefit because he didn't care.

He gave her a big tip. She took the money, and he said nothing as he left the room. She wasn't sure what to think about him. She didn't mind his roughness as long as she knew it was coming.

She also didn't mind him calling her Maria as long as he left her another big tip. She just had to make sure that Judy didn't find out about the tip, or she would take it. He became one of Suzette's most loyal customers.

He felt so good that he whistled all the way home. America wasn't so bad after all. He just needed to find the right outlets for his needs like he did tonight.

He enjoyed using his fists and beating other people; he was a fighter after all. That was when he felt the most alive.

Tomorrow was Nunzio's birthday, and Enzo and Jesse expected him for dinner. He would have to buy a present for his nephew in the morning. What does one get, he wondered, for a six-year-old boy?

Scary Time in Steubenville

It was 1934, and Angelo and Nina had been back in Steubenville for a couple of years. Their trip to Italy was a bittersweet memory. Theresa was growing up quickly, and Nina was still praying for another child.

Lena and Benny started a family, and Nina was thrilled to be the godmother to baby Rosemarie. Nina spent time in Weirton helping Lena once the baby was born.

Since the end of Prohibition, the previous December, Vincenzo Santucci was hard at work expanding his hold over Steubenville. Many bars opened back up, and his illegal activities began to boom again. Vincenzo's illicit activities weren't the only thing that worried the people of Steubenville.

The residents of Steubenville were all on edge because there was a murderer on the loose. Someone was attacking and killing men employed at the mill near Mingo Junction. Mingo Junction was a small village south of Steubenville.

The murders occurred at night and involved men who worked the midnight shift. The local newspaper had dubbed him the Phantom Killer. It was the talk of the town.

Nina was thankful Angelo worked across the river, in Weirton, and not Mingo. She was also grateful he didn't work the night shift. Like everyone else in town, she prayed the police would catch the killer soon before anyone else died.

Because she didn't want any harm to befall her daughter, Nina would not allow Theresa to run around the neighborhood like many other kids. Theresa, at ten years old, became quite used to entertaining herself.

She spent many lonely hours on the porch of the Seventh Street house playing with paper dolls while the neighborhood kids ran along the streets and alleys playing. At first, the kids asked her to play, but they didn't anymore because they knew she wasn't allowed.

Theresa was unhappy that she was an only child. She didn't understand why Mama didn't have any more babies. Maybe Mama wouldn't be scared to let her play with the neighbors if she had a sibling.

One of her favorite neighbors, Lillian Farchione, was only a couple of years younger, and they liked to play dolls and hopscotch together. Lillian had older sisters and an older brother who never had time to play with her, so she spent time at Theresa's house whenever she could. Nina would make little sandwiches and cookies and serve the girls on pretty China plates.

By the middle of summer, the killer had shot four men at the mill. Three had died, and the fourth man, paralyzed by the bullets that hit him. Morale among the employees at the mill was very low. Men were calling in sick, so they didn't have to report to work.

Facing low morale among the workforce, the mill offered a large reward for the arrest and conviction of the person responsible for the shootings. The police were working hard to solve the case.

A suspect was finally arrested and put in jail at the end of July. The man proclaimed his innocence, but the killings stopped. That Fall, he was found guilty of murder during a trial that garnered plenty of media attention.

The Phantom Killer was an Italian immigrant who worked at the Mingo plant and lived near Beatty Park. Everyone in Steubenville was glad the killer was brought to justice, and life went back to normal.

As the years passed, Theresa learned to ask her father first if there was something she truly wanted to do. She reasoned that if Papa said it was okay, then Mama would allow it.

When their neighbor, Jesse Pagano, asked if she could babysit, Nina's first instinct was to say no. In Nina's eyes, Theresa was still a child. However, Angelo had interceded and said that she could. He told Nina that Theresa was mature for her age and that babysitting the neighbors' children would be a good experience.

67

Since Angelo overruled Nina, Theresa babysat Nunzio and Rosemary Pagano on occasion. The children were well behaved, and Theresa enjoyed earning her own money.

At twelve, Theresa wanted to go to the city swimming pool with Yolanda, Dora, and Mary. All the local kids would be there, so she asked Papa if she could go. She was not a good swimmer, but, she reasoned, how would she ever learn if Mama never let her go. Zia Domenica had purchased a family pass for the summer and took the girls almost daily.

Angelo loved to swim and gave Theresa lessons the few times he had taken her to the lake. Mama didn't know how to swim and only got her feet wet along the shoreline when they had gone to the lake. Theresa was elated when Papa interceded on her behalf and forced Mama to let her go to the pool.

Her figure was blossoming, and she was turning into a beautiful young lady. She ran into her bedroom and put on her swimsuit before Mama could change her mind. Papa would bring her to Zia Domenica's house when she was ready. Zia Domenica was going to the pool with them. Her friend Lil would be there too with her siblings. It promised to be a perfect summer day.

Mama made most of their clothes and had made Theresa a pretty pastel coverup to wear over her blue swimsuit. Zia Mary, one of Mama's sisters, worked at a factory in Scranton and sent her bolts of fabric and boxes of sewing notions, no longer needed at the factory. Papa had purchased a used sewing machine for her, and Nina spent many hours sitting at the machine, making clothes for her daughter.

Papa was yawning as she entered the living room of their home on Seventh Street. She noticed that he seemed to be tired a lot lately. Theresa knew Mama was trying to get him to see a doctor, but he didn't want to go. She had heard their heated discussions more than once, but they always changed the subject whenever she entered the room.

Angelo had been working hard lately to earn extra money to buy the house where they lived. The elderly couple who owned it had never returned from the old country.

The husband passed away, and the wife decided to stay in Italy. She had no desire to come back to America. Living in America had been her husband's dream. She wrote and asked if Angelo and Nina wanted to purchase the house. They immediately said yes and were in the process of agreeing to terms.

Before they left the house, Mama gave her a thermos of fresh lemonade, a salami sandwich, and an apple in a paper bag. She gave Theresa some money to pay for her entrance to the pool and a treat at the pool's concession stand. Theresa was thrilled to be going. She promised to listen to Zia Domenica as they left the house.

Theresa and her cousins spread out a blanket at the pool, sat down, and excitedly talked about boys, their new favorite subject! Domenica sat on a chaise lounge, not too far away, reading the magazines she had brought. Soon the girls decided to go into the pool and were having a grand time when a couple of boys came over and started talking to them.

The boys asked if they would watch them dive into the pool's deep end, and the girls migrated to the deep end to watch. One of the boys kept smiling at Theresa and told her she was pretty. He was flirting with her!

Theresa's cheeks turned bright pink. Right at that moment, a girl shoved Theresa right off the side of the pool and into the deep water! "Quit flirting with my boyfriend!" shouted the girl.

Theresa had been taken entirely off guard and immediately panicked in the water. She felt like she was drowning. A lifeguard immediately jumped into the water to grab Theresa and pull her out. Embarrassed by the incident, Theresa wanted to go home. She hated to be the center of attention.

Domenica and the girls took her home immediately. Domenica relayed to Nina what happened at the pool. Nina was livid. Her precious daughter had almost drowned, and she had been unable to shield her from harm.

She argued with Angelo when he got home from work. They never argued much, and the incident had upset them both. That night in bed, they promised to always listen to each other with respect.

A Sick Husband

Nina had not gotten pregnant again, and frankly, she had given up hope. She knew deep down that Angelo was sad about it, but whenever she brought up the issue, he would say he was already the luckiest man in the world because he had her and Theresa.

She had recently undergone some testing with Dr. Barducci, and there was nothing physically wrong with her. Now she was determined Angelo should get tested when he was feeling better.

Nina was worried about him. He was tired all the time and had lost some weight. When she first mentioned it to him, he laughed and told her she imaged it.

When they came back to America, he had been able to get his job back in the mill. He was trying to work extra shifts to purchase the house on Seventh Street. But Angelo came home so exhausted he had begun to take naps in the evening instead of spending time with them.

When he did have energy in the evening, he spent his time with Theresa learning about America. A couple of months before, as an assignment in school, she had written a report on immigration and citizenship.

"Papa, why haven't you ever applied for citizenship? Don't you want to be an American?"

"Of course, I want to be an American citizen, just like you and your Mama, but I was always busy working to do anything about it. We'll go tomorrow and get the application. Will you help me study?"

"Of course, I will, Papa."

The next day, they picked up and completed his citizenship application. He promised his daughter he would become a citizen as they walked to the post office to mail the application. He loved his wife and daughter so much, and the small family they had become was his whole world.

Angelo knew Nina still occasionally cried when she did not fulfill her hopes of becoming pregnant again. He tried to reassure her he was happy. She seemed so fixated on having more children that sometimes he thought she didn't pay much attention to the child they did have.

Theresa was so much like him that sometimes she gave her mother a fit. She was a fun-loving, carefree child who only wanted to fit in with the other children around her. Nina, however, did not always let her play with them. She was so worried something would happen to Theresa that she was very strict with her.

Angelo was the buffer between them. When Nina told her no, Theresa often turned to her father to plead her case for going to the Saturday matinee at the theatre, going roller skating, or going to Islay's for an ice cream sundae on a hot summer day.

It wasn't that Nina didn't want her child to miss it, but her fear of some harm befalling her kept Nina from allowing Theresa to do many things most children took for granted.

Theresa found that she had a passion for baking, just like her mother. After the local swimming pool incident last summer, Theresa spent much of her time in the kitchen of their Seventh Street home learning to bake. It was a bonding experience for both mother and daughter, and they enjoyed it immensely.

Angelo was thrilled to see them bonding over something they both loved to do. He found himself sampling cream puffs, tiramisu, and his personal favorite, blueberry scones, on any given day. The women in his life loved to create desserts; it was a wonder he didn't weigh three hundred pounds! He was losing weight instead of gaining it.

He didn't have the heart to tell them everything seemed to have a metallic taste to him anymore. He always seemed weak and tired, more often than not, and he was having bouts of nausea. He was also having trouble sleeping and getting muscle cramps. He figured he had the stomach bug that many of the guys from the mill seemed to have recently.

Maybe he should relent and see a doctor after all. It would put Nina's mind at ease. It seemed that she was always worried about him. She had gone to Church with Domenica to sing at a funeral Mass. He would tell her to make an appointment with the doctor when she got home.

Domenica and Nina were walking home after the funeral Mass when Tony's friend Gino pulled up next to them in his taxi.

"What are you ladies doing out on the street today? You need to get in the taxi. The streets of Steubenville aren't safe right now."

The funeral Mass was for one of Vincenzo Santucci's men who had been shot to death by a rival faction, and Vincenzo was on the warpath to get revenge for the killing. Two other cars sped by as he told them this, and men in each vehicle fired shots.

The sound of screeching tires and rapid gunfire rang loudly in the ears of both women as they quickly jumped into the taxi. They screamed as the two cars crashed, and smoke was everywhere.

One car crashed into the pump of a nearby gas station and immediately burst into flames. The other car driver must have gotten shot as he hit a parked car near the church. Two men with guns stumbled out of the back seat and fled on foot.

The taxi sped away from the scene as Gino brought them safely home, but both women were shaken to their core. Nina told Angelo what had happened, and they spent the whole weekend indoors. Nina had never been around violence before, and it affected her greatly. She kept making sure that the doors were locked and didn't allow Theresa out of the house.

Theresa, who was supposed to go to a birthday party with Dora, was upset when her mother told her she was no longer allowed to go. When she pleaded her case to Angelo, he sided with Nina, so Theresa spent the weekend moping about the house.

When they went to bed, Angelo held Nina close and promised to keep her safe. He also told her that he would agree to see a doctor about his health.

After the shooting incident, Nina kept very close tabs on Theresa, only allowing her to go to Yolanda's or Lillian's house up the street. Nina trusted the Farchione family. Their family had come from Pescara, and she felt a kinship with them. She knew their family wasn't involved with the mafia in town.

By the summer of 1938, crime was getting worse in Steubenville, and the Taglieri family prayed that it didn't touch them. A group of twelve local preachers recently formed a vigilante committee to fight the city's vice and gambling.

Domenica and Tony were thinking about moving to another part of town, away from the Santucci family. On the one hand, the Santucci's had lots of security around their house, but on the other hand, Tony didn't want a stray bullet harming his family.

Angelo understood his dilemma. He wondered if they should move as well, but they had just recently completed their house purchase. They were now the proud owners of the red brick house on North Seventh Street. Angelo thought he could keep his family safe by staying out of the way of the Santucci family and their associates.

Benny and Lena told them they should move to Weirton, West Virginia, where they had purchased a small farm a few years before. They were quite happy living on the other side of the river. Benny had a large garden in the backyard where he loved to spend his time when he wasn't working, and Lena doted on their two small children, Rosemarie and Tony.

True to his word, Angelo went to the doctor. Nina wanted to go with him, but he told her no. Doctor John Brown was a tall, thin man with thick glasses and a receding hairline. His office was downtown in the First National Bank building, one of Steubenville's tallest buildings.

Angelo's appointment was on a Wednesday afternoon at four o'clock. He went straight there after his shift at the mill.

Doctor Brown and his nurses were very efficient and ran a battery of tests on Angelo. They told him to come back in a week for the test results. So, Angelo went straight to the doctor's office after work the following week.

He was in the outer room, waiting for the nurse to call his name. He hoped it wouldn't take long to get the results because he was pretty tired and wanted nothing more than to go home and take a nap.

He was just thinking about leaving the office and letting Nina call in the morning for the results when they finally called his name. Doctor

Brown said his kidneys were not working correctly, and it was essential to do more tests. It was not at all what Angelo expected to hear.

The nurse wanted to schedule more tests right away, but Angelo said he needed to check his work schedule to see when he would have time for more tests. He left the office promising to have Nina call the next day to schedule them.

But while walking home, Angelo decided that he was fine and wouldn't have Nina call to schedule anything. He would just take better care of himself.

Once he got home, that plan went out the window. Nina pestered him as soon as he opened the door. "What did the doctor say?" She asked. The look on her face told him that he would have to tell her the truth. He could never lie to his Nina.

"Cara Mia, Doctor Brown said there's something wrong with my kidneys, and he needs me to do more tests. His nurse will schedule them once I get my work schedule for next month."

"What kind of tests? What's wrong with your kidneys? Is it something that will get better with medication? I have so many questions." Nina instantly wanted to go to the public library to look up information about the kidneys.

"Nina, let's let the doctor do his job. I'm sure I will be fine once they figure out what's wrong with my kidneys. Let's keep this just between us; I don't want Theresa to know."

"But she knows that you haven't been feeling well, and she knows you finally went to the doctor," said Nina.

"Well, I'll talk to her about it," answered Angelo. He didn't need both women in his life worried about him. He would find the right words to tell his daughter in a calm voice and not interject any of Nina's fears.

Over the next few months, Angelo went back for more testing and grew even more tired. He finally confided in his boss at the mill about his situation. The boss conveniently asked him to do some office paperwork instead of the manual labor Angelo usually did.

At first, Angelo was offended but then was grateful that he didn't get laid off. The doctor's testing was expensive, and the medical bills piled up. Doctor Brown had called in a specialist on his case, and now he had even more testing to undergo.

Angelo just wanted to close his eyes and rest. As the months passed, his fatigue grew. Even when he slept, he didn't feel rested anymore. He didn't tell Nina, but he was getting pretty worried about his medical condition. What if he didn't get better? What if he died? What would happen to his wife and daughter? These thoughts now plagued him daily. He needed to talk to Tony.

He had Nina ask Domenica, Tony, and the girls, over for dinner one Sunday. After a nice dinner, while the girls were busy and the wives were cleaning up, he would share his concerns with Tony. Tony was like a brother. He could trust Tony.

Sunday finally arrived, and it took all of Angelo's energies to get out of bed and dressed for Mass. After Mass, the two families planned to go to their favorite park down by the river for a picnic. Nina took one look at Angelo and wanted to cancel their plans. She tried to take him to the hospital instead, but he was hearing none of it. So off to church they went. Luckily, St. Anthony's was only a few blocks away.

After Mass, instead of having a picnic on the river bank, Nina suggested going to their house. Seeing how weak her brother was, Domenica readily agreed and said the girls wanted to listen to Theresa's new record on her turntable. They all went to the house on Seventh Street.

Once there, Tony suggested retiring to the living room while the ladies set out the food. "Angelo, you need to level with me about what's going on with you."

"Tony, I have something called chronic nephritis. It's a kidney disease, and I'm afraid I'm dying. Doc Brown and the specialist say that my kidneys are not working properly and will soon shut down completely."

"They said the disease is too far gone. Nina doesn't know that part. She thinks Doc Brown and the specialist are working to cure me of the disease. I don't have the heart to tell her that's not the case, although I think she senses it."

"Tony, I need to ask you something important. When I'm gone, will you help Nina? She's pretty strong, but she will need help." Angelo held his breath as he waited for an answer.

Tony shook his head in disbelief. "Angelo, stop. You aren't going to die. You just have a disease that the doctors need to treat. You'll be fine."

Angelo sighed, "No, Tony. I'm not going to be fine. I have six months to a year, according to the specialist. I need to get my affairs in order. I need to know that you'll watch over Nina and Theresa."

"They are the most precious things in the world to me. I'll never grow old with my sweet Nina or watch Theresa fall in love and get married. I'll never get to see my grandchildren. These are just facts that I must face."

"I have a small life insurance policy that should help, but there are mounting medical bills. Maybe Nina can take in boarders, and their rent will help her get by. Hopefully, she won't have to get a job unless she wants to. I wish I had more saved for her, but we used it to buy the house. How she loves this house!"

"Please, tell me that you and Domenica will help her out."

"Angelo, please don't talk like that. We're going to see our daughters marry into good Italian families and have kids that we can spoil. We're going to make and drink wine and eat lots of pasta in our old age. You and I are going to be Tatones together."

"Tony, please, just answer me. Will you take care of my wife and daughter? I need to know they will be fine after I'm gone."

"Of course, Angelo. I will help Nina and Theresa always, I promise."

"Thank you, Tony. I know they will be in good hands. That makes all of this more bearable."

"Angelo, come, let's go have a glass of wine. It's good for the body," and the two men drank a glass of their favorite wine. Angelo could no longer enjoy the taste but drank it anyway.

That night as he tried to rest, Angelo felt as if someone had lifted a weight from him. He knew that Tony and Domenica would help his wife and daughter when he was gone. They would not be alone; Tony would help and protect them. That thought helped.

The holidays came, and Angelo cherished every minute he could with his wife and daughter. Deep down, they all knew it would be their last as a family. On Christmas Day, Angelo didn't have the energy to go to Mass. He sat by the small pine tree that Nina and Theresa had gotten from the gas station lot next door to their house. The owner delivered it and put it up in the stand for them.

He worked as best as possible and went home to rest on the days when nausea got too bad. Doctor Brown told him to live life as best as he could. He said Angelo would know when it was time to go to the hospital.

Life in America

L ife in America for Bruno was eventful. Vincenzo gave him more and more responsibilities within a few short years as he proved his loyalty to the Santucci family. In those years, he became one of Vincenzo's most trusted henchmen, killing and disposing of anyone Vincenzo deemed an enemy. He didn't mind getting his hands dirty.

Not only did he run the Café, but he now also ran a bar called The Westwood Tavern. It was directly across the street from the Café and had an apartment upstairs. Bruno moved into the apartment. He finally had a place of his own in America.

Enzo and Jesse frequented the Café with their three kids, but Jesse would not let the youngsters enter the Tavern. Jesse never stepped foot in it. Enzo, though stopped by the Tavern frequently to talk to his brother about business.

Enzo seemed a bit jealous of Bruno's carefree lifestyle. Bruno could do whatever he wanted; Enzo had a wife and kids to look after. Enzo had family obligations.

The truth of the matter was Bruno was jealous of Enzo. He had a wife and family, but his enemies viciously took them from him. The death of Maria and his child left him cold and cruel.

Now, among the mob in Steubenville and the surrounding area, his ruthless reputation was beginning to grow. He often used his fists to coerce someone to pay their proper debts or see things his way.

This reputation for cruelty led him to be arrested by the city cops recently. The cops tried to get him to spill the beans about Vincenzo Santucci, but Bruno wouldn't.

The police charged him with the illegal sale of alcohol on a Sunday. He went before one of the local judges in Santucci's pocket and ended up with a warning and a three hundred dollar fine. That was peanuts to him.

Another time, he beat up a bootlegger from Kentucky. The bootlegger had tried to increase the price of whiskey Bruno had ordered for the Tavern. Bruno beat him so brutally that he died from internal injuries on his way back downriver.

At Judy's place, he was no longer allowed to ask for Suzette. A few months before, he beat Suzette so severely when he was in a dark mood that she had to be taken to the hospital with two black eyes and a broken rib.

Vincenzo heard about this and was not pleased. Judy and Vincenzo made Bruno pay for Suzette's hospital expenses and a vacation to the coast as part of her recovery. He paid those expenses and promised Judy never to hurt another one of her girls. Most of them were afraid of him, anyway.

Enzo and Luca told him he should settle down, but he didn't. Vincenzo was growing weary of Bruno's bad habits.

Bruno also had the habit of picking up whores off the streets. He would bring them up to his apartment through the bar's back entrance, give them liquor, and then take advantage of them in his apartment. Sometimes Bruno beat them as well as just used them for sex. Then, Rocco Bricola, his head bartender, would dump the girl somewhere in West Virginia, right across the river from Steubenville.

One of those whores fought back as Bruno tried to attack her. She cut Bruno with glass from a broken whiskey bottle. The whore slashed at his nose, kicked him in the groin and ran out of the apartment. Half-naked, she ran through the bar and out the front door before anyone could stop her.

Bruno had blood all over his face and couldn't chase her in front of his customers. She ran to the nearby railroad tracks and hopped on a train going by at the time. No one in town saw her ever again.

Rocco took him to the hospital, where he received four stitches. He never returned to get the stitches out but had Enzo remove them. He refused to tell the hospital staff what had happened.

Bruno turned to alcohol when he missed Maria. He lost control of himself when he drank and usually fought with other patrons. He was frequently involved in fights either at the Tavern or any of Vincenzo's other places in town. Vincenzo regularly smoothed things over because Bruno was one of his best henchmen and had married his cousin's daughter.

One Saturday night, Bruno drank at the Globe Café on Market Street. He insulted the waitress because she refused to serve him more alcohol; he was already drunk. He got very loud and obnoxious, and the bouncer told him to leave. At that point, he became belligerent and yelled at the waitress again, calling her a whore. The bouncer threw him out.

He started towards home but was intercepted by the waitresses' husband and a friend. They had been sitting at the bar and heard his insults. They dragged him into an alley and beat him up, slashing him with a razor.

The police found him bloody and half-unconscious in the alley. They took him to the hospital, where he received six stitches to close a couple of gashes on his face and side. He also had a broken nose. The police questioned him at length, but he refused to tell them why or with whom he fought.

By early 1939, Bruno was well known by the police and judges in Steubenville and the liquor control department in town. Again, Luca told Enzo that Vincenzo was tired of smoothing things over for Bruno.

Either Bruno settled himself down, or Vincenzo would be forced to do something drastic. Luca said Vincenzo had talked to Bruno, but Bruno was not heeding Vincenzo's warning.

Enzo knew what that meant. If Bruno did not settle down, Vincenzo would whack him. Enzo knew that he needed to do something. He immediately talked to Jesse about it. Jesse thought they needed to find a wife for Bruno, someone like Maria, who would soften his hard edges. Enzo agreed.

The problem was, who could they get to marry him? Most of their friends were married and had children.

The Hospital

Angelo had severe bouts of nausea and vomiting daily by the Spring of 1939. Now his legs and feet were swollen most of the time. He could no longer go to work, so he took medical leave.

He tried to ignore the pain and discomfort as he willed his body to keep functioning. He was determined to live to see his daughter's fifteenth birthday in July. Angelo marveled at what a beautiful and sensitive young woman she was becoming.

Theresa had asked to have a small party with her cousins and a couple of friends from the neighborhood. Nina had told her no, but Angelo had told his daughter she could have the party. He wanted to cherish what little time he had left with them. So together, they made plans for her special day.

By June, though, Nina had to take him to the hospital. He was in horrible shape. The doctors were not surprised to see them. They admitted him immediately and gave him some pain medication to make him comfortable. As Nina looked at her husband, she could no longer hold back her tears. She would not leave her husband's bedside.

The medication took away some of the pain but also made him sleepy. Nina sat by his bed and stared at his chest, making sure it moved up and down, making sure Angelo was still breathing.

For the past three months, she had begged him to go to the hospital, but he was adamant in his refusal. She had gone to the library by herself after his diagnosis and read everything she could about his disease. She knew his prognosis was not good.

Nina canceled Theresa's planned birthday party; she had enough to deal with already with Angelo's illness. Theresa didn't mind that much; she worried about her parents. Theresa didn't realize how severe her father's sickness was; he always hid it from her. She also had never seen her mother look so lost and helpless.

Theresa sat in the corner of her father's hospital room and prayed. She was so quiet that Nina and the hospital staff forgot she was there. Seeing her father in the hospital bed brought back vague memories of her Tatone in Italy.

She heard the grim news of her father's condition from the doctors and nurses who came into the room. As reality set in, Theresa realized her father was dying, and soon she and her mother would be alone in the world. She knew her mother would need her to be strong.

For several weeks, their lives took place within the sterile walls of Angelo's hospital room. Tony and Domenica came by as much as possible. They tried to get Nina to leave, but she would not. The hospital staff brought an oversized leather chair for her to sleep in because she would not leave Angelo's side.

In contrast, Nina forced Theresa to go home with Tony and Domenica. She did not want her daughter to witness Angelo's suffering. Theresa did not want to leave but only left because her father told her she must. Angelo tried to get Nina to go too but was met with a steely resolve in Nina he didn't know she had.

They spent his waking hours talking about the past, and Nina changed the subject whenever Angelo tried to talk about his death and his family's life without him. Nina did not want to even think about it. The hospital staff sent a social worker to talk to them, but Nina shooed him out of the room.

Theresa's fifteenth birthday was a beautiful sunny day full of promise. She spent the day at her father's bedside, listening to the machines beep as they monitored his vital signs. He woke up as soon as she walked into the room. His smile was so full of love Theresa and Nina forgot he was sick for a moment.

"Happy Birthday, my sweet girl. I have a special gift for you." He told her to open the drawer of his hospital nightstand. Inside was a small black box.

Her hands shook as she lifted the box out of the drawer. It was a jewelry box. Papa had given her jewelry before, but he had been sick for so long she wondered how he found the time to purchase a gift for her.

"My love, inside that box, is something very special to me, and I want you to have it."

Theresa opened the box and found Papa's wedding ring inside. She looked at it quizzically; she didn't understand. "Papa, I don't understand. Why are you giving me your wedding ring?"

"Cara Mia, it's a symbol of the love your mother and I share. I'm giving it to you, so you will know how much I love you. I won't be of this world much longer, and for that, I'm very sorry. But I want you always to remember your Papa loves you very much."

"Oh Papa, I love you too, and I will never forget how much you love me," she said through her tears.

Angelo spent the day talking about how much he loved his family and about how much he would miss them when he was gone. He apologized to Theresa for not becoming an American citizen. He probably never would. Theresa told him she loved him and that it didn't matter.

Nina realized that day he was living on borrowed time. She had some things she had to do. She told the nurses she had an appointment early the following day and wouldn't be at the hospital until the next afternoon.

The next day, she sent Theresa to the hospital and promised to be there in the afternoon. After Theresa left, Nina sat at the kitchen table by herself with a hot cup of coffee. She wrote a letter to her mother-in-law telling her about Angelo's disease. She knew that Angelo would probably die before his mother got the letter, but it was proper.

Then, she called her parents and gave them an update on his health. They were shocked and promised to pray for Angelo. They told Nina they would travel to Steubenville if she needed them. She assured them there was nothing anyone could do but pray.

Next, she sat and looked over their finances and bills. Angelo had always taken care of those things, and Nina had no clue how to decipher any of them. She knew they still owed money on the house. She also knew there were a lot of mounting medical bills.

She made a list of questions to ask Angelo. She hoped to get them answered without him realizing what she was doing. She could also ask Tony for help, but she wished to do things herself.

She looked around her home on Seventh Street and cried while thinking about all the memories the house held. After a while, she washed her face, changed her wrinkled dress, then called a taxi to take her to the hospital.

A week later, the doctors had to increase Angelo's pain medication. It made him unsteady for long periods and kept him sleepy. All Nina and Theresa could do was sit by his bedside and pray.

Their parish priest, Father Paul, came by and prayed with him. He told Nina she could call him no matter the day or night if she needed anything. Father Paul would miss one of his favorite parishioners. Angelo was always the first to volunteer his help with church projects.

Several hours after the priest left, Angelo took his last breath. Nina and Theresa were at his bedside. Mother and daughter clung to one another as they cried for the man they loved. The nurses gave them their privacy to say goodbye.

A Loving Goodbye

Mama, we need to go now," said Theresa. The nurses had given them an hour to themselves with Papa. "The nurses want to come in and take care of Papa now. We need to go and talk to Father Paul. He'll help us."

Nina didn't budge. She sat on the side of the bed, just holding Angelo's hand. It was turning cold. His hands were never cold. She was the one who always had cold hands, and Angelo always warmed them.

Theresa grabbed her mother's hands now. She was talking, but to Nina, her daughter's voice seemed so far away instead of right next to her. Nina didn't want to move. She didn't want to leave; Angelo needed her.

"Mama? Mama, can you hear me? The nurse is talking to you."

"Mrs. Taglieri, I need you to sign some papers for me," said a nurse in white. "Please come to the nurse's station with me to sign them." Nina didn't know how long she had been in the room.

"No. I can't leave Angelo. He needs me."

"Dr. Brown is here and will take care of Angelo for you," answered the nurse. And as she said that, he entered the room.

"Nina, it's okay. I'm here now. I'll take good care of Angelo for you. You and Theresa need to go home and get some rest. You have a couple of long days ahead. Would you like me to call anyone for you? Do you have a way home?" Dr. Brown held her in a quick embrace.

Nina realized everyone was looking at her. She never liked to be the center of attention. "Thanks, but you don't need to call anyone. Theresa and I are fine. We need to go. We have to see Father Paul at St. Anthony's. Thanks, Dr. Brown, for taking such good care of Angelo. Theresa and I are most appreciative."

Nina kissed her husband one last time as she brushed away the tears that threatened to fall. "Come, Theresa, we need to go now."

Theresa touched her father's hair and moved her hand to his cheek. She loved her father with all her heart, and now it was broken. She didn't want to leave him either but knew that she must. Theresa leaned over one last time and whispered in his ear, then kissed her Papa goodbye.

They left Angelo's room and took the hospital elevator to the first floor. As they departed the elevator into the lobby, they collided with a man in a dark suit and hat. He was not watching where he was going even though he seemed to be in a big hurry. Nina almost said something to him, but the look on his face was intimidating.

"I'm so sorry, sir, we weren't watching where we were going. My Papa just died, and we need to go to St. Anthony's Church." Theresa managed to say. Theresa, who was like her father in so many ways, apologized to the man as she picked up his hat for him. It had fallen off his head during the collision.

He looked as if he would bite her head off when he realized they both had tears streaming down their faces. Something about them looked off, and he felt charitable, even in his current circumstance.

As he took his hat from her hand, he recognized the look of grief on each of their faces. He knew exactly how they felt. Her words filtered through his brain.

"Allow me to apologize," he answered. "My name is Bruno Pagano, and I'm sorry for your loss. Please, allow me to drive you to the church; it's on my way home."

Surprisingly, Nina let the stranger drive her and Theresa to St. Anthony's. On the way, he told her he was looking for a new cook for his restaurant, the Roma Café.

Nina thanked him for his kindness and got out of the car. All she could think about was that her life as she knew it was over.

After evening prayers, Father Paul left the church and saw Nina and Theresa getting out of a car. He knew before he even reached them that Angelo had died. His heart went out to them as he gathered them into his arms. Grief consumed them.

"Nina, I just said a rosary for Angelo. He's at peace now and no longer in pain. Come into the rectory with me."

The three went into the church rectory, where the housekeeper made tea. Father Paul called the Stellano's to tell them the news since Nina was too shaken up. Tony said he'd come at once to get them, and Domenica would go directly to the house.

While they waited for Tony to arrive, they discussed the details of Angelo's funeral. Nina was surprised to find out he had already discussed his wishes with Father Paul. She was also surprised to find out he had purchased a cemetery plot. Angelo had taken care even in death, so Nina would not have to worry about such things.

As they were finishing their tea, Tony came into the rectory. He gathered Nina and Theresa into an embrace. "I'm so sorry about Angelo. Please know I will take care of you both. He was like a brother to me, and I loved him very much."

The three of them cried together, then Nina wiped away her tears. She wasn't sure about what lay ahead for them, but she knew she would never know the same type of love that Angelo had shown her for the past sixteen years. She had to be strong for Theresa.

She hoped someday her daughter would find that same type of love. "Let's go home. We have much to do before the funeral."

Tony drove them home to Seventh Street, where several neighbors had already heard the news and delivered food to the house. It seemed that all the neighbors on Seventh Street had loved Angelo, and they all had kind words, as well as expressions of sympathy, for Nina and Theresa. Nina hugged and thanked them all.

Domenica was at the house and heartbroken. She didn't want Nina and Theresa to be alone. She loved her brother deeply and felt like she had lost a part of herself as well. She told Nina she would stay with them for a few days.

Over the next several days, there was a wake and a funeral for Angelo. Members of her family came to town to show their love and support. Nina felt as if she was on autopilot. She said and did what was expected but felt like she was in a dream or watching a movie.

Many former coworkers of Angelo's from the mill attended services to pay their respects. Everyone had a story of how Angelo had touched their lives positively. Nina had no idea who half of them were but thanked each of them for their kindness.

Domenica and Tony never left her and Theresa's side, and Father Paul stopped by several times to check on them.

Nina and Theresa clung to each other for support and strength at the funeral. It was a perfect sunny day. The pews of St. Anthony's Church were full as Father Paul spoke eloquently about Angelo. It was a beautiful send-off for a lovely man.

Chance Encounter

I n the summer of 1939, Bruno's cook, Filomena, had a heart attack and was in the hospital. Elena, the assistant cook, stepped in and took over the kitchen. Bruno was thankful until he ate some of the food she had prepared. It was terrible! Bruno needed to find a new cook and fast.

He decided to stop by the hospital and ask the cook for her recommendation. Hopefully, she knew someone who could fill in until she was better. Filomena was gravely ill, and her family didn't expect her to make it out of the hospital.

Great, he thought. The cook was no help, and her family had all but thrown him out of the hospital room. He'd make them pay for the way they treated him. His temples began to twitch.

He was in a foul mood as he exited the elevator and collided with a petite woman and a young girl. He was about to bite their heads off until he noticed they were both in tears. The girl apologized and said her father had just passed away, and they were going to St. Anthony's Church.

"I'm so sorry for your loss. My name is Bruno Pagano, and I'd like to help you. Please let me drive you to the church; it's on my way home." Surprisingly, Bruno had instant compassion towards this mother and daughter.

On the way there, he learned the mother's name was Nina Taglieri, and the girl, Theresa. Nina's husband had just passed away from kidney disease.

He told them his cook had a heart attack, and he needed to find a new one for his restaurant, the Roma Café. He asked the woman if she knew anyone looking for a job. She just shook her head. He dropped them off at the rectory, and she thanked him for the ride.

Later, he decided to visit Enzo and Jesse to see if they had any ideas about who he could hire. As he parked on Seventh Street near their house, he noticed several cars parked along the street. Many people were going into a place right down the road with food. What was going on?

Rosemary opened the door for him and promptly vanished from the room. He wondered why she always disappeared when he was there. Jesse came into the living room and greeted him. She seemed out of sorts. "What's going on? Why was it so hard to find a spot to park?" he asked.

"Our neighbor Angelo passed away today. Many people from the church have been stopping by the house to pay their respects and deliver food. I was just finishing a pan of lasagna to bring over to Nina. What can I do for you? Enzo isn't home yet. Did you need him?"

"Did you say your neighbor's name is Nina? Did Angelo die of kidney disease? Do they have a daughter named Theresa?"

"Yes, Nina and Angelo Taglieri live down the street with their daughter, Theresa. They are lovely people. Theresa sometimes watches the kids for us. Why do you ask?"

"Because I met them earlier today as I was leaving the hospital. Filomena had a heart attack, and I was there to see when she'd be back to work. Her family all but threw me out of the room."

"Nina and her daughter collided with me as I got off the elevator. I drove them to St. Anthony's. I wonder if she would like to work for me temporarily."

"Well, right now, she's in mourning and can't think about anything. Although she is an excellent cook and baker."

Just then, Enzo came through the door and was surprised to see his brother. "Ciao, Bruno! To what do we owe this honor? Why don't you join us for dinner? How about some vino?"

"That sounds good, Enzo. I could use a good homecooked meal." The brothers retired to the backyard with a glass of wine. It felt good to be together. Jesse told Rosemary to set another place for her Zio Bruno at the dining room table.

Enzo and Bruno made small talk during dinner while the children were at the table. Jesse said she received a letter recently from Father Guido, their brother. Guido wrote that he was beginning to get headaches like their mother. He planned to see a doctor about them. The brothers hoped Guido would be fine.

As soon as dinner was over, the children disappeared, and the men had a cigar and several glasses of wine in the living room. They were both feeling no pain.

Enzo told Bruno that he was worried about him. He knew that Vincenzo was growing tired of the trouble that always followed Bruno.

"Bruno, you need to find a wife, someone who will be there for you and love and support you. I know you were heartbroken when you lost Maria and the baby, but you need to move on. Maria would want you to be happy."

"Enzo, I'll never be able to replace Maria. She knew the true me and still loved me. I'll never find anyone like her again. Besides, I need to find a cook first and foremost."

"If I don't have a good cook for the restaurant, then I won't have any customers. If I don't have customers, then my restaurant closes. The restaurant is the cover for the gambling rooms; you know that. Vincenzo will not be pleased if my gambling rooms don't make money for him. I'm already in hot water with him for the way I treated Suzette."

"I understand all that, brother; I was talking about you. Everyone needs someone."

"I disagree, Enzo. I need to go. Please tell Jesse I said thanks for dinner. Too bad she can't come work for me as my cook."

As he left his brother's house, Bruno noticed many people were still down the street at Nina's. He would give her a couple of weeks and then talk to her about the job. He somehow felt a kinship with her, and he couldn't understand why. Maybe it was because they had both lost a spouse.

Life Without Angelo

Two weeks after Angelo's funeral, Nina sat alone at the kitchen table. She stared at the stack of bills on the table that she needed to pay. The bills were simply not going to disappear because she couldn't pay them. Nina knew she must do something to earn some money.

Tony had stopped by yesterday and asked how she and Theresa were doing. She told him, okay, but that wasn't the truth. They were existing and going through their daily routines as expected. But, in reality, they felt numb; they missed Angelo immensely.

Luckily, it was still summer break from school, and Theresa spent her days moping about the house and listening to music on her turntable. In other words, she was a typical teen.

When Tony asked about the bills and finances, Nina lost. Tony told her he had a plan that may help them both. He asked Nina how she would feel if he and his family moved in with them.

They desperately wanted to move away from the Santucci estate on Eighth Street. Tony said it would be a bit crowded, but he could pay the household bills and mortgage for Nina if they moved in together.

Nina said she would think about it and talk to Theresa. She said she'd let him know soon.

As she sat at her kitchen table with a cup of coffee and a stack of bills, she prayed to Angelo for guidance. Having them move in would give her some support, and the money they paid in rent would help her pay off the medical bills. She thought it would be a viable solution to her current problem, and Theresa would be happy to have her cousins around.

She could give Tony and Domenica her bedroom. She hadn't been able to sleep there since Angelo passed. She could move into the small bedroom, and Theresa could share the other large bedroom with her three cousins.

With them paying rent, maybe she could manage the medical bills. Theresa was excited about the prospect. She loved her cousins, and it would be good for her and Nina to have others around. The Stellano family moved in with them a week later.

A month after Angelo's passing, Bruno Pagano called on Nina to offer her a job as a cook at his restaurant, The Roma Café. Nina found out he was the brother of Enzo Pagano and his wife Jesse, one of her neighbors on Seventh Street. Theresa occasionally was called to watch their three children. They were from Calabria and seemed nice.

Nina politely declined but thanked him for the offer. She currently had to deal with too many things. Bruno told her he understood. "If you change your mind, just let Jesse or Enzo know. They know where to find me."

Tony was coming home from work as Bruno was leaving the house. The two men were civil to each other, but that was all.

Tony went directly inside. "Why was that man here? What did he want? I've heard about him. He's bad news."

"He offered me a job as a cook at his restaurant. I declined the offer. I've never had a job before and don't have any skills," answered Nina.

"Well, I think you should stay far away from him. I think he's connected to the Santucci family; I've seen him going to Vincenzo Santucci's house before."

"Well, since I turned down the offer, I don't think we'll see him again."

"I certainly hope you're right."

As the heat of the summer began to fade, they all adjusted to life on Seventh Street. Domenica and Nina took turns cooking, and Tony helped Nina sort out all the bills. The girls were happy being together, and Theresa felt like she had siblings for the first time.

One morning, as Theresa and Yolanda walked home from the grocery store, they discussed the future. Yolanda had just enrolled in the local beauty college to become a beautician. She and Theresa had talked about it for hours on end. Theresa wanted to register as well. They both loved hanging out at La Rosella's Beauty Salon.

"Theresa, you aren't old enough to enroll; you're not sixteen yet," said Yolanda.

"If I quit school and go there now, I'll be able to help my mother pay off Papa's medical bills."

"Zia Nina will never go for that. She'll tell you to stay in school."

"The bill collectors are starting to hound us, and we don't have the money. If I quit school, I can get a part-time job sweeping the floor and laundering the dirty towels for Miss Rosella. I've already spoken to her. She said she would hire me."

"It sounds like you have a plan already in place. Have you talked to your mom yet?"

"I'm going to talk to her this evening, right after we get back from Zia Lena's. We're going there for dinner."

"Well, good luck. Zia Nina has always been pretty strict. I can't imagine her letting you quit school."

Later that day, Nina and Theresa took the bus from Steubenville to Lena and Benny's house in Weirton. Lena had invited them for dinner. They made small talk on the way over.

Theresa could tell that the stack of bills they still owed preoccupied her mother's mind. She knew her mother spent many nights staring at those bills and crunching numbers at the kitchen table.

Lena and Benny lived with their two children in a farmhouse overlooking the steel mill on top of the hill. Benny still worked at the mill and tended his prolific vegetable garden in his spare time.

"Nina, the men still talk about Angelo and how much they miss him at the mill. I walk into the office and expect to see him, only to remember he's gone."

"Yes, Benny. I still wake up in the morning and expect to see him next to me in bed. It's still so hard to believe he's gone; I miss his soothing voice."

"Oh, Nina," said Lena, "we miss him too. We know he left you with a lot of medical bills, and we wish we could help you out, but we don't have much ourselves."

"It's okay, Lena. Tony and Domenica are helping as much as possible, and I received a job offer recently. I'm thinking about accepting it."

"Who offered you a job? What type of job is it?" asked Lena.

"It's a position as a cook at a restaurant. You know how I enjoy cooking. I'm thinking about accepting the job."

As they were on the bus back to Steubenville, Theresa asked her mother about the job offer. "Mama, I didn't know you were considering that man's offer."

"Well, I wasn't until I saw the look of concern in Benny and Lena's eyes. I don't want anyone to worry about us. I do like cooking, but I've never gotten paid before to do it."

"Tony said I should have nothing to do with Bruno Pagano, but Enzo and Jesse seem nice. You've been to their house before, Theresa. What do you think of them?"

"They seem nice, Mama. Jesse is a good mom, and Enzo has some type of office job. The kids are well-behaved. They never mention their Zio Bruno, though, so I don't know about him."

"Mama, I need to ask you something important. I want your permission to quit school to enroll in a cosmetology school like Yolanda. It's what I truly want to do."

"I've talked to Gina Rosella at La Rosella's Salon on Market Street. She'll hire me to help out at her shop part-time. I'll be able to learn so much while working there. It will help me with beauty school. Please, Mama, the money I make there can help with household expenses or help pay Papa's medical bills. I know we still have a lot of bills. I want to help."

"Theresa, I don't know what to say. School is important, and you need to finish it. It's what your father would want."

"But Mama, if we both get jobs, then we can pay off the bills, and the bill collectors will stop hounding you. We'll be able to honor Papa by paying his debts and make our way in the world.'"

"Cara mia, let me think about it for a few days. When do the classes start, and how much does it cost?"

"Oh Mama, classes start next week. If you let me do this, Miss Rosella will let me start at the salon as soon as possible. She said she'd work with me on the cost. She said Papa once helped her complete some renovations at the shop for free. Please, Mama, I truly want to do this."

"I know who she is, Tre. Let me sleep on it. I'll give you my answer tomorrow."

That night as Nina lay in her bed, she thought about how she had once begged her father to let her get a job. Maybe now was the time to get a job and make her way in the world. She had a daughter to think about and support.

They could pay the bills and keep their house if they both got jobs. She prayed she was making the right decision.

Tomorrow she would go to the Roma Café on South Sixth Street and see Mr. Pagano about a job. She would also let her daughter go to beauty school. Tomorrow would be a day of new beginnings.

Part Two

New Beginnings

The sun rose early the next day. Nina felt strangely renewed as she got out of bed. She was an unemployed widow with a teenage daughter, a broken heart, a large house, and a mountain of debt, but she was a woman with a purpose.

She showered and dressed before anyone else arose and made breakfast. Domenica came into the kitchen as Nina pulled fresh blueberry scones out of the oven. They smelled heavenly.

"Nina, those smell delicious! They look like they came from the Steubenville Bakery. What's the special occasion?"

"Well, it's a day for new beginnings. Theresa will enroll in beauty school, and I hope to get a job. I will see Bruno Pagano this morning and ask if that cook position is still available. I'm taking him a batch of fresh scones. They were Angelo's favorite."

"Oh my, these are delicious," exclaimed Domenica. "Angelo said you were a good baker, but these are incredible!"

"Thanks, Domenica. I hope Mr. Pagano is impressed. I do need that job. I have a mountain of bills to pay off, and Theresa needs money for school. I have to work to make ends meet. You and Tony have been a great help, but it's not enough."

"Oh, Nina, I'm sorry to hear that. If we had more to give you, we would. I hope you get that job if it's what you want. I can do all the housework, cooking, and laundry here. That way, you don't have to worry about those things."

"Thanks, I appreciate that. I don't know how Theresa and I would have made it through the past couple of months without you and Tony. I truly love you like a sister."

"I feel the same way. I felt it the first time I laid eyes on you, and you picked up Yolanda with such love on your face. I may have lost my only brother, but I gained a dear sister."

Tony entered the kitchen and wanted to know who had gone to the bakery for fresh scones. Nina told him she had made them, and she planned to go to the Roma Café to see if the cook position was still available.

Tony was not happy when she said this. He was starting to voice his misgivings when the girls entered the kitchen.

"Mama, have you made your decision yet? May I enroll in beauty school," asked Theresa?

Theresa wanted to know if Nina had made a decision. Nina gave her permission to quit school and follow her dream. It was one of the happiest days of Theresa's young life.

She and Yolanda ran back to the bedroom to get dressed. They had to go and see Miss Rosella. Nina was going with them to make sure everything would work out. She wanted to see the place where Theresa would work. It was not too far from the Café she hoped to find work.

Before Tony could talk her out of her decision, she left the house with Theresa and Yolanda. She was determined to get a job today.

La Rosella's Salon was on Market Street near the center of downtown. Nina had never been there to have her hair done, but she knew the Rosella family from church. Julio and Jeannie Rosella ran the beauty school, and their daughter Gina ran the salon.

Gina was a few years younger than Nina, with short curly brown hair and blue eyes. She dressed like she had just stepped out of the pages of a magazine, always wearing the latest fashions and with perfect hair and nails. She made Nina feel frumpy.

Nina was a bit apprehensive about walking into the salon and school. She knew that Gina had flirted with Angelo many years ago, even though she knew he was married. Julio had been Angelo's barber.

Gina was unlocking the doors to the salon and saw Nina and the girls as they rounded the corner. She felt bad now that she had flirted with Angelo when he completed some renovations for her father, even though she knew he was married. He was so handsome, and besides, she wasn't the only female who flirted with him. His daughter resembled him.

"Ciao, ladies. You're out and about early today. What can I do for you?" She said as they entered the salon.

Simultaneously Yolanda and Theresa both started talking until Nina held up her hand and told them to give her a private moment with Miss Rosella. The girls instantly sat and started looking through the stacks of fashion magazines everywhere in the salon's waiting area.

"Mrs. Taglieri, I'm so sorry to hear about your husband's passing. I'm sorry about everything else as well, you know, the flirting. What can I say? I was young and foolish; I hope you know that nothing ever happened."

"Gina, thanks for your kind words. Please, call me Nina. I know nothing ever happened. Even though our marriage was arranged, Angelo and I loved each other, and I'll cherish those memories for the rest of my life."

"I came to talk to you about Theresa enrolling in beauty school and working here part-time. How old does she have to be to enroll? Will her work hours be flexible enough for her to study when needed? Will she get paid for her work?"

"Nina, I know that Theresa isn't quite old enough to enroll, but I'm willing to bend the rules for her. She and Yolanda have often stopped by to watch the beautician's work. She has a natural flair for doing hair."

"Her work hours will be flexible so she can attend classes. We take a hands-on approach to learning. Working here will give her lots of experience that the other students won't get. Of course, she will earn a fair wage, plus any tips from the customers. It's an excellent opportunity for her. Will you let her enroll?"

"Yes, it's what she wants to do, and I believe in her. Thank you for giving her this opportunity, Gina. Is there anything I need to sign?"

"No, just have her come in tomorrow morning at eight o'clock sharp. I'll give her a smock to wear over her clothes so they don't get ruined."

Nina left the salon to walk a couple of blocks to the Roma Café, and the girls stayed to watch Gina give a perm to her first customer of the day.

As she got closer to the restaurant, Nina felt a bit nervous. She had never before applied for a job. She had not even called Mr. Pagano to ensure he would be there or even inquire if the job was still available.

The Roma Café, on south Sixth Street, occupied the ground floor of the large square building on the corner. The other three floors of the building housed apartments.

A brightly painted ornate sign hung over the restaurant doorway. Large glass windows on either side of the entrance showcased the round tables and booths inside. There was also a long bar against one wall with several stools underneath it.

A couple of fenced-in bocce courts were sandwiched between the restaurant and some railroad tracks. Directly across the street from the restaurant was a tavern.

A bell jingled as the restaurant door opened. Nina was surveying the area and didn't realize that someone was watching her.

"Good morning. If you are here to eat, we aren't open yet," said a thin young man with a dirty white apron tied around his waist.

"Oh, hello," answered Nina. "I'm not here to eat but to see Mr. Bruno Pagano. Is he here?"

"Yes, but is he expecting you? He had a very late night, and he's not really in any shape to see anyone. Are you selling something? What do you have in that basket that smells so good?"

"May I come in? It would be better to answer your questions inside instead of out on the street."

"Oh, of course. I'm sorry. Please come in. My name is Carlo, and I'm the dishwasher here. I will get Mr. Pagano for you. What is your name?"

"I'm Nina Taglieri, and I've come to inquire about the cook position. Is it still available?"

"I'm afraid the position is filled," answered Carlo.

"Carlo, that's not completely true," said Bruno as he entered the room. "Please, bring the usual, for us both. Ciao, Mrs. Taglieri, this is a surprise. Please, have a seat, and Carlo will bring us some coffee and a Danish."

"Thank you, Mr. Pagano," answered Nina. The table was not very clean, but she sat where he indicated. "I came to inquire about the job, but it seems that I'm too late."

Carlo arrived with two steaming cups of dark black coffee and a plate with a couple of cheese Danishes. He set a plate in front of them and asked if she needed cream and sugar. Nina declined either one. The coffee smelled good, but the Danish looked old.

Nina opened the basket to show the fresh blueberry scones. "Would you like a fresh scone? They were my late husband's favorite."

Bruno eyed the scones and immediately said yes. They were so moist that he licked his fingers as he devoured one. "Mrs. Taglieri, did you bake this? It's delicious!"

"Yes, I did. I thought you might want to sample something that I made. However, if the job is no longer available, I guess I'll buy a newspaper on my way home to look at the job postings. Maybe there is another restaurant in town looking for a cook."

"I do have someone cooking temporarily, but I would love to have you fix dinner for me tonight. If the meal is as good as this scone, then the job is yours."

"Bruno," interrupted Carlo as he refilled their coffee cups, "we need someone to cover the day shift. My mother just called to say that my Nonna is sick, so she can't help you out today."

"Well, are you interested in cooking today? I can show you the kitchen, and I'm sure there's an apron somewhere in there you can put on over your dress."

"Yes, I'm interested," answered Nina. "Just let me call home to let my daughter know I won't be home until dinner. I don't want her to worry."

Nina surveyed the large kitchen. It had all the modern conveniences, and the appliances were so shiny they sparkled. She thought about her tiny kitchen at home and just sighed.

"Mrs. Taglieri, may I call you Nina?" Bruno had watched her face as she surveyed the expansive kitchen. "I hope you can find all that you might need. If not, just ask Carlo."

"Oh, yes, please call me Nina. I've never seen a kitchen so large. I hope I don't disappoint you, Mr. Pagano."

"My name is Bruno. Please call me Bruno. I'll let you get started. Elena, the assistant cook, and waitresses will be here shortly. They'll do whatever you need them to do."

"Mr. Pagano, I mean, Bruno, what do you mean, assistant cook?"

"The waitresses take the orders and deliver them to the kitchen. Then the assistant cook looks to you for direction on what to do. Once the order is complete, she rings the waitress that it's ready to go to the table."

"Here's our current menu. We always have wedding soup, minestrone, and pasta e Fagioli, along with sausage and meatball sandwiches. Do you think you can handle that?"

"Of course. Well, I'd better get started if I need to make all of that for lunch."

A half-hour later, Nina found herself giving Carlo a list of groceries that she would need to make everything. He promised to be back soon. In the meantime, Nina met Elena, the assistant cook, and Carmela and Caterina, the waitresses. They welcomed her to the Café.

The batch of scones she had brought quickly sold out, with customers asking for more. She was secretly thrilled as she made another batch and a batch of cream puffs for good measure.

True to his word, Carlo returned with everything she requested, and Nina had everything ready by eleven o'clock. The lunch crowd began to trickle into the Café, and Nina was busy cooking spaghetti, gnocchi, and ravioli. She was so busy cooking that she forgot to eat.

By midafternoon, Bruno came into the kitchen to see how she was doing. Elena mentioned to him that Nina had not taken a lunch break. He immediately set a place at the small break table in the kitchen and told Nina she must take a break. He asked her what she wanted to eat, and when she couldn't decide, he put a plate of steaming pasta in front of her.

He sat down next to her and told her many customers complimented him on the food today. He said that had never happened before, and he wanted her to continue as head cook at the Café. She thanked him and said yes, she was excited to be the new head cook of the Roma Café.

A few hours later, she walked home. She was tired but also exhilarated. She and Theresa were both starting new chapters in their lives.

The Roma Café

Life for Nina changed the day she decided to accept the job offer from Bruno Pagano to work at the Roma Café. She soon found herself working long hours most days. Theresa didn't mind because she also worked long hours at the salon. Mother and daughter spent time together on Sundays and got caught up with each other's lives.

Theresa was learning much from her job at La Rosella's Salon. She learned how to wrap a perm, create finger waves, and apply makeup like a pro. Gina made sure she washed the hair of all the wealthy ladies that came into the salon. That way, Theresa earned good tip money. Nina was proud of her daughter and told her so.

Nina was still learning about managing the kitchen of a busy restaurant. Elena and the waitresses were reserved around her, but Nina didn't mind. She liked to cook and felt comfortable in the expansive kitchen.

Bruno told her business had picked up because everyone loved her cooking. He was accommodating and made sure Carlo got whatever she needed each day.

The waitresses noticed Bruno seemed to spend more time than he used to around the kitchen. They tried to steer clear of him most of the time, but that was becoming harder and harder to do. He made the staff uncomfortable.

One evening at the beginning of October, as Nina finished her shift, an early season snowstorm fell fast and hard. Nina was walking out of the back door of the café when she slipped and fell.

Carlo was washing the huge soup pots at the kitchen sink and heard her fall. He rushed to her side and helped her back into the kitchen.

"Nina, are you okay? Did you hurt yourself?"

"No, I'm pretty sure I'm fine but thank you for your concern. I didn't realize it would snow today, and I didn't wear my boots. I slipped on the snow in my shoes."

Bruno had just entered the kitchen as she was answering Carlo. "What happened here?"

"Nina fell as she stepped out into the snow."

Bruno was surprised to find he was genuinely concerned about Nina's well-being. Generally, he didn't care about his employees unless they didn't do their jobs, then he treated them poorly until they quit.

He surveyed her thin dress and light coat, both threadbare. She didn't have a scarf or gloves.

"Well, you certainly aren't dressed to go out in the snow and walk home. Let me drive you there."

"Thanks, but I'll be okay. I didn't know it was going to snow today. I will be fine walking home."

"Nonsense. Carlo, start my car. Nina, I'm going to drive you home, and I won't hear any more about it. I don't want my favorite cook getting hurt or sick."

Carlo started his car, and a few minutes later, Nina was seated on the passenger side. Bruno drove her home and even helped her to her front door.

Tony and Domenica were concerned when they saw Bruno helping her to the house. Nina thanked him for the ride and said she would be fine. She hated being the center of attention.

As she hung up Nina's coat, Domenica asked, "What happened? Why did he drive you home?"

"I'm fine. I fell as I left the restaurant. Bruno got concerned and drove me home."

"Are you sure you're fine?" inquired Domenica. "You seem flustered."

"Yes, I said I'm fine," answered Nina. She just wanted to soak in a warm bath.

"I don't like him. I wish you didn't work at his restaurant," said Tony.

"Well, Tony, he gave me a job when I needed one and has been very kind to me," retorted Nina. "I don't want to hear anything negative about him."

Nina left the room and went upstairs. It had been a long day at the restaurant, and she didn't want to argue with Tony. She just wanted to take a warm bath and go to bed.

When Nina arrived at work on Monday morning, a small package with her name scrawled on it was on the kitchen counter. She opened it and was surprised to see a lovely scarf with a pair of gloves to match. The muted blue material was thick and soft. As she tried on the gloves, Bruno walked into the kitchen.

"Oh, good. You found the package I left for you."

"Bruno, these are lovely, but I can't accept them."

"You certainly can. I can't afford to have a sick cook. I would lose my customers, and my business would suffer. I consider it an investment in my business."

"But I can't accept such an extravagant gift from my boss. The others will talk, especially after you gave me a ride home the other night."

"I don't care what they think or say, Nina. You and your daughter are in a tough situation, and I'm in a position to help. Let me help you in this small way."

"Well, thank you, they are lovely, and I will think of you when I wear them."

The holidays were difficult for Nina and Theresa, even with the Stellano's at the house with them. They were both struggling with their feelings.

Nina felt lonely and isolated, especially when she saw how happy Tony and Domenica were. She felt cheated that she had lost Angelo.

Theresa loved and missed her father but was busy with the excitement of her new life. She loved going to beauty school and working at the salon; every day was a new adventure. Theresa didn't realize her mother felt so alone.

Bruno spent the holidays with Enzo, Jesse, and their children. He found himself wondering what Nina was doing down the street more than once.

He couldn't understand why he kept thinking about her. She was, after all, just one of his employees.

On the Brink of War

Steubenville was no different than the rest of the country. In the fall of 1939, the war was all anyone in the country could think about after Germany invaded Poland. Most people believed America would enter the war; the only question was when.

War was a major topic of discussion at the Roma Café. Several regular customers engaged in heated discussions daily, and Bruno had to break up the occasional fight.

Since the holidays, Bruno tried to keep his distance from the Café, staying mainly at the Westwood Tavern across the street. He figured if he didn't see Nina, he wouldn't think about her, but that wasn't the case.

Bruno found himself wondering what Nina was doing whenever she wasn't at work. He began wondering if she was seeing anyone. Several of his patrons had asked him if she had a man in her life. He only grunted at them in reply.

Jesse seemed to always mention something about Nina to him whenever he saw her. She began to frequent the Café more often since Nina became the cook. She informed Bruno that Nina's relatives had moved in to help pay her late husband's high medical bills.

One evening, Jesse and Enzo came to the Café and insisted that Bruno join them at their table. They spent the whole time talking about how delicious Nina's cooking was and how she was such a nice person.

"Enzo and I have two extra tickets for the theatre this weekend. Please join us," stated Jesse. "Nina might like to go; you should ask her."

"I haven't been inside a theatre since I dated Maria," declared Bruno. "Jesse, you need to back off. I'm a different man than I was back then. Besides, I'm not interested in dating anyone."

"Well, think about it, Bruno. You need to do more than just work. You need a suitable social life."

Bruno just glared at her. He didn't need Jesse trying to fix him up with Nina or anyone else.

The following day at the Cafe, Bruno had to break up another fight between a couple of drunk customers. One of the men found his way into the kitchen and began badgering Nina.

Bruno saw red as Carlo yelled for him. He went into the kitchen in time to see the man grabbing Nina and trying to force himself upon her.

It was as if a switch had gone off in Bruno. He was suddenly transported back in time to when Maria had been kidnapped and abused. Bruno violently grabbed and punched the man. He continued his assault and only stopped when he heard the sound of Nina crying behind him.

He shoved the man out the kitchen door and told him never to come back. The man ran away. The waitresses heard the commotion and ran into the kitchen, but Bruno shooed them out.

Bruno turned and embraced Nina, and she instantly began to cry again. Her whole body shook as she cried in his arms. He held Nina close and thought about kissing her, but Carlo was still there.

"Carlo, bring me a bottle of red wine and two glasses."

Carlo returned with the wine and glasses. He poured some wine into each glass and told Nina to take a drink.

"I don't drink," answered Nina.

"Take a sip. It will help calm your nerves. You're shaking like a leaf," stated Bruno as he handed her a glass. Nina drank some wine.

"I, I need to get back to work. You have hungry customers," she answered. Her hands were shaking so badly he grabbed the glass and put it on the counter.

"Don't worry about the customers. Elena will handle the rest of your shift. I'm taking you home." His temples were throbbing, and he was surprised by how protective he felt towards her.

As he drove her home, he asked if she would like to go to the theatre with him this coming weekend. He didn't even know what was playing and had never been there before, but he wanted to take her someplace special. He told her they would be going with Enzo and Jesse, and he wouldn't take no for an answer.

At first, Nina didn't answer him. Maybe it was the incident or the effects of the wine, or perhaps it was his strength, but Nina decided to take a leap of faith and told him yes, she would go.

A few days later, she wished she hadn't said yes, as she stood before her closet, trying to decide what to wear. She had never been to the theatre, and she had no idea how to dress.

Theresa, who seemed so worldly lately, told her mother she needed a new dress. She had seen pictures in the magazines at the salon of what was in fashion now, and Nina had nothing fashionable in her closet.

A new dress was not an option, so Nina decided on a simple black sleeveless dress. Theresa applied a bit of makeup and did her mother's hair. Once Theresa finished, Nina hardly recognized herself in the mirror. She was only in her mid-thirties, but she felt so old.

Bruno picked her up, and they stopped up the street to pick up Enzo and Jesse. Tony glared at her as she left the house. He did not trust Bruno at all.

The evening flew by quickly, and Nina found she had enjoyed it. Bruno had been a perfect gentleman, and she enjoyed the company of Enzo and Jesse.

In the weeks that followed the Café incident, Bruno was very watchful of everything that happened there. The staff noticed he was very vigilant, which put everyone on edge.

Carlo, the only employee allowed to enter the back rooms without permission, was also on edge. He usually ushered the men into the back rooms for Bruno. The men allowed to enter lately were only Bruno's most loyal customers.

The waitresses were even instructed not to enter the occupied rooms. Bruno was extra cautious since there was a new county prosecutor in town.

The prosecutor was working with a vigilante committee to investigate many local bars and restaurants for any form of vice. Bruno, who was on thin ice with Vincenzo lately, didn't want to get caught.

Nina was very nervous and skittish since the kitchen incident. She jumped at the least little sound. One day Carlo dropped a large soup pot in the deep sink, and the noise scared Nina, causing her to drop a pan of meatballs she was just taking out of the oven.

Many of the meatballs fell onto the floor. Nina was upset because there wasn't any other meat in the refrigerator to make a fresh batch.

She figured Bruno would be upset because meatball sandwiches were part of today's special. Maybe she could have Carlo go to the store for more beef and pay him out of her wages. She was finishing cleaning up the mess when Bruno came into the kitchen. He wondered aloud why there were no meatballs in the pot of sauce.

She explained what had happened, and he just pulled money out of his pocket and instructed Carlo to hurry back with the meat needed. Then he took Nina by the hand and led her to the back room where he usually had a poker game going. She had never been in the back room.

"Nina, don't be scared. I'll protect you from anyone who dares to bother you."

Then he pulled her close and kissed her. It started quite innocently as a way to calm her nerves but quickly escalated to a deep hunger within him.

Nina was shocked by the feelings the kiss evoked. She wasn't quite sure how to respond, but at that moment, she knew she shouldn't be in a room alone with Bruno. It would appear improper. Just then, Elena knocked on the door and said Carlo was back from the store.

Feeling confused, Nina immediately went into the kitchen and made another large batch of meatballs. She didn't say anything else to Bruno or any of the kitchen staff. She worked her shift and quietly walked home.

Bruno was surprised by his feelings and went across the street to the Tavern; he needed a drink. He didn't want to have feelings for Nina, but somehow, he did. After several drinks, Bruno told Rocco to send a whore up to his room. He needed to get the image of Nina out of his mind.

Nina wasn't a beauty like his precious Maria, but she had an inner core of strength and goodness like his mother, Rosa. He admired the fact that even though life had dealt her a harsh blow, she was determined to make a life for herself and her daughter.

A knock at his door interrupted his thoughts. He opened it, and a girl in red lingerie entered the room. Her face was all painted up. Bruno barely looked at her as he shoved her to the bed. In his drunken state, he tried to get an erection but failed. The whore attempted to arouse him but was unsuccessful. He couldn't get the picture of a frightened Nina out of his mind for some reason.

Finally, he yelled at the woman to stop and leave his room. The whore laughed as he zipped up his pants. She demanded cash, and he threw some money at her as he shoved her out the door.

He drained the bottle of whiskey on his dresser and passed out on the bed.

Matchmakers and Mobsters

Enzo and Jesse were determined to play matchmakers after their evening with Bruno and Nina. They tried to include Nina and Theresa in whatever they were doing. When Bruno questioned them, they said they were merely trying to be good neighbors.

Because of their efforts, Jesse's dad, Luca, intently watched Bruno and Nina's interaction. Aided by his daughter's prompting, he agreed it would be a good idea for Bruno to marry Nina. Bruno needed a wife who could help keep him out of trouble.

Luca was finding it harder to smooth things over with Vincenzo, where Bruno was concerned. It was time to give Bruno a push. It was time for Vincenzo to visit the Roma Café.

One day, Luca and Enzo mentioned to Vincenzo that business at the Café had picked up, and profits were good because of Bruno's new cook. Vincenzo wanted to meet her, so they went to the Café for lunch.

Carlo was shocked to see his Zio Vincenzo walk through the doorway of the Café. He was very nervous and almost dropped the tray of dirty dishes he was carrying. He managed to take care of them and then snuck across the street to the Tavern to summon Bruno.

"Bruno, I don't know why, but Zio Vincenzo and Luca Salvatore just walked into the Café. You need to come over and see what they want."

"What? Vincenzo and Luca are at the Café? Did you seat them? Did they ask for me?"

Bruno got up abruptly, straightened his suit, and hurriedly followed Carlo across the street, back to the Café.

"Ciao, gentlemen. To what do I owe this great honor? Why have you chosen to have lunch at the Roma Café today?"

"Ciao, Bruno! Luca and Enzo keep telling me what a wonderful cook you have here at the Café, so I decided to see myself. We'd each like a bowl of the Pasta é Fagioli and a meatball sandwich."

"Certainly, coming right up."

"And Bruno, we'd like you to join us for lunch," said Vincenzo.

Bruno went into the kitchen and had both waitresses in an uproar with his quick orders to serve Vincenzo and Luca.

He joined them for lunch and was surprised that they didn't want to discuss business but only raved about the food. They wanted to meet the cook. Luca told Carlo to have Nina come out.

Nina was nervous about being summoned to a table. She wondered what was wrong with their meal. She nervously wiped her hands on her apron and hurried to the table where Bruno and Luca were seated along with a large husky man wearing a dark suit.

The husky man demanded, "Are you the cook who prepared this lunch?" He had a thick Italian accent.

"Yes, I am, sir. Is there a problem with your lunch?" She looked nervously towards Bruno.

"Yes, it's too delicious! People have stopped going to my restaurant and now come here to eat. I must have the recipe for this delicious Pasta é Fagioli!"

"I'm sorry, sir, but I don't understand."

Bruno chuckled, "Nina, don't worry. Vincenzo and Luca are jealous because you are the cook here and not at their restaurant. They loved your soup and the meatball sandwich. I told them they should try your cannoli. Please, don't give them your secret recipe!"

"I'm Vincenzo Santucci. Nina, it's nice to meet you. You are an excellent cook," stated Vincenzo with a smile.

"Thank you, sir. It's nice to meet you, but I'd better get back to the kitchen. I need to finish making the sauce for the chicken cacciatore that is this evening's special."

After she left, Vincenzo and Luca got up to go. They had accomplished what they set out to do. On the way out the door, Vincenzo told Bruno that he was no longer allowed to set foot inside any of Judy's salons anymore.

Luca told him he might want to consider getting married instead. He might want a new wife who cooked delicious meals.

As the months passed, Nina found herself courted by Bruno. They always made sure to keep things professional when she was at work. Nina didn't want anything to happen that would make her lose her job. She was finally getting the bills under control and didn't spend each night worrying whether a bill collector would show up at her door.

Nina and Bruno were both lonely people who had lost a spouse they loved. They found a kindred spirit in each other. On the anniversary of Maria's death, Bruno, who usually got drunk until he passed out, instead went out to dinner with Nina this year.

She sat quietly and listened to him as he talked for hours about his beloved wife. He didn't tell her about Maria's connections to the family or what he did to her kidnappers. She just listened and didn't judge. Bruno felt at ease when Nina was around. He found it easy to talk to her.

Tony continued to clarify that he disliked Bruno and that Angelo would not want her dating him. Nina just told him to mind his own business. Secretly, she was beginning to resent Tony's assumption he could control her life.

Domenica tried to stay neutral about the situation. She wanted Nina to be happy, but she didn't trust Bruno. Domenica had seen him coming and going around the Salvatore property before and surmised he was a part of the local mafia.

Nina knew Tony and Domenica didn't like Bruno, but they didn't know him as she did. She wanted them to all get along, but Tony flatly refused. He swore Bruno was corrupt.

In July, Bruno got four tickets to the theatre for Theresa's birthday. He took Nina, Theresa, and her friend Lillian. Afterward, they went to dinner at the Fort Steuben Ballroom. It was the most exclusive place in town. Theresa and Lillian were so excited.

Tony was furious when Nina and Theresa went out that night. Bruno invited Tony and Domenica to join them at the Ballroom, but they declined. Nina tried to change their minds, but they said no.

They ran into Theresa's boss, Gina, at the Ballroom. Gina was with Rocco Bricola, Bruno's main bartender. She was surprised to see Nina with Bruno; she knew him by reputation.

When Nina went to powder her nose, Gina followed her into the room.

"Nina, I'm surprised to see you with Bruno Pagano. How do you know him?"

"He's my boss at the Roma Café. We have gone out several times now."

"Well, he may be your boss, but Rocco says he's very ruthless and dangerous. In my opinion, you should be very careful around him."

"Gina, I didn't ask for your opinion, but Bruno has been a perfect gentleman around me."

"Fine, Nina, just talk to Rocco someday when Bruno's not around. He'll tell you some things about Bruno that may make you change your mind about him."

"Maybe I will, but for now, I want to go celebrate with my daughter."

The rest of the evening, Nina kept thinking about her conversation with Gina. Bruno interacted naturally with everyone and was especially chatty with the coat-check girl.

As Bruno dropped off the girls at Lillian's house, Nina watched as he interacted with Antonio and Santina Farchione. They didn't fear him. Maybe Gina was just jealous, thought Nina.

A month later, as he dropped her off after one of their dates, Bruno mentioned he had to go to New York the following week on business. He and Enzo would be gone for about a week, and he would miss her.

He said he wished she could go with him, but he knew that was impossible. She wasn't the kind of woman who would go away with a man who was not her husband.

To his surprise, he admitted he had feelings for her. She told him she had feelings for him as well. Bruno promised to bring her a present from New York.

Bruno and Enzo were carrying out a special mission for Vincenzo. It was the kind of task that could only be handled by a couple of his most trusted men.

Vincenzo's brother-in-law, Vinny, was skimming money from the gambling operation in the county's southern part. Vincenzo had lost quite a bit of cash before Enzo figured out precisely what Vinny was doing with the books.

Vincenzo and Luca devised a particular plan to handle Vinny. They were going to get rid of him, but they had to do it away from Steubenville and make it look like an accident. Vinny was his wife, Mary's younger brother, and her favorite. She would be mad if she knew that Vincenzo was planning to have him whacked.

The plan was to have Vinny and Enzo attend a top-secret meeting in New York with another mafia family's head accountant. Vinny and Enzo were supposed to learn some creative accounting tricks to fix the books to suit the family's needs better. Bruno was only going to provide security for the men while there.

Vincenzo's orders for Bruno were to whack Vinny during the trip and make it look like an accident. Bruno and Enzo planned to get Vinny drunk and have him accidentally fall in front of a train at the train station one night. They ruled out anything messy like a shooting or stabbing as they didn't want to dispose of any evidence.

They would back up each other's story that the three of them had a few after-dinner drinks at a strip club before going to grab a train at Grand Central Station back to their hotel. They would tell the police that a drunk Vinny had lost his balance and fell onto the tracks.

After the accountant's third and final day of meetings, Enzo suggested going to a place uptown with strippers and the best pasta in New York. Bruno quickly agreed, and by then, Vinny was ready to cut loose. He wanted to paint the town and spend some cash, so they took a train uptown.

After a couple of hours at the joint, they left, and Bruno and Enzo pretended to be drunk. Vinny was drunk, and he also had drugs in his system that Bruno conveniently slipped into his drink when he wasn't looking.

As they waited on the platform in the dark of night, it wasn't hard to give Vinny a slight shove as a train came rushing by. The few bystanders did not notice anything unusual. All they saw was a drunk man lose his balance and fall onto the tracks in the path of an oncoming train. The two other travelers were convincingly devastated by his "accident."

Two days later, Bruno and Enzo were traveling home with the body of their friend, Vinny, brother-in-law of their boss, Vincenzo.

On the way home, Enzo and Bruno talked about the future. Bruno admitted he had feelings for Nina. She needed a husband, and he needed a wife. Enzo told his brother to marry her.

Bruno pulled out a box from a jewelry store in New York. One day, he had gone while Enzo and Vinny met with the accountant and picked out a ring for Nina. She wasn't Maria, but he was tired of being alone. Bruno would ask her to get married once they got back to Steubenville.

Enzo was happy for his brother. It was the answer to his and Jesse's prayers. He only hoped Nina would soften Bruno's dark edges as Maria had done. Maria had been wild, though he wasn't sure Nina was. He wondered if Nina would be able to handle his cruel brother.

When they arrived back in Steubenville, Bruno asked Nina to go out. He picked her up in his sedan.

It was a beautiful sunny day in mid-September, and the leaves on the trees shimmered in shades of goldenrod and red as they drove out to the country. They drove to Jefferson Lake, where Bruno parked, and then pulled out a large picnic basket from the trunk. He had packed a picnic lunch for them.

Nina was surprised and helped him set out a red and white checkered tablecloth to sit and serve sandwiches piled with prosciutto, capicola, and provolone cheese on semi-hard Italian rolls. There was also a plate with assorted cheeses, grapes, and olives.

They drank a bottle of chianti and then switched to prosecco with cannoli. They were both feeling pleased with themselves. It was the most wine Nina had ever consumed, and she was feeling carefree.

"Nina, it's so good to be here with you. I missed you while I was in New York. Did you miss me?" He kissed her.

"Bruno, of course, I did. I'm glad you're back."

"When I lost Maria, I thought my life was over. I didn't care about anyone until the day you walked into the Café with those wonderful scones. I think about you all the time, and I want you. I know it's only been a year since your husband died, but I want us to get married. Will you marry me?"

Nina listened as he poured out his feelings. She didn't feel the same type of love she felt for Angelo, but she certainly felt safe in Bruno's arms. Maybe her love for Bruno would grow as it did for Angelo.

"When Angelo died last year, I thought my life was over. I never expected to meet and have feelings for another man. You gave me a job when I was desperate for work and have treated me with respect and kindness. Yes, Bruno, I will marry you."

As the world around them seemed to be falling apart, with countries fighting against one another, this man had become a part of her life and made her feel safe. The man before her was not ruthless and dangerous but gentle and kind.

They decided to get married in early November. Since they had both been married before, they decided to keep things simple. There would be a quiet ceremony at St. Anthony's, followed by a small dinner party at the Fort Steuben Ballroom. They would live in the house on Seventh Street.

Nina completely forgot about her conversation with Gina La Rosella. She never asked Rocco Bricola about his boss.

Kindred Spirits

Nina's happiness was short-lived after the picnic. At home, the news of her engagement to Bruno stunned Theresa and Domenica. Tony was infuriated. Domenica had never seen her husband so angry.

"Nina, Angelo asked me to watch over you, and I haven't done a good job. I've let him down. I should have never let you go to work at the Roma Café. I demand you tell Bruno you made a mistake! You need to quit there today."

"How dare you demand anything! I told you before, Tony, you aren't my father or brother. Because you're a man, you think you can control me, well, you're mistaken."

"You can't marry Bruno; he's ruthless and dangerous. He's a member of the mafia in town, and I refuse to let you marry him. Capisci?"

"Tony, you have no right to talk to me like this in my own home! I will work where I want and marry whoever I want. How dare you speak about my fiancé that way. Bruno is a respected businessman in the community. Besides, we are kindred spirits."

"You are no longer welcome here. You need to get out of my house as soon as possible."

She told them once she married Bruno, he would be moving into the house on Seventh Street, and they would have to find somewhere else to live.

Domenica tried to calm Tony. She was surprised Nina was marrying Bruno and shocked that Nina would make them move out after they had moved in to help her.

The turn of events shook Theresa. She loved Zia Domenica and Zio Tony, and her cousins were more like sisters.

Conflicting emotions tore at Theresa. She was surprised her mother had agreed to marry Bruno, but she had also seen how happy her mother had been these past months since they began dating. She wanted her mother to be content.

The Stellano's moved out two weeks later. Tony and Nina barely saw one another during that time. He felt he failed to keep his promise to Angelo. Deep in his heart, he knew Bruno was corrupt, and he had been unable to keep Nina from him.

Domenica felt like she was losing a family member. She talked to Nina and promised that even though they were moving out, Nina could always count on Domenica to be there if she ever needed anything.

On a cold and blustery Friday in early November, Nina married Bruno. She wore a simple navy-blue suit with white accents. Theresa was her maid of honor and wore a cornflower blue dress with white trim. Both looked lovely. Bruno wore a navy-blue suit with a white shirt and a cornflower blue tie. Enzo, his best man, was dressed the same.

The ceremony was on a Friday afternoon at St. Anthony's Church. Lena and Benny, Jesse and Enzo, and their children were the only guests as Father Paul married them. Tony and Domenica and their girls were nowhere in sight.

It was a simple ceremony, and Nina was shocked when Bruno placed an elaborate ring with a massive diamond on her finger. She was now Mrs. Bruno Pagano.

Earlier in the day, she had taken off the slim gold band Angelo had given her. She lovingly placed it in a box along with several photos of her and Angelo. That box was on the top shelf of her closet.

Angelo would always be in her heart. She would always love him, but now he was part of her past, and Bruno was her future. Bruno made her feel safe and secure with America about to enter the war and the future's uncertainness.

After the ceremony, everyone went to the Fort Steuben Ballroom for dinner. Dino Crocetti, a local boy with good looks and a smooth voice, entertained the crowd. Dino worked in the gambling casino attached to

Vincenzo's restaurant. Everyone said Dino was trying to break into show business.

Luca and Vincenzo were also at the Ballroom having dinner with their wives. Luca was relieved to see Bruno and Nina walk in as husband and wife. He hoped Bruno would settle down now that he was married. He and Vincenzo both went over to congratulate the happy couple.

The celebration and evening flew by in a blur. Nina was surprised by how much alcohol Bruno consumed. Enzo pulled him aside at one point and mentioned he might want to slow down a bit.

For his part, Bruno just continued to drink. The newlyweds were driven home by Enzo and Jesse at the night's end. Theresa was spending the weekend in Weirton with Benny and Lena.

Bruno got sick as they entered the house and threw up all over the living room carpet. Nina helped a drunk Bruno up the stairs to bed. As she helped him remove his shoes, he got sick again. This time she quickly grabbed a small wastebasket for him. After he threw up, he apologized to her. He said he usually held his liquor and didn't know why he was sick.

Nina went to the bathroom and returned with a cool, wet washcloth and put it on his forehead. She was surprised to find he was burning up. He had a fever. She helped him strip down to his underwear and ordered him into the bed. He quickly passed out.

She changed her clothes and gathered Bruno's soiled clothes from the bedroom floor. She carried them to the basement and put them in the laundry tub to soak. Then she went to the living room, where she began to scrub the soiled carpet. Hopefully, it wasn't ruined; she couldn't afford new carpet.

Two hours after she put Bruno to bed, she climbed the long flight of stairs back up to the bedroom. Exhausted, she put on a nightgown and climbed under the sheets. She said her prayers and fell asleep.

A few hours later, Bruno woke her up. His sweating soaked the bedsheets. His fever was gone.

"Nina, these sheets are soaked, and I can't sleep like this. You need to put clean sheets on the bed."

"I'm sleeping. I'll change the sheets in the morning," Nina murmured as she turned over to go back to sleep.

Bruno shoved her off the bed and onto the floor. "I said, you need to put clean sheets on the bed, now!" His tone was one she had never heard from him before. His eyes blazed, and his temples throbbed.

"Get off the floor, and get the sheets. You aren't sleeping now."

Her side hurt from the fall, but she got up and put fresh sheets on the bed. He watched her with his arms crossed.

"Now, take off that nightgown and get in bed. I want sex."

Nina looked at Bruno, wounded by his abrupt tone. She removed her nightgown as he stood and watched. She got under the fresh sheets and waited for her husband.

He removed his underwear and climbed into bed on top of her. He looked at her closely from head to toe and then kissed her. She tried to kiss him in return. She was a bit repulsed because he still reeked of alcohol, but she wanted to please her husband.

He entered her a bit roughly and was done quickly. He fell back to sleep immediately, and she went to the bathroom and brushed her teeth. She put her nightgown back on, climbed back into bed, and drifted off to sleep.

The following morning, she woke up to find Bruno cooking bacon and eggs in the kitchen. He had a pot of coffee already made and had two plates set at the table. In the center of the table was a vase of fresh-cut roses.

"Good morning, Nina. You're just in time for breakfast. Bacon and eggs are the only things I know how to cook. I hope you like them."

"Thank you for the beautiful flowers," she answered. She winced as she sat down at the table. Her side was still sore from her fall. She bruised easily.

"I'm sorry about last night," he said. "I didn't mean to ruin our wedding night. After my business meetings today, I'm going to come home and make it up to you."

"It's okay, Bruno. You didn't mean to get sick. I'm glad you are feeling better. I'll make us a nice dinner and some cannoli for dessert. I know you like it."

"That sounds great," he said as he got up to leave. "I have a busy day and won't be home until dinner time. Carlo will be by later with my clothes. I trust you will be able to launder everything and put it all away."

"Of course; have a good day."

After he left, Nina cleaned the kitchen and scrubbed the living room carpet again. Carlo came by right after that with several suitcases full of Bruno's clothes.

Nina spent the day laundering Bruno's things and putting them all away. Several of his suits would need to be dry cleaned, so she set them aside with thoughts of dropping them off next week. She had just put fresh bread into the oven to bake when Jesse stopped by.

"Nina, what beautiful roses! How's my favorite newlywed today?"

"Thanks; I'm fine, Jesse, just a bit tired. I unpacked and laundered all of Bruno's clothes."

"Well, I just had a call from Enzo saying the guys will be a bit late getting home and figured you would want to know. I'm so happy for you and Bruno. He seems so much happier lately."

"Thanks. I can't believe how much my life has changed in a year. Last year I was very depressed because of Angelo's passing. I was worried about the future, and now I have a decent job and a new husband. Bruno and I are kindred spirits."

"Do you think you'll still work at the Café?"

"Well, I just assumed I would still work. We never talked about me not working. I enjoy it a lot."

"Well, now that you're his wife, I'm not sure Bruno will want you to work at the Café. I guess we'll find out. Well, I must go; I have errands to run before Enzo gets home."

"Thanks for stopping by, Jesse."

A couple of hours later, Bruno came home drunk and in a bad mood. Whatever business he and Enzo had to do, had turned out badly. He was opening kitchen cupboards and slamming them shut. He yelled out for Nina.

"Here I am, Bruno. What's wrong?"

"Where's the whiskey in this house? I need a damn drink!"

"I don't have any whiskey, only some cooking wine."

"What do you mean, you don't have any whiskey. I need a stiff drink!"

"Bruno, I think you've already had enough to drink. Why don't we sit and eat dinner instead? Then I'll make us some coffee. We can have it with our dessert." Nina put her hand on Bruno's arm to try and guide him to the dining room table where she had dinner waiting.

"Don't tell me what to do," he said as he roughly grabbed her hand, wrenched it, and then pushed her away.

She fell into the kitchen table and bruised her side again. Tears filled her eyes, and she cried out in pain and shrank away. Confrontation and rough treatment were foreign to her.

He immediately changed when he heard her painful cry. He straightened up and went into the dining room. "Come, Nina, let's eat; I'm hungry."

She followed him into the room, and they ate dinner in silence. He tried to be tender towards her that night in bed, but it wasn't really in his nature. He took her quickly and promptly fell asleep.

The next day was Sunday. Nina got up and dressed for church. Bruno told her she could go, but he was not. He said he didn't believe in religion. Nina went to Mass and sat with Enzo and Jesse. Tony and Domenica were there but did not speak to her.

When she got home, Bruno was gone. She assumed he was at the Tavern. She missed her daughter. Nina made a pot of wedding soup and prepped some chicken parmesan. Then, she waited for Theresa to come home.

Theresa arrived home early in the afternoon, and they spent time enjoying each other's company. Theresa thought her mother looked happy, but she noticed a black and blue mark on her mother's arm that hadn't been there a few days ago. When she inquired about it, Nina just brushed her off, saying she bumped into the kitchen counter.

Just then, Bruno arrived in time for dinner. He carried in a case of whiskey and made himself a drink. He complimented Nina on the

125

chicken parmesan at dinner and said she should make it for the Café this coming week as a special. She said she would be happy to do so.

They all had a comfortable evening together, and Theresa watched the interaction between her mother and Bruno. It seemed something was off, but she couldn't figure out what. Theresa prayed her mother was happy.

Nina and Bruno quickly fell into a routine of working at the Café, spending time together, and spending time with Enzo and Jesse. Nina enjoyed their company, but she missed Domenica and Tony more than she let on. Bruno noticed and told her she shouldn't waste her time on them.

They had found a house on the hill in the LaBelle section of town. Theresa was a frequent guest there. She saw Domenica and Tony more than her mother in the first weeks of Bruno and Nina's marriage.

Theresa divided her time between working at the beauty salon and spending time with her cousins and friends. Jesse had urged her to give the newlyweds time to get to know one another better, but she missed her mother and her bedroom. She expected to spend the holidays at home with her mother.

Nina missed her daughter, too, and was anxious for Theresa to come back home. Christmas was coming, and she wanted to have Theresa home where she belonged.

When she brought up Christmas and having Theresa home, Bruno said he wanted to have Nina all to himself for just a bit longer. Nina was determined; however, her daughter would be home for good soon.

She was beginning to think she didn't know her husband at all. He seemed like a different person at times, and she was never sure which Bruno she would encounter each day. Sometimes he was kind, gentle, and attentive, and other times he was mean, nasty, and rough.

At Christmas time, Theresa did go home. Nina and Bruno welcomed her with open arms. Bruno liked Theresa and wanted to be a good stepfather. He enlisted Jesse's help in shopping for presents for Nina and Theresa. He wanted their first Christmas together to be special.

They spent time with the Pagano and Salvatore family on Christmas Day at Jesse's house. Bruno was very generous to Nina and Theresa, lavishing them with many gifts. He seemed disappointed in the handmade gifts and small trinkets Nina and Theresa gave him. They could not afford much.

On New Year's Eve, Bruno and Nina hosted a party at their home on Seventh Street. Nina did all the cooking and spent the evening refilling platters of hors d'oeuvres and cleaning up spills and messes while Bruno paraded around playing host to people that Nina didn't even know. Late in the night, he started gambling with a few guests. Nina went to bed in the wee hours of the morning when she could no longer keep her eyes open.

She woke up abruptly when a naked Bruno ripped off her nightgown and entered her roughly. She tried to move but realized he had tied her to the bed. When she asked him to stop, he just slapped her across the face and told her to shut up. He reeked of alcohol, and his eyes were glazed as he took her. She squeezed her eyes shut to block out his face as he used her body.

The following day, when she woke, he was not in bed. Her whole body hurt. Her wrists had marks on them where he had tied her up, and she had a red spot on her cheek where he had struck her. She gingerly got out of bed and showered. Tears ran down the drain along with the hot water as she tried to cleanse her body and mind of what he had done to her body the previous night.

After she dressed, she began the task of cleaning the house. It was in shambles from the party, and she knew she must have everything immaculate upon his return or pay the price if it wasn't. She also knew Theresa was coming home in time for dinner. She had spent the night at Domenica's.

Nina must have everything back to normal before either of them got home. Even as her body ached, she knew she must scrub the house from top to bottom.

Joan McGlone

It was 1941, and as the war raged on half a world away, Nina was beginning to realize that she was in a war herself. She was at war with her new husband, and he had all the ammunition. She would quickly have to learn how to do battle against him, or she would lose herself.

A Big Surprise

As the months passed, Theresa noticed her mother changing before her very eyes. She seemed to always have a mark or bruise on her arm or leg, and she was very skittish. Whenever Theresa inquired about her bruises, she would shrug it off as a clumsy accident at work.

Nina always seemed tired anymore. She was constantly picking up after Bruno, who left things everywhere. She worked long hours at the Café and tried to keep the house spotlessly clean.

If he entered a room that wasn't clean, he expected her to drop whatever she was doing and clean the room immediately, even if he made the mess. If Nina dared to say anything, he would scowl at her and criticize her until she was near tears.

He had a voracious appetite for sex, and Nina wasn't used to his rough handling. Angelo had always been caring and gentle. Bruno's hands were always coarse, and he didn't seem to care about her feelings at all. In bed at night, he would degrade her in ways she never knew existed.

One evening he came into the bedroom carrying a shiny spittoon. He placed it on his side of the bed. When Nina asked him what it was for, he chuckled and told her it was his piss pot. She looked at him quizzically. He told her he didn't like going all the way down the hall at night to use the bathroom. From now on, he would use the spittoon, and Nina, as his wife, would have to clean it each morning.

Nina opened her mouth to discuss the offensive spittoon with Bruno but thought better of it. She realized if she argued with him, he would only take it out on her in other ways.

She had several bruises on her arms and legs where he had hurt her already, and she was just too mortified to say anything to anyone about the rough treatment she received from her husband.

Joan McGlone

One morning in late April, as she was just about to pick up the foul-smelling spittoon, she felt as if she would throw up. Bruno said he left a wonderful present in it for her. The sneer on his face as he told her turned into concern as she passed out on the floor.

He grabbed her and quickly laid her on the bed. Her face was as white as the starched sheets covering the mattress. He shook her, and she slowly came to. She threw up all over him and the bed as she sat up. She was immediately petrified of what he would do. She didn't know why she had passed out or why she had thrown up. She was usually never sick.

The look on her face told him she was about to throw up again. He promptly carried her to the bathroom, where she threw up again. Damn, he didn't want to deal with a sick wife.

He left her in the bathroom, hugging the toilet. He angrily changed his clothes back in the bedroom and tore the sheets off the bed, dumping them on the bedroom floor. He had no idea where she kept the bedsheets. When he carried her back to the bed, he just covered her with a blanket.

Bruno emptied the spittoon and left it in the bathroom for Nina to scrub when she felt better. From the bedroom doorway, he told her he would get Elena to cover her shift at the Café. He left the house in a foul mood.

A few hours later, Theresa arrived home from work to find her mother asleep on the bed and a smelly mess on the floor. Theresa took the soiled sheets and washed them, then took a slice of toast and a cup of tea to her mother.

When Theresa went back into the bedroom, Nina woke up and told her daughter what had happened. She drank the tea but just nibbled at the toast; her stomach was still queasy.

Theresa helped her get cleaned up and remade the bed. By mid-afternoon, Nina felt a bit better but still had no appetite.

At dinner time, Bruno arrived home to find Nina still in bed.

Theresa heated some soup for them and then went to her room. Bruno sat in the living room by himself in a bad mood, having a few drinks. He didn't want to sleep in the same bed as Nina if she was sick. He left the house, gambled, and slept in his old apartment above the bar.

Nina awoke the next day and felt the same. This time she made it to the bathroom before throwing up.

As she sat on the floor in the bathroom, a thought dawned on her. It was a tiny seed at first, but as she sat and thought, a small smile broke out on her face. Nina needed a doctor to confirm it, but she thought she might be pregnant.

Theresa made her tea and toast again before leaving for work.

Nina thanked her daughter but said nothing to her about her thoughts. Once she was alone in the house, she called and asked if she could stop by Dr. Barducci's office.

As Nina got ready, she began to hum. She felt sure she was right. She had been exhausted the past few months, she couldn't remember when her last cycle was, and her breasts felt fuller.

Dr. Barducci was surprised to see her so pale and thin. He examined her and confirmed her suspicions. He told Nina she would need to take it easy with this pregnancy. She needed to rest more often since she was in her thirties, especially with her medical history of miscarriages.

He said the baby was due around Thanksgiving.

Nina left his office on a cloud. She had tried for so many years with Angelo to have another baby, but it never happened. After being married for just a few months, she was pregnant with Bruno's child. How would he react upon hearing the news? Would he be happy? Would she be able to carry this baby to term? Did he even want children?

Lost in her thoughts, she collided with a slender man in quite a hurry and fell. He was coming out of the Diamond Cigar Store carrying a paper bag. The bag fell, and paper receipts scattered all over the ground. The man let out a loud curse.

"Dammit, woman, you should watch where you're walking!" He said as he tried to retrieve all the scattered papers. It was Rocco Bricola, the bartender at the Westwood Tavern.

"Oh, Rocco, I'm so sorry, I wasn't watching where I was going. Please excuse me."

"Nina, I'm sorry. I didn't realize it was you who bumped into me. Let me help you up. Are you okay?"

"I'm fine. Let me help you gather those papers."

"It's okay; I can do it. Where are you headed in such a hurry? Bruno told me you were sick. He spent the night in his old apartment above the bar."

"So, that's where he was last night. I wasn't feeling well, but I'm much better today. I'm headed to the Café to see him."

"I don't think he's there right now. He and Enzo had to run an errand for Luca. Why don't you go home and wait; I'm sure he'll be there soon."

"Well, okay. I'll go and fix a nice dinner. Tell Bruno to bring home a nice bottle of wine."

"I'll tell him, Nina. You take care now."

When Nina got home, she took a short nap and then made a pan of lasagna, a salad, and some fresh bread. The table set, she waited for Bruno to come home. She caressed her belly and prayed to God she could carry this baby to term.

Theresa came home while waiting, and Nina told her daughter the news. She was happy for Nina but also concerned about her past medical history.

Theresa ate a quick dinner and then went to Lillian's house to spend the night.

About twenty minutes later, Bruno came home and was surprised to find Nina waiting for him in the living room. She looked pale but said she was feeling better. He was glad.

She told him she had dinner ready. He had a busy day and was hungry. He noticed that she seemed a bit different, but he couldn't imagine what it was. She was in an excellent mood. They ate dinner, and he noticed that she only sipped her wine.

"Nina, you asked me to bring home a nice bottle of wine for dinner, but you've only taken a sip of it. What's going on? This wine is expensive," he said as he drained his glass and poured himself another drink.

"Bruno, I know we haven't talked about it before, but I didn't think it was possible."

"What are you talking about, Nina? What haven't we talked about?"

"I went to see Dr. Barducci today; I'm pregnant. We're going to have a baby."

Bruno choked on his wine. "What? You're pregnant!"

"Yes. After the miscarriages I had before, I didn't believe it was possible to get pregnant, but I am. The doctor said I need to be very careful this time around because of my medical history and age."

"Nina, I don't know if I can go through that again. Maria got big and fat, lost the baby, then died."

"Bruno, I don't know if I will be able to carry this baby to term, but a baby is a gift from God, and I will accept whatever God has in mind for me. You told me Maria was kidnapped and tortured. That's why she lost the baby and died."

"That's right, and I'm going to make sure you and the baby are protected. You'll stay home and in bed. Jesse will come over to visit you. I'll bring you whatever you need. Nothing is going to happen this time around. I will not lose this child."

"Bruno, with my medical history, there are no guarantees, but I'll stay home and in bed to protect this baby."

Bruno held her in his arms and promised to be a better husband. He was finally going to be a father.

Old Fears and A New Life

The summer flew by rapidly, and now the fall colors were all around. Bruno made sure Nina remained at home by having Carlo watch over her. He stayed in the spare bedroom and doted on Nina.

Theresa felt uncomfortable around him, so she spent most of the summer and fall at Domenica's when she wasn't working at the Salon. She was starting to date Lillian's older brother Eric. Nina approved of him since she knew the family.

Bruno was very protective of Nina, and he hovered over her as much as she would let him. He was thrilled as her belly grew rounder and rounder. He was sure the baby was a boy. Nina hoped so, for his sake. She followed the advice of Dr. Barducci in all things and prayed she would have a healthy baby.

Jesse and Enzo were frequent guests at Nina's home on Seventh Street during that time. They both remembered hearing how overbearing Bruno got with Maria when she was pregnant. They wanted to keep Bruno grounded and make sure Nina was okay. Luca made certain Bruno's jobs remained local so he wouldn't be out of town when it came time for Nina to deliver.

After enduring a few months of morning sickness, Nina felt healthy and protected. She spent most of her time just lounging around the house. She taught Carlo some simple recipes in the small kitchen of her home. He idolized Nina and became very protective of her. He often interceded on her behalf when Bruno began to pick on her. Bruno knew better than to harm Carlo, though, as Vincenzo's favorite nephew.

On Thanksgiving Day, Jesse cooked dinner at Nina's house. Everyone was there, and Nina, who felt like a giant balloon, had no appetite. She didn't want a house full of company; she just wanted to be alone. Bruno told her to quit being selfish.

As the day wore on, Nina felt more uncomfortable and began having contractions. Jesse noticed at once and made everyone leave. Bruno took Nina directly to the hospital's labor and delivery department. Nina prayed for an easy delivery and a healthy baby.

Dr. Barducci arrived at the hospital and butted heads with Bruno when he told him he couldn't smoke in the waiting room. Bruno made a big fuss and threatened the doctor. Bruno didn't like being told what he could and couldn't do.

The doctor had security promptly escort Bruno out of the hospital. He was furious and vowed to make the doctor pay dearly.

Nina had difficulty laboring with the baby; her contractions were very hard. After several hours of arduous labor, Dr. Barducci finally gave her a shot to relieve some of the pain, and a few hours later, she gave birth to a healthy baby boy.

Bruno was allowed back in the hospital only after promising not to smoke inside. He walked into the room as Nina held the baby for the first time. He was relieved to find both Nina and the baby doing well. He had been worried he would lose another wife and child.

While Nina rested from her labor, Bruno held his son and vowed to give him the world. Overcome with emotion, he cried. Finally, he had a family. They named the baby Giovanni.

A week later, Bruno and Nina brought the baby home to their Seventh Street house. The news on the car radio was awful. Japan had just attacked Pearl Harbor; America was now at war. Bruno told her he would keep them safe. Nina prayed he was right. She wondered how the war would affect them all.

Nina was finding it hard to bounce back from Giovanni's delivery. Dr. Barducci said it was due to her miscarriages, age, and rough delivery. He recommended she not have sex until healed completely. Instantly that caused a lot of tension in the Pagano household.

Bruno needed sex, so he met with Vincenzo and asked if he was allowed back in Judy's place on Water Street. Vincenzo permitted him to go to one of her new venues, a Steam Room on Washington Street, only if he promised not to hurt anyone. He quickly agreed; of course, he didn't tell his wife.

Nina slept on a cot next to the baby's crib for the first few months of Giovanni's life and tended to him there. Bruno wasn't too happy he slept alone, but she told him that she could keep the baby from waking him up during the night.

Bruno tried hard to be kinder to Nina. After all, she was the mother of his precious son. He thought the boy was perfect in every way and spoiled him. The unruly boy was the spitting image of his father.

Since she had the baby, Nina had not returned to work at the Café. The business suffered a bit, but Bruno worked harder to increase his gambling profits. He regularly hosted gambling nights in the back room of the Café.

One sultry evening in July, Bruno and Enzo were gambling with a couple of drifters they thought were just passing through town. Both of the men turned out to be federal investigators working undercover. They were trying to get dirt on Vincenzo and the mafia in Steubenville. When Bruno realized it, he pulled out a gun and shot one of the men before attacking the second one.

The second investigator became very talkative after being worked over by Bruno's fists. He said they were trying to identify and arrest members of the "Black Hand Gang," running the illegal gambling in Steubenville. The feds knew Vincenzo Santucci was the ringleader and were building a case on all of them.

Bruno brutally beat the man and got as much information out of him as possible, then finished him off with a shot to the head. His temples pulsed like crazy. Bruno's efforts left him exhilarated; he felt so alive. Violence was like an aphrodisiac to him.

He badly wanted to beat someone else but needed to get rid of the two bodies on the floor of his gambling room. He was raw; his nerves were on high alert, and he needed to settle down.

Enzo, Rocco, and Carlo had been with him throughout the entire episode. Now they all worked together to dispose of the bodies.

"Bruno, you need to calm down. If you go home to Nina in this state, you might do something you'll regret," said Enzo. "You should stay in your old apartment tonight."

His brother was right. Pretty bloody from the incident, Bruno decided to spend the night in his old apartment above the Tavern. If he went home in this condition, he might hurt Nina.

"Carlo, go fetch me some clean clothes, and tell Nina I won't be home tonight."

Nina knew better than to ask why Carlo had come by for clean clothes at three o'clock in the morning. She was secretly glad her husband would be spending the night elsewhere. He was typically rough on her when he came home drunk. Those were the painful times that hurt if she didn't comply with his wishes.

Oh, after a beating, he would sometimes apologize, but more often than not, he made her think she deserved the abuse and punishment he doled out. It was getting harder and harder for Nina to hide such things from her daughter.

Theresa finished beauty school and was now a beautician at La Rosella's, starting to build a clientele of her own. She knew deep down that Bruno abused her mother, but her mother denied it every time she asked.

She didn't know what to do about the abuse in her own home. She missed her father terribly and prayed that Bruno would not harm her mother each night. She wanted to talk to Zia Domenica about it but realized that it would only make things worse for her mother.

She also thought about talking to Father Paul after Mass but didn't know if that would do any good. So, she just gave her stepfather the cold shoulder. He wasn't happy with her anyway since she was dating Lil's brother, Eric.

Bruno wanted her to date Vincenzo's son, Dominic Santucci. Theresa remembered him from their school days. Dominic was mean and nasty and considered himself better than everyone else. There was no way she wanted to have anything to do with him.

A few years older than her, Eric was tall, dark, and handsome. Theresa was falling in love with him, and she was confident he felt the same way. Her Papa had known and liked his family. Papa had been a good judge of character. He had also told them to stay away from the Santucci family. She still remembered many things that Papa had said, even though her mother seemed to forget.

The ring of the telephone interrupted Theresa's thoughts. It was Eric asking her to go out this evening. He said he had some information to share with her. As she got ready, she wondered what the news could be.

Eric, it turned out, was drafted to serve in the Army. He was going to war. He told Theresa he wanted to fight to make the world better for all people. Theresa was afraid he would go and never come back but kept her fears to herself. She promised to write him daily but knew that that wouldn't be possible for Eric.

They spent as much time together as they could before he had to leave for basic training. Several local guys were going. Lillian's boyfriend, Romeo, was also going. Theresa and Lil knew they would be spending a lot of time together, praying for the safe return of their boyfriends and all the other soldiers.

The time soon came for Eric to leave for basic training. It was November 1942, and Theresa felt like her life would never be the same. To help distract her, Nina had enlisted her help in organizing a birthday party for Giovanni, who was turning one. It gave Theresa something else to do.

Once Bruno found out Theresa was planning a party for the birthday, he soon took over. The once simple party became something else. Held at the Ballroom, it was more than a bit extravagant for a one-year-old. The guest list consisted of mostly adults Bruno knew. Dino Crocetti even stopped by and sang happy birthday to the toddler.

Bruno was happy with the turnout. Theresa didn't even know half of the people there, and no one noticed when she left early with Lil. Nina spent the time trying to remember the names of all the guests. She would have a lot of thank you notes to write and send out.

Giovanni had missed his afternoon nap and was cranky. Soon after the cake and ice cream were done and presents opened, Nina took Giovanni to a dim corner of the room and finally got him to take a short nap. As she watched the festivities unfold before her, she realized the crowd was all associates of Bruno's. Nina also noticed he was doing a lot of drinking. She wished he wouldn't.

Nina wished she could end the party and take the baby home. But she knew that wasn't what Bruno wanted, so she tried her best to soothe her young son. He was teething and pretty uncomfortable with all the activities around him. She wasn't sure how much longer the party would last. She looked around for Theresa but quickly realized she was gone.

Before long, Bruno was drunk, and she knew then she had a long night ahead. If she were lucky, he would just use her body for sex and then pass out. However, if he felt someone slighted him during the party, he would take it out on her. She wondered what abuse lay ahead. She hoped Theresa was spending the night at Lil's house.

Around ten o'clock, a card game started. Nina decided it was time to go home. She called out to Carlo for help since Bruno was playing cards. Rocco drove her and the baby home once they piled the gifts into Bruno's vehicle.

At the house, Rocco insisted on unloading everything for her. There were two huge stacks of opened presents just inside the front door. He ensured she was settled and then drove back to the Ballroom in Bruno's car. Rocco, she thought to herself, was always kind to her.

Theresa was already home and asleep in her bed. Nina worried about her daughter more than she let on. She prayed Theresa would marry a man who made her happy, a good man like her father.

Nina put Giovanni to bed and decided the stacks of presents could wait until morning. She washed her face, brushed her teeth, and pulled on her favorite nightgown. She fell asleep as soon as her head hit the pillow.

In the wee hours of the night, Nina heard Bruno come into the house, slamming the front door. She heard him loudly curse as he stumbled over the heaping stacks of birthday presents. She knew then it was going to be a rough night. Should she try to appease him or pretend to be asleep? Either way, she knew trouble lay ahead.

He lumbered up the steps and threw open the bedroom door. He reeked of alcohol and tobacco. Nina lay in bed quietly with her eyes closed as she heard him shed his clothes. He pulled the covers off of her and threw them onto the floor. She rubbed her eyes and pretended she was just waking up. His temples were throbbing, and his eyes were as black as coal as he looked at her.

"Get up, Nina! You have some explaining to do."

"Bruno, please quiet down, or you'll wake up the baby. What's the matter?"

"You neglected our guests at Giovanni's party. You were rude to them leaving early, and now you will pay the price."

"But Giovanni was tired and cranky. I wanted to get him home and to bed. You know he's fussy if I don't keep him on a schedule."

He grabbed her by the arms and shook her violently. His fingers dug into her skin, leaving bruises she would have to try and hide. He was furious because she had left the party with Giovanni.

As he slapped her across the face, he told her she made him look like a fool because she didn't socialize with his friends at the party. With a smirk on his face, he asked her why. Then, without waiting for an answer, he ripped her nightgown down the front. He greedily pawed at her breasts and squeezed her nipples until she whimpered in pain. He smacked her again, then shoved her to the floor and took her crudely as he pinned her arms above her head.

The assault seemed to go on forever, but in fact, didn't last long. Nina endured it all in silence. She knew better than to speak up. She prayed neither of her children heard the abuse.

After his sexual appetite was satisfied, Bruno got up and filled the piss pot before climbing into bed. Within minutes he was snoring.

Once Nina heard him snoring, she gingerly got up off the floor. She silently went to the bathroom, sat on the floor, and cried. Then just as silently, she cleaned herself up. When she came out of the bathroom, she was shocked to see Theresa standing in her bedroom doorway with tears streaming down her face.

Silently, Nina hugged her daughter and told her to go back to bed. Now was not the time for discussion. Nina had to get back to bed before Bruno realized she was gone.

The next day after Bruno left the house, Theresa confronted her mother about the abuse.

"Ma, I know Bruno hits you. I've seen your bruises and heard your cries. Why do you let him abuse you? Why don't you leave him?"

"I wish I had an answer for you. Bruno doesn't mean to hurt me; he loves me. It's just that he gets angry and mean when he's drunk. It's the alcohol."

"I don't care if he claims to love you, Ma. It's not how people show love. Papa loved you and never hit you. Bruno is sick and needs help; he needs to stop drinking."

"It doesn't happen very often. I'm fine."

Theresa disagreed but didn't want to argue with her hurting mother. "Ma, please, I'm begging you, please leave him."

"You don't understand. I have to consider Giovanni. For better or worse, he's my husband; I can't leave him." The subject was closed.

War on Two Fronts

T he next few years were a blur for Nina. While the world was at war, she endured her own within her marriage. Nina had to admit that her brother-in-law Tony had been right all along. Bruno was not the kind, caring person she thought he was, but rather a member of the mafia in town.

For the sake of her children, though, she tried very hard to make her marriage work. She tried hard to please Bruno and turned a blind eye to his drinking, gambling, and cheating. She did his bidding and endured physical and verbal abuse because he was her husband. She didn't have a choice.

She did her best to insulate Theresa and Giovanni from his ugly ways. She cleverly learned how to hide her bruises from everyone. She never spoke an unkind word about Bruno because she never knew who was listening. Instead, she spent her time raising her young son and listening to her daughter fret about her love, who was off fighting in the war.

Giovanni was spoiled terribly by his father and did whatever he wanted. He stole things from his sister's room, just for fun, and then lied about it. Nina had a difficult time maintaining order in her own home. Giovanni was a holy terror; if he didn't get his way, he threw a tantrum until his parents gave in. Bruno always sided with his son; the boy was incorrigible.

In 1944, Nina received word her mother succumbed to pneumonia. She and Theresa went to Scranton for the funeral. Bruno was too busy to go and forbade Nina to bring Giovanni to the funeral, so Jesse agreed to watch him. They were gone for a week when Bruno called and demanded she come home immediately. The boy missed his mother.

At the same time, the Allied forces invaded Normandy in France to liberate it from Germany. Nina and Theresa prayed for Eric's safety and the safety of all the Allied forces. Theresa didn't know he was in Corsica, Africa, feverish and sick with malaria at the time. He was not part of the most massive seaborne invasion in history, but that invasion laid the foundation for victory. They prayed daily for the defeat of Adolf Hitler and his men.

On the home front, Theresa tried hard to ignore Bruno. She spent as much time away from home as she could. She and Lil volunteered at the USO to help the war effort. They worked clothing drives, delivered flyers, wrote letters, and did whatever they could to shorten the war's length.

Nina devised a way to warn her daughter when Bruno was drunk or angry at home. Whenever Theresa went out in the evening and was ready to come home, it was safe to go inside if the light was on in the living room window. But if the light was out, Theresa knew Bruno was home drunk.

Those were the nights she stayed either with Lil or her cousin Yolanda. Both girls knew enough not to ask any questions. Theresa was very grateful.

Over the years, Theresa tried hard to get her mother to leave Bruno, but Nina always refused. Bruno tried to be a good stepfather but didn't know what to do. He still wanted her to go out with Dominic Santucci, but she always refused. She hoped her refusals didn't cause her mother any abuse, but she loved Eric.

By the end of World War II, in the fall of 1945, Giovanni ruled the roost and was quickly learning how to manipulate his parents. He pretty much did whatever he wanted. Everyone let him have his way, except for Theresa. She tried to hold him accountable for his actions.

She was more than a bit miffed at her mother. Nina had been very strict with her, but Giovanni could do just about anything. She felt the double standard was wrong. Theresa remembered her childhood all too well with a mother who always told her no. No didn't seem to be in Nina's vocabulary where Giovanni was concerned.

It's not that Theresa disliked her little brother; she just didn't have much time for him. She spent all of her time between work, volunteering for the war effort, and writing letters to Eric.

Now that the war was finally over, Theresa couldn't wait for Eric to be discharged from the Army and return home. It was all she could think and talk about.

Giovanni knew where Theresa had Eric's letters stashed away in a hatbox on her closet shelf. She yelled at him whenever he went into her room. He was determined to get his hands on the letters even though he didn't know how to read.

He frequently went into her room and played with her cosmetics whenever she wasn't home. Somehow, she always knew when he had touched her stuff. It frustrated her immensely.

Once Giovanni began school, Nina went back to work at the Roma Café and under the ever-watchful eye of her domineering husband. If anyone at the Café showed her attention, she paid for it at home.

Once a handsome customer asked to speak to the cook, so the waitress got Nina from the kitchen. "Are you the person who made my delightful meal?" he asked. "You are as pretty as your culinary creations are delicious."

"Yes, sir, I am the cook here," Nina answered as she blushed at his compliment. "I'm glad you enjoyed your meal."

"How would you like to come and cook for me at my new restaurant in Pittsburgh? You would have free reign of my kitchen and a staff of a dozen assistants. I'll pay you double whatever your boss is paying you here."

"Thank you, sir, but I work here for my husband, and I cannot accept your offer." Nina nervously glanced around and saw Bruno watching her intently. Storm clouds instantly appeared in his eyes. Quickly she nodded politely to the man and turned to leave the table, but he grabbed her elbow and repeated his offer.

Again, she declined the offer just as Bruno came to the table. "Excuse me, sir, why did you ask to speak to my cook? She's busy and needed in the kitchen." Nina excused herself and quickly fled.

A few moments later, Bruno came into the kitchen, grabbed her hand, and pulled her into the gambling room. Once there, he locked the door and shoved her against the wall.

"How dare you openly flirt with a customer! How dare you entertain thoughts of leaving the Café!" He sneered as his temples began to pound. He gathered her hair in his fists and started pulling it.

"I wasn't flirting with anyone, and I would never leave the Café. I like working here with you. Please, Bruno, let go of my hair; you're hurting me."

He just laughed and pulled harder. Nina had learned the signs and knew he was thinking about how he could hurt her here at the Café with employees and patrons very close by.

"Please, not here. Let me show you how much you mean to me. I love you," Nina said. She began kissing Bruno and caressing him through his trousers.

Over the years, she had learned how to stroke his ego. She knew the best way to defuse the situation was to submit to him. So, Nina began removing her dress as she told him she loved him and would never leave him.

As she shed her clothes, his anger subsided a bit. He liked it when Nina was subservient to him. It made him feel superior. He unzipped his pants to take what she offered. He leaned her over the gambling table and thrust himself inside her as he made a mental note to make her pay for the incident later.

Afterward, he left the room with a smug look on his face. Nina told him she would go back to the kitchen after getting dressed. Alone, Nina sat and hugged herself; she felt like she belonged to the devil himself. She winced as she put her dress back on and combed through her hair with her fingers. Nina wondered what she ever did wrong in life that led her to her current situation.

In the kitchen, she learned Bruno had gone across the street to the Westwood Tavern. Carlo said Bruno's mood seemed black. Nina just nodded and went back to work. The sex she had just given him wasn't enough. She wondered what awaited her at home this evening and prayed she was strong enough to endure it.

Later at home, Nina suggested that Theresa have dinner and a sleepover with her friends. Theresa took the hint and quickly left the house. After dinner that night, Bruno told Giovanni he was going on an overnight adventure with Carlo. The boy was thrilled; he idolized Carlo.

Nina was surprised to hear this and was just about to ask a question when someone knocked at the door. It was Carlo who had arrived to gather Giovanni. He nodded to Bruno but didn't look at Nina at all. As quickly as he had appeared, Carlo and Giovanni were gone.

Bruno sat at the table and glared at Nina. She could feel his anger growing.

"Bruno, I don't understand why you are so angry. I certainly didn't know that man, and I didn't invite him to the restaurant today. You should be flattered he liked my cooking so much that he wanted to hire me. I cook for you every day." As she spoke, his temples throbbed. She should stop talking.

"I made your favorite cannoli for dessert. Would you like some now or in a little while?"

Again, he glared at her, then finally spoke.

"Nina, you sicken me. How dare you speak of that man in my house! How long have you been playing me for a fool?"

"I don't know what you are talking about. I don't know the man and have never seen him before. I don't even know his name."

Bruno just shoved the dishes off the table and onto the floor, making a huge mess. "Clean this mess up right now," he said as he stood. "I'll be right back, and you better have everything done," and he strode out of the room.

Nina quickly cleaned up the mess and did the dinner dishes. She was just putting the last pot away when he walked into the kitchen. He took her hand and led her to the basement door.

"Go downstairs and wait for me there."

She opened the door and lifted her hand to turn on the lights. He smacked her hand and told her to go down in the dark. She nodded her head and looked down into the dark cellar. Her heart skipped a beat as she stumbled down the steps but caught herself before she fell.

She stood in the dark at the bottom of the steps waiting for Bruno. She had no idea what was going to happen. He appeared as a silhouette at the top of the stairs, and it looked like he had something in his hands, but she couldn't tell what. He struck a match and lit a candle as he proceeded down the steps. He closed the door behind him. She could see the fury in his eyes as he approached her. For some reason, she shivered.

He motioned for her to go under the steps where there were wooden shelves along the wall to store her canned goods and preserves. She noticed there was a small table there and something on the floor. Near the table, he shoved her from behind, and she went falling onto the concrete floor. He kicked her in the stomach, and she cried out in pain. He had never done that before.

"You disgust me, Nina. You acted like a puttana today, so I'm going to show you how men treat a puttana."

He grabbed her arms and jerked her up and around by the hair. "You are my wife, my property, and you shouldn't act like a puttana around other men." He said through clenched teeth as he hit Nina across the face. He tied her arms together with a rope and shoved her forward onto the table. He hit her back and buttocks several times using his belt while calling her a puttana.

Nina finally cried out in pain and pleaded for Bruno to stop. Her backside felt like it was on fire. He stopped his assault.

"Are you done acting like a puttana? Are you going to straighten up and act like my wife?"

"Bruno, I am your wife. I don't know why you think I acted like a puttana, but I am not one. You should know I love you, and I belong to only you and no one else," she said through her tears.

"I'm sorry that man flirted with me, but it's not my fault. You are the only man for me. What can I do to prove that to you? You say you love me, but yet, you beat me. Is this how you show your love?"

Her words resounded in his ears, and he put the belt down. He untied her arms and held her in an embrace. She trembled in fear and pain. She usually just took his abuse in silence. She had never spoken back to him before.

"Nina, I do love you; that's why I got so angry when I saw you talking and flirting with that man. Puttanas flirt with men; ladies do not. I had to teach you a lesson. You are mine, and I will never let you go. Promise you will never leave me."

"I promise I will never leave you." She said through her tears. "Please, let's go upstairs to bed. You are my husband, and I want to show you how much I love you."

Later that night, after the untiring sexual demands of her husband were satisfied, he fell asleep. Nina lay awake, sore and aching from today's abuse. She shed silent tears as she began to pray.

She prayed to God Bruno never found out she had just lied to him. She had begun to realize that she would need to find the courage to leave him if she wanted to survive.

Nina needed to save some money so she could get away from him. She decided to skim a couple of dollars from Bruno's household money each week. He would never know.

She'd hide the money in a safe place where he would never look. She finally fell asleep dreaming about a future without Bruno and his abuse.

A Family Wedding

On a cold and snowy early December day, Theresa nervously checked and rechecked her reflection in the mirror as she touched up her red lipstick. Her hair and makeup were flawless, and her dress was the latest fashion. She didn't know why she was so nervous that Eric and his parents were invited to Sunday dinner.

Mama and Santina Farchione were long-time friends and knew one another well. Theresa, however, was anxious about what type of mood Bruno would be in during the visit with Eric's parents. She prayed he wouldn't get drunk or be rude. She learned never to expect too much from her stepfather.

She also hoped her seven-year-old brother behaved himself. Giovanni always had to be the center of attention.

She had an idea why they were coming over but didn't want to get her hopes up too much. She and Eric talked a lot about the future, and she felt confident he was giving her an engagement ring for Christmas in a few weeks. However, certain formalities had to take place. Eric must ask her mother and Bruno for permission to marry her, and the parents must meet to discuss the formal announcement.

She and Eric didn't care about any of that. They just wanted to get married as soon as possible. Since Eric had returned home from the military a few years ago, they had both been working hard to save enough money to get married.

Eric had been a mechanic in the army and quickly got a job when he got home, but a mechanic's salary was deemed unacceptable in Bruno's eyes. He told Theresa he would not give his blessing for her to marry a "grease monkey."

Since that day, Eric worked hard to get a job on the railroad. They finally hired him in the fall of 1947, and Theresa was so proud of him. Bruno would have to give his blessing now.

A knock on the door broke into her thoughts.

"Theresa, Eric, and his parents are here," announced Giovanni from her doorway.

"Thanks, Giovanni," she answered. "Remember, if you behave today, I'll take you to McCrory's and let you pick out whatever comic book you want."

"Okay, but only if you let me get two comic books and some candy."

"You drive a hard bargain, but it's a deal, buddy." She answered as they went downstairs and into the living room.

"Ciao, Mr. and Mrs. Farchione. I'm so glad you can join us for dinner today. Mama has outdone herself and made her special chicken cacciatore for us."

"Theresa, my dear, you look beautiful as always," answered Antonio Farchione. "Doesn't she, Eric?"

Eric had pulled her close when she walked into the room and given her a quick hug. His eyes shone when he looked at her. The feelings they had for one another were quite evident.

"Well, now that we're all here, let's go into the dining room and have a toast to our families," announced Bruno. Nina quickly agreed, and the group moved to the next room. Nina was thrilled to see Bruno acting like a gracious host.

Last night, he argued he was unhappy with Theresa's choice of beaus. He proceeded to go on at length about Dominic Santucci until Nina said Theresa did not love Dominic but Eric. Nina reminded him about their lunch with Eric at the Fort Steuben Ballroom two weeks before.

Eric had invited them to lunch while Theresa was at work and had asked their permission to marry her. Nina said yes immediately, while Bruno grumbled. By the time lunch was over, Bruno grudgingly gave his consent. Eric had won him over.

Bruno was now starting to warm up to the idea since he had no other choice. Deep down, he knew that Theresa didn't need his permission but was treating him with respect as her stepfather. Nina had done a great job raising her.

He saw their wedding as an opportunity to show everyone what a wonderful husband and father he was. So, he would throw his stepdaughter a grand wedding, whether she wanted one or not. That would earn him big points with Vincenzo since he valued "la famiglia" above all else.

The dinner was a huge success, and Bruno played the doting stepfather. He said he would spare no expense for the wedding of his lovely stepdaughter. Nina sat in amazement at his change of heart. Just a few months ago, he told Nina he wouldn't pay for any part of a wedding for Theresa unless she married Dominic.

After dessert and espresso, Antonio and Santina thanked them and departed, thrilled that Eric was marrying Theresa. Soon after, Giovanni left with Theresa and Eric. They headed to McCrory's, a local five-and-dime store. As promised, they were going to buy comic books for Giovanni.

Bruno left to check in on the Tavern, and Nina went into the kitchen to clean up the mess from dinner. Once she was alone, Nina said a prayer of thanksgiving that everything had turned out so well. She had just finished cleaning up when Theresa and Giovanni returned. Her two children were her whole world. She would sell herself to the devil to protect them and keep them safe.

A few weeks later, Theresa and Eric got engaged on Christmas Eve. They set their wedding date for October. That gave Nina enough time to plan a bridal shower and a wedding.

That winter and spring flew by quickly as everyone was busy making plans for the wedding. Bruno fumed over Theresa's wedding gown's cost but had to admit she looked radiant in it. Nina kept her dress very simple, and Bruno wanted to know why.

He wanted her to buy something extravagant, but she stood her ground and kept the simple dress. After almost ten years together, he still didn't realize his wife didn't like to bring attention to herself.

On a chilly Saturday morning in March, while Nina was busy cleaning the house, there was a knock at the door. She had been scrubbing the kitchen floor on her hands and knees when Giovanni said, "Ma, there's a lady here to see you. She said she couldn't come in but wants you to meet her on the front porch."

Nina was curious and went to greet the visitor. It was Domenica. The two women hugged each other fiercely. It took all of Nina's resolve not to cry in front of her former sister-in-law. She wanted to ask her in but knew Domenica would not agree to go inside. Instead, they sat on the front porch glider and talked while holding hands.

"Nina, I hardly recognize you. You look so thin and tired. Are you okay?"

"Domenica, you are a sight for sore eyes. You haven't changed at all. I'm okay. Thank you for allowing Theresa to stay at your home all those times. My life has changed so much since I lost Angelo."

"Nina, she's my goddaughter as well as my niece. I'd do anything for her and you. I came to tell you my mother passed away in Italy a few months ago. She sent this necklace to you. She wanted you to have it." Domenica pulled out a delicate gold necklace with a tiny solid gold heart on it. "Angelo bought it for her a very long time ago."

"Oh, Domenica, I'm so sorry to hear that. How are you doing? Are your sisters okay?"

"I'm fine. Both sisters decided to move to Australia. They don't want to come to America. I'm fine with that. I did want to give you this necklace. It's yours to keep or do whatever you want."

Nina looked at the necklace; it was simple in its beauty. It made her heart hurt as she thought about Angelo. He was such a handsome, loving, and kind man. Her life with him was a distant but beautiful memory.

"I'll give this to Theresa today. It belongs to her," she said as she put the necklace in the pocket of her dress. "It's so good to see you. Are you sure you can't come inside?"

"No, I must go now; Tony doesn't know I'm here. I love and miss you, Nina."

"I love and miss you, too, Domenica. Theresa is getting married in October, and I want you and Tony to be there."

"I already know. Theresa visits often. I want to be there for her, but I can't promise it just yet. You'd better get back inside before you catch a chill. I pray for you and Theresa every night." Before Nina could respond, Domenica was off the porch and halfway up the street.

Nina went inside and made herself a cup of tea to warm up. She missed Domenica so much it hurt. Nina couldn't wait for Theresa to come home from work so she could give her the necklace. She knew Theresa would cherish it.

Since that day, Nina decided to go to the A&P store for her groceries on Saturday mornings around nine o'clock. She remembered that Domenica shopped there on Saturday mornings. They invariably ran into each other and exchanged pleasantries before continuing their separate ways. They even managed to have lunch together one day at DiFederico's Spaghetti House without either husband finding out. Each encounter made Nina feel good about herself.

At the end of July, Nina hosted a bridal shower for Theresa, held in a banquet room at the Fort Steuben Ballroom. Nina wanted it to be a simple affair, but Bruno insisted that she include many of his associates' wives. Nina and Theresa were both appalled when Judy Jordan walked in, along with a few of her girls. They were not on the guest list, and many other guests began to murmur loudly.

Judy walked straight up to Theresa and Nina. "Congratulations, Theresa, on your upcoming marriage. Your future husband is very handsome, right girls?" They chuckled and said they were disappointed they didn't know him.

Judy continued and directed her comments to Nina, "We are well acquainted with your husband, though. He's the one who told us to come. You're a strong woman to put up with him."

Nina wanted to crawl under a table and cry. She didn't know what to say to the woman before her.

"We're not staying. We just wanted to give you a present." And with that, she pulled out a beautifully wrapped gift for Theresa and an envelope for Nina. "Let's go, girls."

A mortified Nina thought the shower was a disaster, but Domenica instantly announced that lunch was ready and games would follow. Nina shot her a look of gratefulness, and Domenica just winked.

Nina shoved the envelope into her purse. Theresa was afraid to open the gift, but it turned out to be a beautiful crystal vase from The Hub, the nicest department store in town.

Bruno asked if she liked his surprise guests as they went to bed that night. Nina didn't answer him at all.

The next day, as Nina was cleaning up some things, she remembered the envelope Judy had given her. She retrieved it from her purse.

Inside were ten $100 bills and a note that read:

Dear Nina,

You don't know me, but I pray for you nightly. Yes, I do pray.
I know you must disagree with my career choice.
However, you must realize that sometimes you don't
always have a choice in life.
You must be a strong woman to have married a man like Bruno.
I know life for you must be very difficult at times.
This small gift is for you to use when you've had enough of him.

I hope it helps.

Sincerely,
Judy

Nina put the note and money in her secret place. Her funds were growing.

When the time came to send out the wedding invitations, Nina made sure the Stellano's were on the list. After all, they were Theresa's godparents and Zia and Zio, and Theresa wanted them there. She knew Bruno was mad, but she stood her ground with him.

Bruno was furious that Nina included them. He intensely disliked Tony and made no bones about it. However, she would not back down on the issue. She told Bruno he could beat and abuse her all he wanted, but the Stellano's would receive an invitation and be welcome to attend their niece's wedding.

In the end, Bruno grew tired of the argument and allowed the invitation to be sent. Nina had paid a heavy price, though. He beat her so severely she feared she had a cracked rib.

She gingerly wrapped her ribs up on the wedding day and wore the plain, loose-fitting dress Bruno hated. She hoped no one would notice how slowly she walked; every step caused her pain.

Nina believed everyone would focus on the bride and groom. She prayed her daughter was so excited about the wedding that she wouldn't notice anything wrong.

The smile on Theresa's face when she saw Domenica and Tony sitting in a pew at St. Anthony's Church that day was well worth the beating. Theresa was happy they were there.

Nina had kept her promise to her baby daughter. On a sunny and crisp autumn day in 1948, Theresa married Eric, the man she loved. She looked beautiful in her ivory satin dress with lace accents, and he looked handsome in his jet-black tuxedo. They made a stunning pair. Lillian was the maid of honor, and Yolanda and Dora were bridesmaids.

Her brother Giovanni was not a part of the wedding party. Bruno was furious about it, but Theresa stood her ground and reasoned he was too young to be a groomsman and too old to be a ring-bearer. She said if he was an altar boy, he could be a part of her wedding. Father Paul obligingly offered to train him; however, he refused to attend the classes.

Bruno got so drunk at the reception that he passed out, embarrassing Nina. Rocco was tending the bar and told Enzo when it happened. Enzo and Jesse took Bruno home, and Rocco promised to bring Nina home safely after the reception.

His girlfriend, Gina, wasn't happy with the thought of taking Nina home after the reception. She threw a fit and started causing a scene until Rocco took her aside and quietly talked to her. Whatever he said seemed to calm her down, and she left the reception by herself.

Everyone gathered around Eric and Theresa at the end of the evening and sang, *"Let Me Call You Sweetheart."* After a couple of quick goodbyes to their family, they left.

Nina had tears of happiness in her eyes when Rocco came to take her home. Her daughter was married. Sensing she was sad, Rocco suggested they grab a nightcap before leaving. Nina didn't know what awaited her at home, so she agreed.

It turned out Rocco was an excellent listener and knew precisely what type of man Bruno was. Nina poured her heart out that night, and Rocco just listened. When she finished speaking, the tears began to flow. He just held her hand and let her cry. He told her she deserved better, and he prayed she would find the strength and courage to leave her husband someday. His kindness and compassion touched Nina.

As he dropped her off on Seventh Street, she wished again she had the strength to leave her husband. She knew it would take a firm resolve on her part to make it happen. She didn't know if she had it within her.

Trust Issues and Threats

T he day after the wedding, Bruno was livid. He was angry because he had passed out and even more enraged when he found out Rocco had brought Nina home. He pushed her down into the basement again, and this time gave her a black eye along with several bruised ribs.

Nina had enough and decided to go to the police. She would tell them about all of the abuse, making Bruno stop. The following day, while he was at work and Giovanni was at school, Nina walked to Steubenville's police station downtown. She wore a babushka on her head with oversized dark sunglasses on her face. Her coat hung sadly on her thin frame.

Several officers were processing a group of Judy's girls for illegal prostitution. The desk clerk didn't even look up at her when she told him she wanted to speak to someone about her abusive husband. The clerk told her to take a seat.

One officer glanced her way, and she thought he looked vaguely familiar. She must have seen him at the Café before. He smiled at her, stood, and motioned for her to come with him. She assumed he would take care of her. He brought her into a room at the end of a long hallway; a metal table and chairs were inside.

The officer smiled again at her, kindly. "I'm Officer Pete Smith. Have a seat; I'll be right back." A few minutes later, he came back with two cups of steaming black coffee. He handed her one as he asked her name.

"Thank you. My name is Nina Pagano, and I want to file an abuse report. My husband beats and abuses me."

"Okay, Mrs. Pagano, are you sure he is abusing you? Are you sure you didn't just fall and hurt yourself? Sometimes ladies, especially ones who are clumsy, are embarrassed when they trip and fall."

"No, officer. My husband likes to beat me. This time he even punched me in the eye." She took off the dark sunglasses just as there was a sharp knock at the door.

Officer Pete got up, opened the door, and Bruno walked into the room. He was seething. He nodded to the police officer.

"Pete, thanks for taking care of my wife."

"No problem, Bruno. I'm glad I was here. You're going to take care of my gambling debt now. Right?"

"Of course," Bruno answered tersely. "Let's go, Nina. We are done here."

The shock of seeing Bruno there left her shaking like a leaf. Nina tried to stand but couldn't make her legs work. Bruno and the officer lifted Nina out of the chair and out the door together. Bruno's car sat idle with Rocco in the driver's seat and Carlo in the back. Bruno shoved her in the car without a word, and they took off for home.

She sat quietly between Carlo and Bruno in the back. She silently pleaded with Rocco to look at her in the rearview mirror, but he did not. Just a couple of days ago, he had shown her compassion after her daughter's wedding. Today, he seemed like a stranger.

At home, Bruno marched her into the bedroom. There he ripped off all her clothes and tied her spread eagle to the bed. In pain from her previous beating a few days ago, Nina could only pray that she passed out from Bruno's punishment. She no longer cared. She was tired of always being afraid.

"Fanculo! What am I going to do with you? Why do you torment me so? Why do you constantly make me want to hurt you?"

Nina said nothing in return. He didn't want her to answer anyway. She had no idea why he was continually hurting her. She just wanted it to stop.

Instead of beating her, he caressed and kissed her naked body. He did it gently at first and then more insistent as if he was trying to give her a massage. "I do love you, Nina. I have since the day you walked into the

Café with those scones looking for a job. You were so vulnerable. We're kindred spirits."

He started to nibble on her body and chuckled as she strained to move away when the nibbles became rougher bites. She was sure he was deliberately callous, even though he kept murmuring he loved her. He was enjoying her discomfort.

Abruptly he got off the bed and stripped off his clothes. As he came back to the bed, Nina saw he was rock hard. He straddled her and shoved himself into her mouth. She almost choked. He moved in and out, enjoying the moistness of her mouth. "That's it, Nina, take me." Then he emptied himself, telling her she belonged to him alone.

Afterward, he left the room and came back with a bottle of whiskey and his cigars. He took a long swig from the bottle and then held it up to her mouth. "Have some whiskey. It's good." She didn't want any, but he forced it down her throat. It burned as it went down; she hated alcohol.

He sat on the bed next to her and surveyed her body. She was thin, and he could see her bones. "You're much too thin, Nina. You should have more meat on your bones with the way you cook. You're a better cook than my mother, and she was damn good."

As he looked at her, he got aroused again. He climbed on top of her and entered her roughly. She wasn't ready and cried out in pain.

He pounded himself into her as hard as he could. As if by doing so, he showed her that she was his to do whatever he wanted. He emptied the whiskey bottle and lit up a cigar. He knew she didn't like him to smoke in bed, but he didn't care.

The tip of the cigar was red hot. On impulse, Bruno placed the end of it on her inner left thigh and quickly removed it. She screamed as it burned her skin. "There; you've been branded now and belong to me. You will always be mine until the day you die." At that point, she passed out.

It was dark outside when she came to, and Bruno held a bowl of broth near her. It smelled wonderful, and she realized she hadn't eaten in a long while. Nina was hungry but couldn't move because Bruno still had her tied to the bed. Her inner thigh hurt, and she remembered he had burned her with his cigar.

"Nina, you need to learn how to be obedient to your husband. Sometimes, you make me so mad that I do things I don't want to do. You are mine, and you'll never be rid of me. You need to realize that." His eyes were black as coal, and his voice devoid of any emotion.

"Everything I do is for you and Giovanni, and I will not have you ruining our life. You must be submissive and do what I say, or someone will get hurt badly. You need to make a choice right now. Are you going to go to the police again, or are you going to be an obedient wife?"

"I choose to be an obedient wife," she whispered.

"Promise me you will never go to the police again. I don't need Vincenzo to find out you were there today. That would be bad for la famiglia. Luckily Pete recognized you."

"I promise, I'll never go to the police again," she whispered again.

"Good, now eat some soup. We won't ever talk about this again."

He untied her and helped her eat the soup. Afterward, he carried her to the bathroom and left her there to tend to herself.

For many months after that, Bruno had his men follow her around closely. She fumed about it but didn't say anything to anyone. She was exceedingly mad at Carlo and Rocco. They both had seen her badly bruised body and black eye and had not helped her.

She stayed away from the A& P store as she didn't want it to get back to Bruno that she spoke to Domenica. She didn't want Domenica to know what had happened; Bruno had broken her spirit. She felt ashamed.

She found herself always looking around to see who was watching her. Wherever Nina went, Bruno's men watched her. Even if she went to Theresa and Eric's apartment two blocks away, someone followed her.

Theresa and Eric settled into married life, and Nina was happy for them. Theresa was soon pregnant and due in July. Nina was thrilled for them. She knew theirs would be a loving household to raise a child.

The months passed by quickly, and they welcomed a baby girl, Angela, into their lives in July 1949. Nina was now a Nonna. As she held her precious granddaughter in her arms, she shed tears of joy. Angelo, Nina thought to herself, look, you have a grandchild. She thought of him many times over the years and often wondered what her life would be like if he were still alive.

The following year, Nina lost her father to stomach cancer. She went to Scranton with Lena and Benny. Bruno was again too busy to go. She stayed with Patsy and his wife, Gert. He instantly knew something was off. Even after all these years, he knew his sister well.

"Nina, please walk to the pond with me. I want to show you how it's grown since you last visited."

As the two of them walked through the field, he stopped and turned to look at her directly.

"Nina, please tell me what's wrong. I know you as well as I know myself. Something is wrong. You're like a scared doe that knows she's about to die."

"I'm fine, Patsy; I'm just sad about Papa. Our parents are both gone now."

"Don't lie to me. I know something is wrong. Lena and Benny told me Bruno is abusive. Why do you stay with him?"

"He's my husband and the father of my son. I can't abandon my child. Besides, he's not always abusive. Lena and Benny should stay out of my business."

"They are only concerned about you, sis. They love you. We all love you and are here for you. You are welcome to stay here in my home with Gert and me. I'll kill him if he comes after you here. I'm not afraid of him or his mafia connections."

She hugged him. "Thanks, Patsy, but I'll be fine. I'm stronger than you think. I have to go back; my kids need me. Besides, I'm going to be a Nonna again in the summer."

"Well, my home is always open to you."

They hugged each other again, and Nina shed a few tears for what was and what might have been. Maybe she should have moved back to Scranton years ago after Angelo died. She would never have married Bruno or had his son if she had.

The years seemed to fly by, and when she felt like she couldn't take Bruno's abuse anymore, she tried to leave him, only to have him find her and bring her back. She lost count of the fractured bones and cracked ribs she suffered from him.

Once, she took Giovanni and went to Scranton to visit, intending to stay. After two weeks, the boy missed his father and friends. He called his Pops and told him where they were. Bruno surfaced in Scranton the next day and forced her to return to Steubenville.

Nina endured a severe beating for that. Bruno even derided her in front of Giovanni. The boy was turning out just like his father. One day when Nina had reprimanded him for not listening to her, he pushed his mother and called her stupid. Nina, who had never raised a hand to either of her children, gave him a spanking with the wooden spoon.

The boy went crying to his father, who only chuckled. "Don't worry, son; I'll take care of your mother."

"Thanks, Pops," answered Gio, and he went to his room to read the stack of comic books his father had just brought him. Giovanni loved comic books and was accumulating a vast collection. He collected everything from Dick Tracy to Flash Gordon to Superman.

Rain or shine, Bruno and Giovanni went downtown together every Saturday morning. Gio would spend hours looking at all the magazines and comic books at the Diamond Cigar Store while his Pops met with Vincenzo, Luca, and Enzo. Bruno let him pick out several comics each week.

From there, they would go up on the hill to Butte Field. The field had a wooden track where Bruno would drink and gamble all afternoon on the races. Giovanni was left to his own devices to wander over to the old stables where he gambled as well by playing marbles or penny-pinching.

Sometimes Enzo and his son Nunzio went with them. Many times, Enzo and Bruno had long discussions about their families.

Over the years, Enzo and Jesse had intervened many times on Nina's behalf. They both desperately wished Bruno would quit drinking. Enzo often reminded Bruno that Nina was a good woman and he should be kinder to her.

Enzo was still finding it hard to keep his brother out of trouble. Their hope of Bruno settling down once he married did not happen. Nina hadn't softened Bruno's sharp edges.

For her own sake, Nina tried to be the obedient wife Bruno wanted. She was subservient to him in all things and endured most of his abuse in silence. Her secret nest egg of money was almost large enough that she could leave him for good.

Her only problem was with Giovanni. He loved his father and would miss him terribly. If she took Gio, then he would, at some point, call his father as he did before. If she left without him, then she would be deserting her son, and she couldn't bear that thought. So, she was in limbo.

One Saturday, as she pulled her coat out of the closet, she noticed a scrap of paper crumpled up on the floor. She had just recently cleaned the closet, so she was surprised that anything was on the floor.

She picked the paper up; it must have fallen out of Bruno's overcoat. He had been acting strangely lately. He had been in a big hurry to get out of the house this morning.

Nina was going to throw the paper away but then thought it might be something important. She opened it and read it. As she did so, her face turned white, and her hands shook.

The handwritten note read:

"Stupido! This is your last warning to settle down.
Do something stupid again, and someone will get hurt. Capisci?"

She dropped the scrap of paper as if burned. To whom did the note belong? Who wrote it, and how did it get into her house? To whom was the threat intended?

Nina shoved the note into her coat pocket. She had to get out of the house and think. She buttoned up her coat and went to the park by the river.

She always liked to go there to think. It was a pretty space with lots of people enjoying nature. It also had lots of wildflowers. She loved to sit on a bench by the flowers and think about her childhood home in Scranton. Those were much simpler times.

It was at the park that Domenica found her about an hour later. She had been out looking for her. Theresa had an accident and was at the hospital. Nina flew off the bench and was on her way to her daughter.

163

An Accident

As she rushed into the room, Nina couldn't believe how pale and lifeless her beautiful, loving daughter looked. Theresa, with the same piercing blue eyes as her father, who was always so vibrant and quick to laugh, now lay unconscious under a hospital bed's crisp white sheets.

Theresa's arms and legs were covered in thick white casts. Several tubes were attached to her body and connected to a couple of ugly, noisy machines. She had fallen down a long flight of narrow stairs in her home, landing on the cold concrete basement floor.

Was her fall indeed an accident or just made to look like one? How long had she lain unconscious at the bottom of the steps before Eric found her? Was Nina the reason her daughter was in this bed? Nina couldn't wait for Theresa to regain consciousness. She desperately needed to know what had happened.

As she looked at Theresa, Nina's thoughts flashed to the sweet baby she had held tenderly in her arms, the precious girl who made her father's eyes twinkle. She thought about the brave teen who put herself through beauty school and then married her best friend's brother.

Theresa was all those things and more. The whooshing sound, made by the massive hospital door opening, shook her out of her thoughts.

"Is Theresa going to be okay? What did the doctor say?" she asked Eric as he entered the room. "Does she have internal injuries?" "Does he know why she's still unconscious?"

Eric wiped tears away from his eyes and looked at Nina. "Doctor Barducci thinks she'll be fine. The shock of the fall caused her to lose consciousness. He thinks she'll come to once her body recovers from that. The ex-rays indicate a lot of bruising and several broken bones, but no apparent internal injuries."

"Thank goodness. Let's pray the doctor is correct. I wonder what caused her to fall. I wish she'd wake up and tell us exactly what happened."

"The doctor said she'll be here for several weeks while her body heals. Then, after that, she'll have lots of physical therapy."

Nina sighed. "I wish I could help you out with the girls, but I'm sure Bruno won't allow it. You know what happens if I disobey him," she said hopelessly.

She felt hopeless and scared. Those were two emotions Nina knew well. She prayed to God Theresa would be fine. Her whole life, she had tried to protect Theresa from harm. Now, Theresa lay lifeless in a hospital bed, quite possibly because of her actions.

No mother should see her child in this condition. Theresa was young and healthy; she would recover and return to her husband's loving arms. She would bounce back quickly. Nina prayed to God Theresa would make a full recovery.

Nina thought about the note hidden deep in the pocket of her old coat. She had found it just this morning on the closet floor. She had been planning to run away again.

The note was a threat that someone would get hurt. Who wrote it? Was it meant for her or Bruno? Was Theresa's fall somehow connected to the note? Nina wasn't sure.

She spent the morning on a park bench, thinking about her life and wondering what to do. It was there that Domenica found her and told her Theresa had been in an accident. Everyone was looking for her.

Nina needed to think about her next move, but the hospital machines' noise made a horrible buzzing sound in her head. She lifted her hand to her head to clear the noise.

Nina realized she was still wearing her wedding ring. Oh, how she hated it. Bruno had chosen the ring because of its' gaudiness. He wanted everyone to see his wealth. She wanted to take it off and throw it away.

She wished many things, but mostly she wished she could take away her daughter's pain. She needed to figure out if Theresa's fall was an accident or if Bruno had caused it as a warning to her. Was he the reason Theresa was in this hospital bed?

She had to find out, but as much as she loved her children, she wasn't quite sure her spirit could survive going back again. But what choice did she have?

Eric believed Theresa's fall was an accident, but Nina wasn't sure. Bruno was very good at making things look accidental.

If Bruno had caused Theresa's accident, then it was done as a warning. How much farther would he go if she didn't go back home? Would he harm someone else? Nina didn't know, but she couldn't take that chance. Bruno, her husband, was evil.

Nina was used to living in constant fear. She knew what she had to do. She had to go home. It was the only way to find out what had happened. It was the only way to keep her family safe.

Suspicions and Strange Actions

Nina went straight home. After seeing Theresa at the hospital, she was shaken to her core. Did Bruno harm her? Was the note somehow connected? She had to figure out what had happened.

Bruno had been acting strangely during the past few months. He came home one evening with his suit ripped and a black eye. He slapped her and told her it was none of her business when she questioned him.

Bruno and Giovanni came home from their Saturday outing as she set the table for dinner. It had become a ritual of sorts for them. She was glad they were so close, but it seemed like Gio was getting the kind of education she wished he didn't get.

Just last week, she had found a foil packet of rubbers in the back pocket of Giovanni's trousers. When she questioned him about it, he said his Pops had given it to him. Good lord, the boy wasn't even a teenager yet!

She had confiscated the offensive item and decided it was time to talk with her husband. Bruno told her to mind her own business. Their son's education was his job, and he would do it as he saw fit. The tone of his voice made her close her mouth just as she was about to argue with him.

As they sat down for dinner, Nina mentioned Theresa had an accident and was in the hospital. She was closely watching Bruno as she gave him the news. He seemed genuinely shocked to hear it.

"What kind of accident? Is she hurt?"

"She fell down a flight of stairs and is in the hospital. She has several bumps, bruises, and broken bones. The doctor said there are no internal injuries, but it could take several months to heal."

"Nina, does Eric need help? We can hire a nurse for Theresa and a sitter for the girls. Whatever they need, just let me know, and I'll take care of it."

He seemed genuinely concerned about Theresa, thought Nina. Maybe she was wrong to suspect him after all. Or, perhaps, he was pretending to care.

"She was still unconscious when I left the hospital. I want to go back after dinner if that's okay with you. Eric hasn't left her side. I'm sure he would like to go check in on the girls at his mother's house."

"Of course, Nina. We'll both go to the hospital. Theresa is like a daughter to me. I'll do whatever I can to help her."

They ate a quick dinner, and Bruno told Giovanni to do the dishes so they could leave. Theresa regained consciousness at the hospital but couldn't remember anything about her accident.

Nina was never more grateful than today for Dr. Barducci. He made sure Theresa received excellent care from the nurses. He said Theresa may or may not even remember what happened. Dr. Barducci told Nina to be thankful her daughter didn't have any internal injuries. Bumps, bruises, and broken bones can all heal, he said knowingly.

Nina spent most of the following days and weeks at the hospital with Theresa while Eric was at work. His mother, Santina, took care of the girls. At first, Bruno was supportive but then grew irritable when it affected his home life. Nina worked hard to juggle everything, but sometimes she couldn't do it all.

Domenica and Lena both offered to help, and Nina was most appreciative. They took turns going to the hospital and spending time with Theresa when Nina couldn't go. Eric spent most evenings at the hospital sharing news about their two daughters, Angela and Jaime. Theresa missed them terribly.

Theresa tried hard to remember how the accident happened, but she drew a blank for some reason. Finally, after a couple of months of rehab in the hospital, Theresa was able to go home. It was a joyous occasion for all.

Bruno had seemed genuinely surprised and concerned for her, so Nina concluded it was just an unfortunate accident.

Many months later, she still was baffled by the note she had found on the closet floor the morning of Theresa's accident. Who was it meant for? Was it sent to Bruno as a warning? Who would be stupid enough to threaten a member of the mob? Or did someone in the mob send it to Bruno?

With everything that happened, Nina forgot to ask Bruno about it. He never said anything, so she never brought it up, but she kept it hidden with the money she had saved. One day she would figure it all out.

Hope and A New Ally

As time marched on, Nina had all but given up on her hopes of leaving Bruno. She worked at the Café and took care of their home. Bruno did as he pleased, and Giovanni followed his father's lead. They were very much alike.

Bruno had a new favorite girl at Judy's and spent many nights away from Nina's bed. She was thrilled. Any night she did not have to service her husband or put up with his abuse was a good night. Giovanni, however, noticed and asked his mother why his father did not come home. She was mortified and didn't know what to tell her son, so she changed the subject.

Later, while at work, she mentioned that Bruno should be more discreet about such things. Bruno just grunted and said he would talk to their son.

One Spring day in 1954, Bruno and Enzo both received an urgent telegram from Calabria. Their brother, Father Guido, lost his battle with brain cancer. Nina watched as Bruno's face changed with emotion. He never talked much about his younger brother. Enzo came over, and the two of them made plans to go to Calabria for the funeral.

"I'm sorry to hear about your brother. Do you want me to go to Calabria with you?" Nina inquired.

"No, I don't. I need you to stay here and take care of the Café." Bruno did not want to talk about his younger brother, the priest.

"Okay, well, don't worry about us. Giovanni and I will be fine while you're gone."

"Oh, I'm taking Giovanni with me. Nunzio is going with Enzo as well. It will be a father and son trip. I'm going to show him the old country where his Pops was born. It will be good for his education."

"Are you sure Giovanni should go? He's still so young. Won't he be in the way?"

"He'll be fine with me, Nina. He's my son, and he's not a baby anymore. It will also give you a chance to see what life would be like if you left me. Gio, I'm sure, would stay with me."

"Rocco can handle the Tavern, so all you need to do is look after the Café. Besides, if necessary, Carlo and Rocco can help you."

Two days later, Enzo and Bruno, along with their sons, Nunzio and Giovanni, left for Calabria. Jesse and Nina didn't know when they would be back. At first, Nina enjoyed the peace and solitude, but running the Café full time kept her busy.

She thought she would spend time with her granddaughters, but Angela got the chickenpox, and Theresa was pretty sure Jaime would get them too. Since Nina had never had them, she opted to stay away. She hoped Theresa wouldn't get them either since she was pregnant again.

Nina worked diligently on the accounts for the Café and made sure all the bills got paid. Rocco came over each day to check on her and helped take care of any problems. The two of them worked well together.

She had forgiven both Rocco and Carlo for the incident at the police station several years back. In her heart, she knew they were doing what Bruno had told them to do. Her husband's abuse was a direct result of his alcohol problem.

During Bruno's six months in Italy, Nina depended on Rocco. It was easy to do.

He had broken up with Gina a few weeks after Theresa's wedding and no longer had a steady girlfriend. Nina took to teasing him that she was going to find the perfect girl for him. They joked about it many evenings while tallying the day's business receipts for the Café and Tavern.

Each night after they locked up the businesses, he walked her home and made sure she locked her doors. They often talked about the businesses and many other matters.

Rocco inquired about her life in Scranton and how she came to live in Steubenville. He was interested in her family and her thoughts about the world in general. He didn't have any family and was fascinated to hear about hers.

Nina found herself starting to compare him to Angelo. He was soft-spoken and kind to everyone. Nina had to admit she was starting to have feelings for him. She couldn't let anyone know, and she couldn't act on them. How, she wondered, did her life ever get so complicated?

One morning, Jesse came by to let her know their husbands were finally on their way home. Enzo had sent a telegram; Bruno had not. As Nina opened the Café, Bruno and Giovanni walked through the door a week later. Nina was glad to see them. She realized she had missed them.

That night Bruno was tender to her in bed. He told her he loved and missed her. He gave her a box, and she opened it to find a small locket. Inside was the picture of a small boy that looked like Giovanni. Bruno said the boy was him as a child, and the locket had once been his mother's. He wanted Nina to have it. It was one of the only things he had left from Rosa. His gesture touched Nina. Maybe, this could be a fresh start, she thought. She wanted them to have a normal life, a typical marriage.

A day later, he came home drunk and in a foul mood. He accused her of cheating on him with Rocco. She denied it, and they argued. He told her his men had watched them while he was in Italy. They reported Nina and Rocco had gotten very close. She told Bruno she never cheated on him.

She acknowledged she spent a lot of time with Rocco while Bruno was in Italy, but they worked for him. Bruno agreed. He knew they spent time together taking care of his businesses but said Rocco had confessed to having feelings for her.

Nina was stunned by his admission. Bruno watched her closely and noticed the change in her expression as he said the words. It was all he needed to see. Bruno knew she felt the same way, and he became furious. She quickly denied having feelings for Rocco, but it was too late.

Bruno beat her and left the house in a rage. He had been a fool to think his men were wrong. Bruno went to the Tavern to confront Rocco, but he wasn't there. While drinking whiskey, Bruno came up with a plan, but he needed Carlo's help to set the trap.

He told Carlo to call Rocco and say that Nina wanted him to meet her at eight o'clock in the parking lot of a local department store the following evening. Carlo told him Nina needed his help in finally leaving Bruno.

Rocco listened and quickly agreed; he didn't question Carlo. Rocco knew Carlo worked closely with Nina daily, so he never suspected anything was off.

Across the bar, Bruno sneered as Carlo relayed Rocco's answer. His plan was now in motion.

Bruno's next call was to a particular cop who was a regular player at his gambling table.

The next evening, Bruno borrowed Enzo's car and got to the parking lot about half an hour earlier than Rocco. He had an unregistered .38 caliber snub-nosed revolver under the seat.

It had no serial numbers, so it was untraceable. The sad part was that Bruno genuinely liked Rocco and considered him a good employee. He would take care of Rocco tonight. It would be a costly lesson for Nina to learn what happens to the people who cross him.

About twenty minutes later, Bruno watched as Rocco's car entered the Mr. Wiggs department store's parking lot. He parked away from all the other vehicles in the lot but not far enough away to cause attention. Bruno waited another ten minutes before he snuck out of his car and quietly made his way to Rocco's car under cover of darkness. Quickly, he shot Rocco twice before putting the revolver in Rocco's left hand. Rocco was dead.

Bruno left the parking lot in Enzo's car, just as Officer Pete Smith and his partner, Joe, were turning in. They were responding to a report of gunfire. Pete was one of the local cops on Vincenzo Santucci's payroll. Bruno was confident the officer would list suicide as the official cause of death of Rocco Bricola. That was what Pete got paid to do.

Bruno drove down to the river and threw away the gloves he had worn before dropping off the car at Enzo's. He needed to get rid of some of his anger, so he went to Judy's. Angel, his new favorite girl there, liked things rough. She was just what he needed this night.

After a night of rough sex, Bruno left and went to his old apartment above the Tavern. He needed to clear his mind. Nina's words rang in his head and haunted his thoughts. If he truly loved her, why did he hurt her so much?

It was a question he couldn't answer. Nina always seemed to get under his skin and irritate him to the point that his temples throbbed, and he felt the need to lash out. As always, he settled things with his fists.

He did love her in his way and always wanted to protect her from others. That was why he had her watched while he and Giovanni were in Italy. He didn't want any harm to befall her. She was the mother of his son, his pride and joy, and his son was his whole world.

The next day, Nina was shocked when the news broke that Rocco Bricola was found dead in his car in the Mr. Wiggs department store's parking lot. The police did not suspect foul play and ruled his death a suicide. Nina had her suspicions about what happened, but she didn't say a word to anyone.

During their investigation of Rocco's suicide, the police questioned Bruno about Rocco's affairs. Bruno stated Rocco had been despondent recently over the breakup with a new girlfriend. He suspected that Rocco had a nervous breakdown.

A month later, Bruno announced they would be moving to the apartment attached to the Café. He said it would be easier for him to keep an eye on his businesses if they were close to them. He told Nina she must either sell or rent out the house on Seventh Street.

Around the same time, Theresa and Eric were looking for a house to rent. With three young girls, their current place just wasn't big enough for their growing family. So, Theresa and Eric moved into the house on Seventh Street as Bruno and Nina moved out. Nina was happy that love would once again fill its walls.

That winter, Bruno was attacked outside the Tavern and beaten badly. Nina wanted him to go to the hospital, but he refused. He said he knew who did it and would take care of things.

She questioned him about his strange behavior, but he wouldn't answer. She asked Enzo if he thought Bruno was acting strangely. Enzo said he hadn't noticed but would keep a watchful eye on his brother.

She thought again about the note she still had hidden in her secret box. Maybe the threat was aimed at Bruno after all. Perhaps it had something to do with his weekly trips to Butte Field Park and the gambling he did there. Lately, he seemed very concerned about their finances and was more paranoid about his surroundings.

As the years continued to pass, Nina resigned herself to the fact she would never leave her husband because she couldn't abandon her son. Bruno was right in saying that Giovanni would stay with his Pops if she left. In his eyes, his Pops could do no wrong.

The one thing that made him different from his Pops was his carefree demeanor. The ladies all found him charming, and he used that charm to get whatever he wanted.

He had charmed his way through grade school by always complimenting the nuns and bringing them his mother's fresh-baked pastries. He told his mother he sold them to buy his favorite comics. Instead, he gave them to the nuns at St. Anthony's in return for passing grades on his report cards.

As a teen, Gio was as devilishly ornery as he could be. He ran around town with his best friend, Remo Santucci, Vincenzo's youngest son. They were the same age.

Gio drank and gambled just like his Pops and spent long hours at Judy's. He told his mother he was playing cards; however, she knew that wasn't the case.

Once he reached high school, he charmed a few bright, quiet girls to do his homework and book reports. As for tests, Remo always had the answers; Gio never asked how he got them.

It wasn't that Giovanni couldn't do the work or that he wasn't smart; it was just easier to get by that way. Besides, it gave him more time to do the fun things in life, like drinking, gambling, and having sex with the girls at Judy's.

One night in the hot steamy summer of May 1956, a young teenager broke into the Café around three o'clock in the morning. He had no idea Bruno and Nina lived in the attached apartment. The troubled teen was trying to rob them.

However, Bruno had heard the noise and attacked and shot the intruder several times. Nina called the cops, and by the time they arrived,

Bruno had shot the boy at least five times. There was blood everywhere, and he was pronounced dead at the scene.

The police questioned both Bruno and Nina. She was visibly shaken by the violence and couldn't answer their questions; however, Bruno recounted the incident in great detail. Nina had to leave the room. She went to the bathroom, where she promptly threw up. Her husband had murdered an unarmed intruder right in front of her without any remorse.

It took several months for Nina to feel safe again in her own home. She was just glad Giovanni had not been home to witness the violence. He had been on vacation with Remo and his family at their cottage on the New Jersey shore. Gio had been thrilled when Bruno told him he could go. They were gone the whole summer.

During his senior year of high school in 1959, Gio applied to several colleges. He wanted to go away like many of his peers. His parents, however, had other ideas. Nina wanted him to go to the local Steubenville college and live at home, while Bruno told him to go to the same college as Remo.

Remo and Giovanni were roommates at West Liberty College in West Virginia, about forty minutes from Steubenville. It was a small liberal arts college. They stayed in a dorm but had their cars so they could come and go as they pleased.

That same summer, Bruno was one of four men arrested and charged with operating a gambling ring in Steubenville. Vincenzo made a few calls and got the charges reduced to minor offenses. Bruno pled "no contest" and got off with just a fine. The judge in the case was on Vincenzo's payroll. A brand-new car was delivered to his home two days after the case went through his court.

Luca told him Vincenzo was not happy during his weekly meeting at the Diamond Cigar Store. Luca told him he better settle down and watch himself. Everyone was growing weary of continually bailing out Bruno.

Bruno instantly recalled the threatening note that had been slipped under the door of the Tavern one night several years back while he was there drinking alone.

He had picked up and read the note, then crumbled it and thrown it into the trash. Who would dare send him such a threat? He would find out and eliminate the person. He fumed as he grabbed the note back out of the trash and shoved it into his coat pocket. Who would be stupid enough to threaten a mafia killer?

He would leave the note with the dead person. He just had to figure out who that person was.

Now, as Luca continued to lecture him, that note burned in his mind. Was Luca the author? Luca was like a father to him. How could that be? Bruno was confused; it couldn't possibly be Luca. He had to find that note and confront him.

The only problem was Bruno couldn't remember what he did with the note once he got home that night. He had been so drunk he blacked out.

Family and the Final Straw

I rish Catholic, John Kennedy, was elected President of the United States in 1960. Together with his wife Jackie, America was in love with the handsome young couple.

Every Catholic family had a picture of the Kennedys displayed prominently in their home. Most girls wanted to look and dress like Jackie, and they wanted their guys to be like Jack. The Kennedys ushered in a new era of politics. Nina and Theresa both loved the Kennedys and prayed for them daily.

Giovanni didn't care for politics but liked the party atmosphere. In the early 1960s, Gio dated a few sorority girls he met on campus during his college years. He and Remo both pledged a fraternity. Life for them was one big party after another. They didn't go home very often during the school year; they were too busy having fun.

Nina and Bruno missed Giovanni terribly. Bruno often drove to campus to have dinner with his son and always brought whiskey and cigars. Nina had no clue he went.

Gio worked at the Westwood Tavern during the summers and spent his free time drinking, gambling, and cavorting with Judy's girls.

One summer, Giovanni met Mary Ann Green, a desk clerk and telephone operator at the Fort Steuben Hotel. She was a pretty blonde with a warm smile and a quick laugh. They began dating. He didn't tell his parents because she was Irish and not Italian. His Pops had been adamant that he marry an Italian girl.

Gio confided in his sister, Theresa. She and Eric had seen him out one night with Mary Ann at the Federal Terrace, a local nightclub. Theresa and Eric were there celebrating their wedding anniversary.

They were surprised to run into each other. Theresa instantly liked Mary Ann and told her brother so. He asked Theresa not to say anything to their parents. He liked her and was frankly afraid of what his Pops would say or do if he found out they were dating.

Theresa understood and promised not to say anything. She and Eric still lived in the house on Seventh Street and had lovingly filled it with five children and a dog. Theresa had quit work to raise their family, and Eric had left his job on the railroad for a better job in a local mill. He worked as an electrician and earned a decent wage to support his family. They were happy.

Theresa and Eric limited their kids' exposure and interaction with Nina and Bruno. Nina loved her grandchildren and wished she could spend more time with them. However, she understood why their parents were so protective. They didn't want the kids to witness Bruno's meanness and abuse. It was just one more thing Bruno had taken from her.

He considered them his grandchildren, though, and insisted on seeing them. But he remained aloof around them. He sensed they were afraid of him, so he gave them money, soda pop, and chocolate bars whenever they were around. Little did he know Nina gave them the same things whenever they were there.

Once a month, Bruno demanded the whole family gather for a large dinner on a Sunday. Rosa used to do it in Calabria when he was growing up. So, Bruno made Theresa and Eric attend dinner along with their kids. Bruno expected Giovanni to join them, although he often made excuses for why he couldn't be there. It was always a stressful affair with edgy conversation at the table.

Sometimes, Nina was able to see her grandchildren on a Saturday afternoon. She took them to the movies or for a walk downtown and even taught them how to bake bread. Nina treasured those days. Theresa's three oldest girls had blue eyes, just like Angelo's. They were close in age and played well together. The younger two, a boy and girl, looked like Eric. Nina's heart was full of love for her grandchildren, but she knew she needed to keep them at arm's length for their own protection.

Lately, Bruno lashed out at everyone when he was drunk. Last week, he threatened one of their renters with a knife in his own apartment. Nina had to intervene, and Carlo helped defuse the situation. Nina told the renter he could have three months' free rent in exchange for not pressing charges against Bruno. The renter agreed. Nina used some of her hidden money, so Bruno would think that the man had paid his rent. He was becoming very unpredictable.

On a crisp afternoon in November of 1963, somebody fired three shots at President Kennedy's motorcade in downtown Dallas, Texas. The President was hurt and rushed to the hospital.

Nina was at Theresa's house on Seventh Street at the time. Theresa was sick and resting on the couch. Nina had come by with chicken soup for her daughter. She watched television with Denise, Theresa's youngest daughter when a bulletin flashed across the screen that the President had been shot and was seriously wounded.

Nina turned the station at Theresa's urging, and newscaster Walter Cronkite instantly filled the screen. He struggled to collect himself as he announced the President was dead. Along with his wife, Jackie, the whole nation mourned the handsome and charismatic President's death.

During that visit, Nina found out Giovanni was dating an Irish girl. Theresa let it slip that Mary Ann was Irish. Nina asked who Mary Ann was. At first, Theresa said no one but then realized Nina should know Giovanni was getting serious about a girl. So, she told her mother about Giovanni's girlfriend.

Nina was happy Gio had found a lovely young girl but also worried about Bruno's reaction. She wondered how he would react to his son dating an Irish girl. Bruno wanted Gio to marry an Italian girl.

The next day, she questioned her son about his girlfriend when he came into the kitchen looking for breakfast. Bruno was not around. She wanted to meet the girl. She told Giovanni he ought to invite her to dinner sometime.

Bruno walked into the room as they talked and insisted Giovanni bring his girlfriend home for dinner.

Much to Giovanni's surprise, his Pops instantly liked Mary Ann. They hit it off like old friends. In 1964, Bruno gave his approval when Giovanni said he wanted to marry her.

Gio and Mary Ann wed a year later and moved into one of the apartments behind the Café. Nina was thrilled to see her son so happy. Bruno seemed to mellow and tried not to drink and gamble so much, but old habits were hard to break.

Mary Ann soon found herself pregnant, and everyone was excited; Bruno, most of all. He swore the baby was a boy and demanded they name him Bruno. Gio and Mary Ann told him they would if it was a boy.

In January 1966, Mary Ann gave birth to a son, and they named him Bruno after his grandfather. Because her labor was difficult, Mary Ann had a cesarean section. Her recovery took longer, and she needed bed rest.

After bringing Mary Ann and the baby home from the hospital, Giovanni went out with Remo. Remo insisted they go out to celebrate the fact that Gio was now a father. Mary Ann told him to go. All she wanted to do was rest as she laid down on the couch. She soon fell asleep.

Several hours later, she was sound asleep when a drunk Bruno barged into the apartment, demanding to see his grandson. He had just gotten back from a job in New Jersey for Vincenzo. Things had not gone smoothly. Vincenzo would not be happy.

"Where's my grandson?" demanded Bruno.

In her post-partum state, Mary Ann was furious that Bruno was demanding to see the baby.

"Pops, what are you doing here? "Come back later." I was resting, and the baby is sleeping," said Mary Ann.

"The bambino, I want to see the baby," demanded Bruno. He was loud and slurring his words.

"Pops, the baby is asleep now. You need to go and let me rest. You can see him tomorrow," answered Mary Ann.

It was not the answer Bruno expected. He demanded again to see the baby, but Mary Ann was adamant that he needed to leave the apartment at once.

An argument ensued, and Bruno pulled out a gun. Mary Ann began to scream.

"Get out of my house right now. How dare you enter my home uninvited and unannounced and demand to see my baby. I will not produce my newborn son for a drunk man with a gun."

Nina and half the neighborhood heard the screaming. Nina rushed into the apartment and cajoled Bruno into leaving with her. "Mary Ann, lock the door behind me and don't let him back in," said Nina.

A drunken Bruno was enraged that he could not see his grandson and argued with Nina. How dare they not let him see the baby! He gave Nina a terrible beating at home and left her with a sprained arm, cracked ribs, and a black eye.

Still furious, he went to leave but slipped and fell, hitting his head on the bar in the Café and losing consciousness.

As she lay on the floor, battered and bruised, Nina thought about how she had endured over twenty-five years of abuse at Bruno's hands. She couldn't take any more.

Nina had reached the end of her rope. She knew she needed to get away from Bruno, or he would eventually kill her.

Through her pain and tears, she dragged herself up the stairs to the bathroom and cleaned herself up. Her whole body hurt as she placed a quick call to Lena.

"Lena, I'm done. I can't take his abuse anymore," Nina admitted to her sister.

"I'm here for you and ready to help. Do you need Benny to come and get you?"

"No, I need to talk to Theresa first. I'll speak to her and then be over. Are you sure it's okay with Benny? If Bruno figures things out before I leave for Scranton, there may be some trouble."

"Nina, don't you worry about us. The sooner you get here, the better. I love you."

"I love you too, Lena. I'll see you soon."

Then Nina called Theresa and explained what had happened. Theresa promised to send Eric for her at once.

Nina quietly packed a small suitcase with a few things and grabbed the box where she had hidden the money she had saved over the years. It is more than enough for a ticket out of town. Nina prayed it was enough to begin a new life, a quiet life away from the monster that was her husband.

She removed the ugly, gaudy ring Bruno put on her finger years ago and dropped it in his piss pot. She vowed she would not be a punching bag for him any longer. A quiet knock on the apartment's back door let her know that Eric was there. Quickly she took one last survey of the Roma Café and left.

The light of the moon, high in the sky, guided their way to Eric's parked car. He was shocked by Nina's appearance but knew enough not to say anything. He quickly stashed Nina's suitcase in the back seat, and they were soon on their way to the house on Seventh Street. Nina needed to speak to her daughter.

Once there, Theresa hugged her mother gingerly and told her she loved her as tears streamed freely down both of their faces. "Ma, I'm so sorry that you're leaving town, but I know you'll be safe in Scranton with your brothers. They will protect you."

"I'll be staying with Uncle Patsy. He won't let anything happen to me, and it will give me a chance to heal. I hope Bruno doesn't cause any trouble for you and Eric. I would never forgive myself if he caused you any harm."

"Ma, don't you worry about us. Eric will protect me. I'm just going to miss you terribly. Promise to call me when you get there."

"I will. The family has contacts within the railroad, so I'm taking a bus to Scranton. It's more open than a train car."

Mother and daughter hugged each other one last time, and then Nina left with her son-in-law.

Eric drove her to Weirton. He hugged Nina and told her that he loved her and was brave.

Lena was waiting for her sister. Nina's appearance was almost too much to bear, and her heart went out to her sister.

"Nina, thank God you finally found the courage to leave Bruno. That man is an animal and deserves to be in jail for what he's done to you. Let me call the police, and you can file charges against him."

"No, Lena. That won't do any good. I tried that once before, and it only got a kind man killed. The police are his friends and would look the other way. I want to rest for a few hours before Benny drives me to the bus station."

"Okay, Nina, if you are sure it won't do any good, I believe you. I spoke to Patsy already, and he'll pick you up at the bus station when you arrive."

"Thank you, Lena. I'll never forget your kindness to me."

Benny took her to the Greyhound bus station in the morning, where she bought a one-way ticket and began her two-day journey to Scranton.

Part Three

Old Threats

In the nine months since she arrived in Scranton, Nina healed from the physical abuse Bruno had inflicted upon her. Her emotional scars were another story. She wasn't sure if she would ever get over the years of abuse she endured.

Patsy and Gert were very welcoming, and she was thankful she had a place to stay. They didn't pressure her to tell them anything about her hasty exit from Steubenville. She wasn't sure if she would ever be ready to talk about the years of abuse she suffered from her husband.

They gave her solitude and told her they were there whenever she was ready to talk. The love they showed one another reminded her of how things were with Angelo. She found herself mourning him all over again.

She spent her days walking the fields surrounding Patsy's farm and enjoying the rolling hills of Scranton again. She visited with her siblings and got to know her many nieces and nephews better. No one asked why she was there or when she was going back. They did inquire about Theresa and Giovanni.

Nina spoke to them about once a week over the phone; she missed them terribly. Even though she felt stronger, she felt like a large part of her was missing. Now that she was in Scranton, she was continually thinking about Steubenville.

Three months after her departure from town, Domenica, her sister-in-law and first friend in Steubenville, passed away. Nina felt awful; she could not attend the funeral or comfort Tony and his daughters. She wished she could be there to hug her daughter as she mourned the loss of her godmother.

Theresa said it was a beautiful memorial and that Zio Tony understood why she could not attend. He was glad Nina had finally left Bruno. She told her mother to stay in Scranton and heal.

Bruno had threatened many people in the days right after her departure. The threat that hurt Nina the most was directed at Theresa and her family. Theresa hadn't directly told her what had happened, but Giovanni did. It wasn't pretty.

While Nina was on a bus to Scranton, Bruno woke up alone and angry. He blamed Giovanni and Mary Ann for not stopping her from leaving. Bruno was furious at everyone because Nina was gone. He trashed their bedroom and fumed when he saw her wedding ring in his piss pot.

He went to the house on Seventh Street and argued with Theresa. He demanded Theresa tell him where her mother was. Theresa shouted she was gone for good and never coming back.

He came towards her as if he would strike her when Eric intervened. He told Bruno he was no longer welcome in their home, and then Bruno threatened them. He was sure they helped Nina leave and knew where she was. Theresa said her mother was finally safe.

His threat prompted Eric to call on Vincenzo Santucci. He told Vincenzo about Bruno's threat. Eric said he was not afraid and would defend his family from Bruno at any cost.

Vincenzo wasn't happy to hear Bruno had threatened his own family. He had Bruno hauled into his private office at the Diamond Cigar Store. Vincenzo told Bruno in no uncertain terms that threatening family was wrong. Vincenzo stated he would personally protect Theresa, Eric, and their family. He expected no harm would come to them.

One of his younger goons beat Bruno and then delivered him back to the Roma Café.

Enzo was waiting for him there, seated at the break table in the restaurant's large kitchen. Enzo knew this was Bruno's last chance to settle himself down. Enzo knew he could no longer intercede with Vincenzo on his brother's behalf.

"Ciao, Bruno. Have a seat; you don't look so good."

"Remember when we were growing up in Calabria, how Mama would sometimes tell us to settle down? Or sometimes Papa would slap us upside the head as a warning? Well, you need to settle down now, capisci?"

"Yeah, I remember wanting to fight back against Papa but knowing I wasn't strong enough then to beat him."

"Do you remember receiving a handwritten note many years ago? It said you should settle down. It said you shouldn't do anything stupid, or someone was going to get hurt."

Bruno's head instantly snapped up, and he looked at his brother directly. He needed to pay close attention to what his brother was saying.

"What? How do you know about that note? I suspected Luca wrote it and slipped it under my door that night. He was always telling me to quit doing stupid things."

"No, Bruno, Luca did not send you that note."

"I don't understand. How do you know Luca didn't?"

"I know, brother, because I sent it. You needed to settle down because Vincenzo was at his wits' end with you. He was ready to have you whacked, but I couldn't bear the thought of losing you. On my behalf, Luca begged Vincenzo to give you another chance."

"But I don't understand, Enzo. Why would you send me a threatening note?"

"Luca told me about his conversation with Vincenzo. I needed to put a scare in you. It was the only way you would settle down. Jesse came up with the idea. You were very wary after you got the note. You settled down a bit, and I was able to smooth things over with Vincenzo."

"Now look at you! You pull a gun on Mary Ann, threaten Theresa and her family, and beat Nina so badly she left. You know how Vincenzo values la famiglia. Yet your damn pride over losing Nina has caused you to lose your standing with him."

"This is your last chance, brother. It would be best if you let Nina go. She is a good woman who loved you, but you beat and abused her to the point her love died. It would help if you settled down, stopped drinking so much, and took care of the responsibilities Vincenzo gave you. If not, neither Luca nor I will intercede on your behalf again."

"I'll see myself out. Oh, and don't bother trying to intimidate me. I've always known your weaknesses. You might think you're tough, but I've always been tougher. Don't make me prove it."

Enzo quietly left as Giovanni walked into the kitchen.

"Hey, Pops. Let's get you cleaned up. Mary Ann is making a pot roast for dinner, and you'll be able to see the baby. He's adorable."

Bruno let himself be led to the bathroom by his son. Once there, Giovanni showed him he had laid out a fresh towel and some clean clothes.

"Come over to the apartment after you freshen up." Giovanni closed the door leaving his father alone.

Bruno was stunned by what Enzo had just told him. He never thought his own brother would threaten him. It was all he could think about as he showered.

Mary Ann gave him the cold shoulder at the apartment until he apologized for his behavior. During dinner, she laid out some new ground rules for Bruno. He was not allowed to enter their apartment uninvited. He had to knock first. He was not allowed near the baby smelling of alcohol. And, he was not allowed near the apartment or the baby with a gun.

Bruno grumbled but agreed to her terms; he had no choice. He was still reeling from all that had happened recently and didn't know what to do with himself. He wanted to be able to see his grandson, his namesake.

He had pulled a gun on his daughter-in-law, beat his wife so severely that she left, threatened his stepdaughter and her family, found out his brother wrote the mysterious, threatening note, and almost gotten whacked by his boss. He desperately wanted a drink of whiskey but knew that wouldn't go over well with his son.

He quietly ate dinner, held his grandson for a few minutes, then said he needed to go. He wanted to be alone so he could process everything.

At home, he fumed while nursing a bottle of whiskey. He was mad as hell at Enzo and Jesse for sending that note. What were they thinking? He decided he would keep a low profile for a few days.

He had almost whacked Luca because he thought Luca was the source. If he had gone through with it, Vincenzo would indeed have killed him for doing so. Vincenzo was already furious with him and told him to take a few days off to reset his priorities.

His priority was finding Nina. He needed her by his side. Somehow, he wasn't as off-balance when she was there. He would use the time to figure out where she went and get her back.

Riding around town looking for her hadn't given him any satisfaction. Theresa knew where she was but refused to tell him. Besides, she and her family were untouchable now that they were under Vincenzo's protection.

He had already asked Gio and was told to go fuck himself. Although he loved his Pops, Gio wouldn't tell him where his mother went. That surprised Bruno immensely because Gio had idolized his father ever since Gio was an infant.

He knew Nina spent time with Domenica and Tony, but he was no closer to finding his wife's whereabouts after sniffing around their place. After watching Domenica for a couple of days, Bruno concluded she didn't know anything about Nina's whereabouts.

His only other option was to watch Nina's sister, Lena. Lena spent most of her time at home. After the third day of watching her place, the Weirton police pulled up to his parked car and told him to get lost. He concluded Lena knew something but hated Bruno for what he did to her sister.

Since there was no trace of Nina around town, he concluded she left and went to Scranton. She had run to Scranton more than a few times over the years. He knew her brothers would protect her if he tried to go there and bring her back.

After that revelation, he settled back into his routine of running the Café and the Tavern. He hired a new cook for the Café and a new bartender for the bar. He also enlisted Gio to help him run both businesses.

A couple of months later, he casually questioned Gio about his mother again. Gio just told him she was gone and never coming back. Bruno threatened to file for divorce. Gio told him to go ahead; Nina didn't want anything to do with him.

So, he decided to contact a lawyer to begin divorce proceedings against Nina. He would make her pay for leaving him. He would leave her with nothing.

Healing Old Wounds

Nina needed to ponder about her future, and for some reason, baking always seemed to clear her head and help her think things through. Maybe it was the thought that you could do several different things if you put the same ingredients together for the dough. You could make a loaf of bread or buns or even use that dough for pizza crust.

You had choices. That made Nina realize she had options too. At least that's what Nina concluded as she pulled the freshly baked bread out of the oven in Patsy's kitchen.

It had been a little more than a year since Nina left her home and family in Steubenville. She still missed her children and grandchildren immensely.

During that time, she realized a telephone was an excellent way to hear about the dances her teenage granddaughters were now going to. However, it was not the right way to convey her current emotions. A muttered "hugs and kisses" over the phone line was quite different than the physical ones; she missed the real thing.

She had missed out on her grandson's first year of life. All the incredible firsts, from sitting up to crawling, walking, and talking, Nina had missed it all. As she looked at the photographs Mary Ann had sent, she realized her grandson, Bruno, was a stranger to her and she to him. She longed to hold him in her arms.

This longing made her very melancholy today, and so she baked.

Patsy and Gert had left at the crack of dawn to go fishing. They would be gone all day. With the thought of a whole day by herself looming before her, Nina decided to tackle her problems head-on.

She knew she was homesick. She desperately wanted, no needed, to go back to Steubenville. As she looked around Patsy's farm, she realized that Scranton, although lovely, was no longer home in her heart. It was the place she had come for refuge. It was the place she had come to heal.

Now healed, she was healthy and strong. She no longer woke up each night from the nightmares that plagued her when she first came to stay with them. Nina was ready to go back home. She planned to take back what she had lost, even if she had to fight her husband for it.

Oh, she didn't want anything from him. What she wanted was to live in peace. She wanted to hug and kiss her children and grandchildren physically. She didn't want to just hear about her granddaughters' dances; she wanted to see them, all dressed up and ready to go. She wanted to see the excitement in their eyes.

She wanted to see her grandson squeal with delight as he toddled around and discovered the beauty of life around him. She didn't want to be a stranger to him.

She quickly tidied up the small kitchen and left the room. At the end of the hallway was the bedroom she had slept in for the past year. She found solitude in the cozy space. It reminded her of the small hotel room she had spent the night in with Angelo when she was first married, how she had been scared of Angelo and leaving her home and family back then.

Now she yearned for her home. She had come to realize home wasn't just a physical place but a feeling you get when you're with those you love. Where ever they are is home. Her decision was made.

Nina took out her small suitcase and packed her meager belongings. She thought of how her mother had helped her pack her meager belongings in her little bag all those years ago when she married Angelo.

Next, she looked at the folded newspaper sent to her by Lena last week. She found a small efficiency apartment for rent on Logan Avenue on Steubenville's north side in the classified section. She called the number.

A man with a deep voice answered the call. His name was Walter Jones, and he owned the duplex on Logan Avenue. He explained that he lived alone on the bottom floor, and the top floor had just become available to rent. The previous tenant had passed away.

He commented that the apartment was spotless. Nina asked about the entrance's security and whether the street was well lit at night. Mr. Jones answered her questions even though he thought them strange. Nina asked him what type of work he did. Mr. Jones replied he worked as the foreman of the custodial workers in the mill.

He asked why she was interested in the lighting and security of the apartment. Those were things about which most people did not inquire. She told Mr. Jones truthfully what had transpired to cause her to leave town.

She told him she was the estranged wife of a member of the mafia in Steubenville. She wished to come back to town to be near her family but promised to stay to herself. She said she understood if he did not want to rent the apartment to her. It would be risky.

She fully expected him to decline her offer to rent the apartment once she told him the truth. He told her once he received a check from her, the apartment would be hers. He said he was not afraid. He said he would protect those who lived in the apartment.

She told him she only had cash. He said he would let her pay in cash. He would tell any other callers that the apartment was no longer available.

She was determined to stand her ground. Bruno no longer scared her. She had faced the demon who was her husband and survived.

Now that she had a place to stay, she called her daughter-in-law, Mary Ann, and outlined her plans. Mary Ann would relay them to Gio.

After that, she only had one phone call left to make. She picked up the phone and called her daughter. Angela, her teenage granddaughter, picked up on the first ring.

"Hello?"

"Hello, Angela, it's Nonna, Nina. How are you?"

"Oh, Nonna, I'm fine. I thought you were someone else calling. How are you doing? We miss you."

"I miss all of you too, dear. Is your mother there? May I speak to her?"

"Of course, Nonna, just a minute." Nina could hear her granddaughter telling her sibling to get their mother. "She's coming now, Nonna. I love you."

"I love you too, sweetheart. I promise I won't talk long to your mother since you are expecting a phone call. Is it a call from a boy?"

"How did you know? Oh, here's mom."

"Hello, Ma. How are you?" said Theresa.

"I'm fine, Theresa. It's good to hear your voice. Listen, I won't keep you; I just wanted to let you know I'm coming home."

"Oh, Ma, you can't go back to Bruno! Not after all he's done to you."

"I'm not going back to him; I'm coming home to be with my kids and grandkids. I'm going to rent a small apartment on the north end of town. Lena sent me the classified ads from the newspaper. If all goes well, I'll be home in a few days."

"But what about Bruno? What happens if he finds out you're back?"

"Your brother promised he wouldn't let Bruno know I'm back. I'm not going to let him stop me from being with my family any longer. I will go see a lawyer if I have to, one from Weirton, not Steubenville."

"That sounds wonderful, Ma. I've missed you so much. Eric and I will help you get settled into your new apartment. I love you and can't wait to see you."

"I love you, too, and hope to see you soon."

Nina hung up the phone and grabbed the paper again. This time she pored over the help wanted ads. She circled several that looked promising. She knew she would need to find a job once she got home. Although large, her stash of cash would not last forever.

She waited for Patsy and Gert to come home. She needed to tell them her plans, now that they were real. She wasn't sure how they would react. Patsy had always been close to her heart, even when they were young. They were born only one year apart, and people often thought they were twins.

They arrived home near dusk with fishing tales to share with Nina. After a late dinner of soup and freshly baked bread, they sat on the front porch. Gert said she needed to get some things done and left the siblings alone together.

"Well, now that we're alone, tell me when you're leaving," said Patsy. He could always read her thoughts.

"What? How did you know? You always knew me so well, Patsy. We're kindred spirits."

"Are you going back to Steubenville? I hope to hell you aren't going back to Bruno. I'd have to go with you and kill him myself."

"I am going back, but not to be with him. I miss my family. I'm going back to my kids and grandkids. Bruno can go to hell for all I care. I'll never go back to him."

"The only good thing to come out of my marriage to him is Giovanni. I pray now that he's an adult with his own family, he'll realize what a monster his father truly is. Mary Ann is a good woman; she'll make sure Gio does the right things in life and doesn't follow in his father's footsteps."

"I hope you're right. How soon are you going, and what can I do to help?"

Secret Homecoming

Nina arrived back in Steubenville in the fall of 1967. She was determined to live her life in peace without any interference from Bruno. Theresa and Eric picked her up at the Weirton bus station. They took her to her new home, the apartment on Logan Avenue, on the north side of town.

She met Walter Jones, her landlord, a tall, muscular, black man. He cut an imposing figure until you saw the deep smile on his face. He greeted Nina warmly and told her the apartment was spotless.

The furnished apartment was at the top of a long, narrow staircase. Walter unlocked and opened the door for her, and Nina walked into a small bright sitting room furnished with a couch, end table, and a small cabinet with a radio on top. The furniture was mismatched but serviceable. A window opposite the cabinet had a view of the street.

A compact kitchenette was next to the sitting room with a sink and sideboard, stove, and refrigerator. A small window was above the sink and next to it were two shelves that held an assortment of cups, dishes, pots, and pans. A small table with two chairs was against the wall opposite the sink. There was just enough room for a person to move around.

On the other side of the sitting room were two doors. One led to a small bedroom, and the other led to an even tinier bathroom. Both were clean. The bedroom had one window that also had a view of the street and boasted a limited view of Nina's favorite park.

She paid Mr. Jones for three months' rent in cash. He thanked her as he handed her two keys, one to the front door and the other to the apartment. He told Theresa and Eric that Nina would be safe here. He left the trio to unpack and get settled in.

Eric checked the locks on the windows and doors and the plumbing and lights. All were in good working order. He carried in the few boxes that held Nina's things, then left mother and daughter alone and promised to come back later to pick up Theresa.

Theresa closed the door and hugged her mother. She felt terrible that the apartment was so sparse. Nina, though, felt safe and at peace. Mr. Jones, she was sure, would help keep her safe.

She chatted with Theresa about how nice it was to be back in the same town as her children and grandchildren. She would be able to see them and hug them whenever she wanted. The apartment, in her eyes, was just perfect.

It was on the second floor so that no one could climb into her windows, and she could see the park that held so many memories.

"Let's start in the kitchen," said Nina. "Put those groceries away in the refrigerator. I'll organize everything else."

"Ma, I have a small cabinet at home in the basement that you can use as a pantry. It should fit nicely in the corner there. I'll have Eric bring it back with him later. Also, you'll need a television for the sitting room. We may be able to find a used one somewhere."

"Don't worry about that; Gio is bringing one over later. Mr. Jones told me he didn't have one here, so Gio is bringing one over from the apartments. Bruno will never know it's missing."

It didn't take long to unpack and organize Nina's things. Mr. Jones stopped by to let her know that Giovanni had called and was on his way over. He would let Gio in once he arrived.

Nina and Theresa were sitting on the couch when Gio arrived bearing gifts. He brought her a television, a lamp, cookware, a jewelry box, and several mementos from the house. She was surprised that Gio had saved these things for her.

He hugged his mother and apologized for never stopping his father from hitting and abusing her. He wished things had been different for them. He vowed he would never be like his father. He promised to be a better son. Nina hugged him as they both cried for what was and what could have been.

Gio told her he would love to stay and visit, but Pops had him working a double shift at the bar, and he needed to get back before anyone noticed he wasn't there. He promised to come back as soon as he could. He told her he was having a telephone installed for her there tomorrow, he would pay for it, and the number would be unlisted.

Eric came by to pick up Theresa a few hours later. Nina thanked them as they left. She climbed the stairs and closed and locked her apartment door. She leaned her head against the wall and let out a sigh of relief; she was finally home and alone.

The tiny apartment was perfect for her, and she felt safe there with Walter Jones right downstairs. It had been a long journey and a long day. She was tired, so she went to bed. Tomorrow would be a new day, and she would savor it.

Mr. Jones knocked on her door the following day. He had two cups of hot, black coffee and slices of angel food cake with berries and cream on pretty China plates.

"Good morning, Mrs. Pagano. I wanted to be neighborly and welcome you here properly. Would you like to have coffee and cake with me? If not, I will understand since you don't know me."

"Good morning, Mr. Jones; please come in. I want to join you for coffee and cake. Please, call me, Nina."

"I will, Miss Nina, only if you call me Walter," he chuckled as he smiled.

They sat in the sitting room and chatted for a while. Nina learned he had lost his wife several years before from breast cancer, and he was a member and elder at the Mount Zion Baptist Church on Seventh Street. He had worked his way up from junior custodian to the general foreman of custodial services at the mill in Weirton.

She mentioned her first husband had worked at the mill in Weirton, and when she said Angelo's name, Walter said he had known him and that he was a kind man. Nina almost burst into tears. Even after all these years, people still remembered Angelo for his kindness.

Walter took his leave then and promised to check in on her again. He said the phone company was coming by to install her new phone at ten o'clock. He told her he would remain in the apartment while they installed it so she could stay unseen in her bedroom. That way, no one would know she was there.

At ten o'clock, true to his word, Walter sat on the couch while the worker installed the phone. When the worker was gone, Nina came out to the sitting room. She now had an unlisted number, which she would give to only a few people.

Once Walter was gone, she locked the door and placed a few calls. First was to her brother, Patsy, to let him know she had made it safely, then, to Lena to tell her the same thing.

Her last call was to Theresa to give her the number. Theresa would let Gio know since Nina would not call the Roma Café or Westwood Tavern.

Nina looked around her tiny apartment and felt comfortable. Theresa was stopping by later with a few things they had forgotten to get yesterday. She was also bringing Nina a newspaper. Nina wanted to begin her job search.

A Loyal Friend

The job search wasn't fruitful, and Nina was beginning to get nervous about finding something when Walter stopped by for a chat one day. The housekeeper and sometimes cook at his church got sick and had to take a leave of absence. He wondered if Nina would be willing to step in for her. It was temporary, but it was something.

She gladly said yes, so she got a part-time job as a cook and housekeeper for Walter Jones' church pastor. She worked four days a week and walked a couple of blocks to the church and back quickly.

As the winter months sped by, Nina spent most of her time in the sitting room of her cozy apartment. She was crocheting afghans for each of her grandchildren. It was something she never had time for previously.

She made a list of each child's favorite colors and happily worked on them. It kept her busy, and she had the noise of the television to keep her company.

The news was rather depressing, though. Once again, America was involved in a war, this time in Vietnam. Nina did not understand all the political complexities of the war and didn't care. She just felt that Americans were dying needlessly. She prayed for the soldiers every night.

On a brisk March afternoon, she had just settled onto the couch to crochet when she heard loud noises coming from the street below. She carefully glanced out the window from behind the sheer curtain. Someone was shouting noisily, and suddenly she froze. She recognized that obnoxious voice. It was Bruno yelling as he walked around the street. He was either already drunk or still hungover and lost his balance as he crashed into someone's galvanized steel garbage can spilling trash onto the street.

"Nina! Nina, I know you live somewhere on this street, and I will find you." Bruno roared, and a couple of dogs barked in reply. "You can't hide from me forever."

An elderly Polish couple carried their groceries home in brown paper bags from the store. They were trying to avoid Bruno but were unsuccessful. He confronted them. Nina could see them talking and gesturing but wasn't sure what they told him. He walked away angrily.

Nina didn't know the couple but passed them on the street a few times. Since she moved in, she had nodded and said hello to them numerous times. She tried to keep her distance from the neighbors, but she was sure these people knew where she lived.

From her vantage point, she could see Bruno leave the street just as she saw her landlord, Walter Jones, walk into view. Bruno stopped him, as well.

Walter seemed like a giant in comparison to her husband. Bruno gestured towards the street. She watched Walter shake his head vigorously and then point in the direction of the park. Finally, Bruno stalked off in that direction.

About ten minutes later, she heard Walter enter the hallway downstairs. Then she heard him knock on her door. She opened the door, and Walter entered the apartment.

"I just had the displeasure of meeting Mr. Bruno Pagano. He said he's searching for his wife, who is sick and dying. He's very concerned she doesn't know how sick she is. He asked me if I had seen her."

"I'm not dying, Walter, unless he kills me. He's brutal, and I can't put up with his abuse any longer."

"I told him I hadn't seen any woman matching your description."

"Oh, Walter, I'm so sorry. You shouldn't have to lie on my account."

"Don't you worry about that, Miss Nina. That man is evil; I saw it in his eyes. I told him to check the park near the bus station. I know you like to walk there, but maybe you shouldn't go to the park for the next few weeks."

"I won't. I have enough yarn here to complete several projects. And the refrigerator is stocked full of food, thanks to my children. Thank you for not telling him where I am."

"I wouldn't let him near you even if he beats down the front door. You are safe here, Miss Nina. That man needs some manners."

"Maybe I should go see a lawyer. I hoped he had given up on me, but it seems he hasn't. I'll talk to Theresa and Gio about it. I just want him to leave me alone."

"Well, I'll let you get back to your work. I meant what I said, though; you are safe here, Miss Nina. I won't let anyone hurt you."

Later that day, Gio stopped by. He seldom did so, and when he did, he only stayed a few minutes. Nina told him about his father's visit to the street. Gio said his Pops was getting more erratic in his behavior, and Zio Enzo wanted to send him away to a hospital in Cambridge to get some help.

Bruno had broken into the apartment of Bill Robinson, one of their current renters, and hit him with a revolver. Bill filed a complaint against Bruno with the police. Bruno countersued for assault, battery, and disorderly conduct. The whole incident was a complete mess, and Gio was stuck in the middle. He had rented the apartment to Bill Robinson against his father's wishes.

Gio didn't know what to do. The stress of trying to keep his Pops out of trouble was causing discord in his marriage. Mary Ann was pregnant again and due in the summer. She was tired of Bruno's shenanigans and wanted to move away from Sixth Street.

Nina told him to do what he felt was right in his heart. It was the best advice she could give her son.

By early April, for the sake of his marriage, Gio decided to go along with his Zio Enzo and get Bruno the professional help he needed.

Enzo and Gio drove Bruno to Cambridge on a Thursday morning. He was snoring loudly on the back seat of Enzo's car after a night of heavy drinking and gambling. He didn't fully wake up until they arrived at the facility almost two hours later.

"Pops, wake up. It's time to get up now."

"What? What's going on? Where are we?"

"We're at a place where you'll get some help. Remember we talked about it a few days ago. You will stay here for a few days, and they're going to help you with your drinking problem. Right, Zio Enzo?"

"Bruno, you'll be fine here for a little while," said Enzo. "It'll be like a vacation. It's what Vincenzo wants."

"But, Enzo, I don't want to stay here. I want to go home. I don't have a drinking problem. I can stop anytime I want."

They ushered him into the facility where the administrator was waiting. They had an appointment. There was paperwork to complete.

Two male orderlies came into the room and escorted Bruno down the hall to another room. An orderly asked him to change his clothes and place his belongings in a clear plastic bag. He began to get belligerent with them. One pressed a button on the wall, and a nurse promptly appeared. She administered a sedative, and Bruno instantly calmed down.

She spoke in a calm but firm voice to Bruno and told him he could rest as soon as he changed. He immediately listened to her and put on the pale blue jumpsuit provided to him.

Back in the office, the hospital administrator told Enzo and Gio they couldn't see Bruno for ninety days once they signed the paperwork to admit him. Gio had mixed feelings but signed the form to admit his Pops. He was doing what he felt was right. His Pops needed professional help.

They left the facility about an hour later. The administrator had given them a tour and an overview of the treatment plan for Bruno. Giovanni prayed it would help his Pops.

A special news bulletin broke into the music radio station they were listening to on the way back to Steubenville. That evening, Dr. Martin Luther King Jr., a leader in the Civil Rights Movement, had been assassinated in Memphis, Tennessee.

A little more than a week later, Nina cooked Easter dinner for her son and daughter-in-law at their apartment on Sixth Street. It was the first time she had been back there in over two years. It felt odd to be there, and she kept thinking that Bruno would walk through the door at any minute.

Right after dinner, she asked Gio to take her home. Gio told her he was at a rehab center in Cambridge, but she still felt strange. There were too many bad memories there. She had enjoyed seeing her two-year-old grandson but wanted to be in her apartment.

At home, she locked her doors and snuggled on her couch as she watched the news coverage of the riots that occurred after Dr. King's death. There was unrest on the streets of Steubenville as well. Nina knew that whatever happened, Walter would keep her safe.

Spring soon turned into summer, and Mary Ann gave birth to another baby boy in July. They named him John. Giovanni was thrilled with his growing family. Mary Ann, however, was still trying to get Gio to move out of the apartments. Their apartment was okay for a couple but not large enough for four.

She began to search for a house. She was also determined to get Gio away from the Café and Tavern on South Sixth Street. The rough neighborhood was not conducive to a growing family. Gio knew she was looking for a house and understood her reasons why.

Since Pops got released from the hospital, he had been hard to be around. He had completed the ninety-day stay at the hospital but still took an occasional drink. The doctors there had told him his liver was dreadful from all the alcohol he had consumed over the years. He was furious at both Enzo and Gio.

They said he needed to quit drinking. He just told them what they wanted to hear so the doctors would release him. Once back in Steubenville, he continued drinking like nothing ever happened.

Bruno's lawyer sent him a certified letter early in 1970. He dropped Bruno as a client and the divorce proceedings he was hired to handle. The attorney was fed up with Bruno and tired of the delays and missed meetings Bruno had put him through.

He didn't care that Bruno had been involved in a vital poker game and couldn't meet him or that Bruno was too hungover to get out of bed. The attorney also had to change a hearing date because Bruno was in a rehab facility. He was tired of Bruno's excuses.

Bruno threw the letter on the floor. After almost three years, he realized that Nina was never returning to him. Bruno knew she lived in an apartment on the north side of town but couldn't locate exactly where. He took a drink of whiskey and realized he didn't care anymore.

He finally accepted that his marriage was over. He felt liberated. He could come and go as he pleased. He could go to Judy's any time he wanted sex, and the new cook at the Café did a pretty decent job; he wouldn't go hungry. He didn't care if the divorce was official or not. Nina was no longer a part of his life.

The New House

Violence was getting steadily worse downtown. Many houses got torn down, and citizens migrated to the city's west end. Whole neighborhoods that had once been vibrant were now suddenly run down or dangerous.

Months ago, Gio and Mary Ann bought a house in a nice neighborhood in the west end of town. It was a large brick ranch home, roomy enough for their growing family. They now lived on Whitehaven Boulevard.

Giovanni found a small house nearby on Chestnut Street for his mother. He didn't want her downtown without him close by. His Pops was still drinking and now was very unpredictable. Nina was reluctant to purchase a house by herself, but Gio would only be one street away.

Mary Ann and Gio's neighbors, Daniel and Dianna Kenton, were teachers. They were looking for a nanny for their three young boys. They offered the job to Nina, and she accepted. The salary would be more than enough to pay for her monthly mortgage.

Nina was thinking about her family when Walter knocked on her apartment door. He had come to say goodbye before going to work. Once again, her meager things were packed and ready to be picked up today. She prayed this would be her last move.

"Miss Nina, I will miss you and our weekly coffee socials. You have been a perfect tenant over these past few years."

"Walter, come in. I will miss you, too. You are welcome to come and visit me in my new house."

"Thank you. You are too kind. I'm not sure your new neighbors would be happy to see an old black man visiting you."

"Walter, you are my dear friend; I don't care what my new neighbors think or say. My door will always be open to you."

"Well, Miss Nina, if you ever need me, you know how to reach me."

They stood in the sitting room of Nina's tiny apartment and hugged. Then Walter left for work. An hour later, Gio and Eric arrived to collect her and her things. She left a loaf of freshly baked bread and a batch of fresh blueberry scones in a basket in front of Walter's door. It was her simple way of saying thanks.

The house on Chestnut Street was immense compared to her apartment. It had a living room, dining room, kitchen, two bedrooms, a bathroom, a full basement, and an attached garage. The best part of the house was the big backyard. It was large enough for a garden and already had several flower beds.

Nina was looking forward to planting a garden and growing vegetables. As she got out of the car, she met her new neighbors, Edward and Helen Greyska. They kindly welcomed her to the neighborhood.

When Nina entered the house, she was shocked to see it fully furnished already. She didn't need a thing. Gio had gone to the house downtown and taken her favorite pieces.

Theresa had already unpacked and put away everything and had also made pizza. Nina found herself surrounded by family; everyone had come to welcome her home. She felt blessed beyond words.

There was still something else to celebrate, as she would soon find out.

"Ma, you know Eric and I have been looking for a new house too. Well, we found the perfect one a few blocks from here on Sunset Boulevard. The owners accepted our offer yesterday. We'll be moving in a month."

"Oh, Tre, I'm so happy for you. How lucky I am to have both of my children close to me. Now I'll be able to see my grandchildren at any time."

After the celebration, Nina thanked them as they left; she did feel happy here. That night as Nina lay in her new bed, she prayed, thanking God for giving her such loving children. Tomorrow she would plant some herbs and vegetables in her new garden.

A month later, Theresa and Eric moved into their new home. Nina had helped her daughter pack up their belongings, and they walked through the house on Seventh Street one last time. The house held so many memories. Nina and Theresa chatted about some of those memories.

It was the house where Nina first found love with Angelo and endured much pain and suffering at the hands of Bruno. It was also the place her children and grandchildren had lived and played.

It was a well-loved house, and now it would be torn down and replaced with an apartment building. As she walked out the door for the last time, Nina felt sad but realized the good and bad memories would always be with her.

At sixty-five, Nina started her new job as a nanny that fall. She was happy to begin this new chapter in her life, living close to the people she loved. The Kenton boys were well behaved, and the professors treated her as part of the family.

With each passing year, Nina was more comfortable in her surroundings when Bruno showed up in her backyard one day. She had been picking herbs in her garden when she heard him say her name. She was shocked to see how old and sickly he looked.

"Nina, is it you?"

She turned around and froze with a basket full of basil, thyme, rosemary, and parsley in her hands.

"Bruno, what are you doing here? You shouldn't be here."

"Don't worry," he said, "I just wanted to see if it was true you lived near Gio and Mary Ann. They brought me out for dinner today. I told them I wanted to walk around the block to work off Mary Ann's delicious pot roast."

"You haven't aged a bit Nina, except for the silver in your hair."

"Bruno, you need to leave now. You aren't welcome here."

"I'm sorry," he said in a low voice. "I'm sorry for everything. I know that doesn't change anything that happened, but I did love you, Nina. I just had a lousy way of showing it."

"I'm dying of liver disease," he continued, "thanks to all the alcohol I consumed during my life. I don't have much time left, and I just wanted to see you once more before I die."

"You need to leave," she said again, just as Gio came into her yard.

"Pops, there you are," said Gio. "You need to come with me. Ma, I'm sorry. I didn't mean for him to bother you. I watched where he was going, and then Johnny asked me to watch him do a trick on his bike. I took my eyes off of Pops for just a minute."

"It's okay, Gio. Just make him leave now. He's not welcome here."

"It was good to see you, Nina, and I meant what I said. Ciao."

Nina watched as Gio led his father out of the yard. Bruno looked frail and sickly. Nina was shaking as she went into the house and locked her doors. The incident made her shiver, so she made a cup of tea. It was 1980, and Nina suddenly felt old.

Six months later, Gio came by to tell her that Bruno had passed away from liver disease. All those years of drinking had caused irreparable damage to his liver. Since they had never actually divorced, Nina was now a widow and owner of the Roma Café and the Westwood Tavern. She told Gio she wanted nothing from Bruno and the businesses were his now.

Nina did say a prayer for Bruno's soul but didn't attend her estranged husband's funeral. At first, she had been grateful to Bruno and even loved him. Then, Nina feared and hated him. Now, she didn't feel anything for him at all.

A month after Bruno's death, Enzo and Jesse knocked on her door. She was surprised to see them.

"May we come in?" Jesse asked. "I promise our visit will be a short one."

Nina held no animosity towards them and welcomed them to her tiny home.

"We want to apologize for all that Bruno did to you. We feel partly responsible for everything since we pushed you two together."

"I accept your apology, although you don't have to apologize for anything. I freely went out with Bruno and married him when he proposed. If I hadn't, I never would have had Giovanni, and my life would have been completely different."

"We tried to scare Bruno and even sent him an anonymous note, many years ago, telling him he needed to settle down, but it didn't work. I should have known better," said Enzo.

Nina was shocked when she heard this. "I'll be right back," she said. She went to her bedroom and returned with an old crumpled piece of paper. She handed it to Enzo. "Is this what you sent?"

"Yes, it is," he answered. "How did you get it? I tried to get Bruno to settle down. We didn't want him to hurt you anymore, but it didn't stop him."

"I found it on the closet floor the day Theresa fell down the stairs. I thought Bruno caused Theresa's accident as a way to hurt and threaten me."

"Gio told us about the night he went to see little Bruno; how he beat you badly, and that was the last straw. I'm sorry we weren't there to stop him." Enzo just shook his head.

"Well, we'd better go. We promised to make this visit quick. We do have one thing to give you. We know you don't want the businesses downtown, but we hope you will accept this instead; it's the least we could do."

Enzo handed her an envelope with her name typed on the front. She opened it to find the deed to her house on Chestnut Street. Her mortgage was gone. She looked at Enzo and Jesse with tears in her eyes.

"Jesse took your wedding ring to a jewelers' and had it sold at auction. The money from the sale was more than enough to pay off this house. We deposited the rest of the money into a bank account for you."

Nina muttered a quiet "Thank you" to them as they got up to leave.

They left her and promised to keep in touch. Nina just sat on the couch to process what had just happened and what she had just learned about the note from so long ago. After all these years, she finally knew that the note was intended for Bruno. It was supposed to stop him from hurting her.

An Unexpected Event

Nina was making bread in her tiny kitchen and talking to her little dog, Lucky. The years had flown by, and she was now retired from her job as a nanny, although she occasionally still watched the Kenton boys. It was April 1985.

Baking was her favorite thing to do and always brought a smile to her face. The warmth of the oven would seep into her bones and make her feel good, and the smell of the bread as it baked was heavenly. The feel of the dough in her hands always brought back heartfelt memories of her childhood.

That late April afternoon was just like any other perfect spring day. The sun was shining, and the tulips, crocuses, and daffodils in Nina's yard were all in colorful bloom. The birds were excitedly chirping as they flew around, looking for twigs to build their nests.

The profusion of color from her flower bed was one of Nina's joys. It reminded her of her childhood home and the wildflowers that grew in their backyard. She loved her little backyard and took great care of the garden and flowers there.

Nina had done her daily chores and had walked the three blocks to her local market to pick up a few groceries. Once back from the store, she had mixed the flour, water, and yeast and worked the ingredients into a dough ball.

She left the dough to rise and took Lucky outside. While outside with the dog, she missed a phone call. The caller didn't leave a message.

Lucky, her dog, was a mutt that had found its way into her heart when she spied him hiding in her backyard a few years before. That day, she had made the ultimate mistake of feeding him the scraps left from her sparse dinner on a cold winter evening.

It had just started to snow when she heard his whimpers out in the backyard. She had gone to shoo him, but his small frame was shaking, and his sad eyes spoke to her heart. He was very timid and looked like someone had abused him.

She knew that look all too well, so she had brought him into the house that night and fed him. She told him he was lucky to have found her and that she would never hurt him. He simply wagged his tail and licked her hand. She laid a small frayed blanket in the corner of her tiny kitchen, where he promptly plopped down and fell asleep.

She didn't have the heart to phone the dog catcher the next day, so Lucky became her new companion. Lucky would sit quietly in the kitchen corner and listen to Nina tell stories of her childhood and happier times with her siblings. He also listened to stories about the years she lived in fear with Bruno. He would simply wag his tail and offer her love.

Lucky especially liked the baking day because the kitchen was warm, and Nina smiled and hummed while baking. She would often give him a special biscuit she had baked just for him.

Nina's life had taken many twists over the years since she left her home in Scranton, Pennsylvania. It was on that fateful April afternoon, while she was in her tiny backyard with Lucky, that her whole world changed again.

Theresa had a freak accident and was taken to the hospital. Somehow, Theresa had fallen in the driveway of her home and hit the back of her head. She lost consciousness, and Eric called an ambulance to take her to the hospital.

Nina and Lucky had just come back into the house when the phone rang again. She picked it up. It was her youngest granddaughter Denise, who was now all grown up and married.

"Nonna, hello. How are you today?"

"I'm fine, Denise. It's good to hear from you."

"Nonna, I'm afraid I have some bad news. Mom had an accident and is in the hospital. The doctors told Dad they needed to send her to Pittsburgh. She has to undergo brain surgery for a hematoma."

"What? An accident? I don't understand. I just talked to your mom last night, and she was fine."

"I know. Mom was with me this morning and was fine when I dropped her back off at the house. She and Dad were painting the trim outside when he heard the tinkling sound of the paint can drop. He went around the house to find mom on the ground, unconscious."

"Nonna, Mark and I are taking Dad to the hospital in Pittsburgh. Do you want to go with us?"

"Of course. I'll be ready when you get here."

"We'll be there soon to pick you up."

Nina sat dumbfounded on her couch after she hung up the phone. She said a quick prayer for her daughter's safety. Then, she changed her clothes and ran next door to ask Ed and Helen to care for Lucky since she wasn't sure how long she would be gone. They said they would and that they would pray for Theresa.

Even though Denise's call was less than ten minutes ago, Nina waited anxiously, rosary beads in hand, by her front door for her granddaughter to arrive. Soon, the dark blue metallic Buick Regal that Denise drove pulled into her driveway with Mark driving. Eric was in the front passenger seat and Denise in the back. Nina climbed in next to her.

The four of them prayed for Theresa the whole way to the hospital. Once there, a nurse led them to a large, dimly lit waiting room despite the sunny day outside. The nurse said that Theresa's helicopter had arrived, and the team of doctors was currently assessing her situation. Someone would update them soon.

Minutes later, the rest of the family arrived. Everyone held hands and prayed for her. A doctor soon informed them that Theresa needed surgery to relieve the pressure on her brain caused by the hematoma. Eric signed the consent forms in his hands. Then began the most extended wait Nina had ever endured. They all joined hands and prayed Theresa's surgery would be successful.

Several hours later, the surgeon came to them. He reported the surgery was a success, but they had to put Theresa in a drug-induced coma while her brain healed. He said they could see her very soon, and the next few days were critical to Theresa's survival and recovery.

They were allowed to see Theresa in the intensive care unit an hour later. Nurses had shaved her hair, and white bandages covered her head.

She had wires and tubes attached to her body, and her skin tone was a pale, pasty grey. Nina, Eric, and everyone else shed tears quietly. They stood by the bed, holding hands and praying for her to recover from her freak accident.

Finally, a nurse told them they had to leave so Theresa could rest. She said they should go home and rest. She promised to call at once if anything changed.

Everyone was in shock. No one felt like leaving but knew they weren't doing any good hanging out in the waiting room. Nina, along with Eric and the family, went back home to Steubenville.

Once there, Nina went into Theresa's kitchen and cooked. She made a big pot of sauce and homemade spaghetti. Nina couldn't remember the last time she had eaten anything, and even though she had no appetite, Nina knew she had to feed her family. It kept her mind from wandering too much.

She reminded Eric of the time, years ago, when Theresa had fallen down a flight of stairs. Theresa had made a full recovery then, and Nina felt in her heart that Theresa would make a full recovery now. They just had to be patient.

Eric moved Theresa to a hospital in Columbus, thinking it was the best place to recover. As the days and months passed, they tried to be patient, but even though Theresa's brain was healing, she wasn't coming out of the coma. Nina was anxious during that time, hoping and praying daily for any news of her daughter.

Finally, a year after the accident, Eric brought Theresa back to Steubenville. Nina was happy that she could now see her daughter every day. She and Eric spent long hours together daily talking to Theresa in the hopes of her coming out of her coma.

Nina was heartbroken. It was so difficult to see her beautiful daughter, lifeless, unresponsive, and lying in a sterile hospital bed each day, but as she told Eric, where there was life, there was hope. They were not giving up hope. They all prayed daily for Theresa to open her beautiful eyes and return to them.

On a gloomy cold morning in late December of 1989, Theresa passed away. An aide had gone into her room to change the sheets and realized that Theresa was not breathing. She instantly paged the doctor. He came in at once. They called Eric right away.

Eric picked up Nina, and they went to the nursing home together. They stood silently side by side as the aide put a clean nightgown on Theresa's lifeless body; then, with tears in their eyes, they said their farewells to her. Both were inconsolable. Nina's beautiful daughter was gone from this life too soon.

Theresa's funeral was beautiful and filled with love, just as her life had been. All those who loved her daughter had turned out and paid tribute to the wonderful daughter Nina had raised. After several long days filled with tears and laughter, Eric dropped Nina off at home.

Now Nina was finally back home with her little dog, alone at last. Nina took off her clothes, lay on her bed, and cried. She hadn't allowed herself to cry this way in years. She had needed to be strong for Eric and her grandchildren. Now that she was alone, the tears came out in buckets.

She prayed Theresa was now with Angelo. Nina was grateful that neither one was in any more pain. Oh, how she missed them both. Nina believed she would be with them again one day.

Full Circle

I t was a lovely day in May, and Nina's flowers were all in bloom. Now, she mostly just looked at them from her bedroom window as she seldom went out into her backyard. Her grandson, John, lived with her now and took care of all the yard work.

She was in her nineties now, and every day, she prayed to God that she was ready to die. It's not that she tried to be morbid; she was just tired and done with life. She had lived a fascinating and full one.

Today was different, though. Nina was up and dressed early. She had something important to do.

Angela was on her way to pick up her Nonna to go shopping. She didn't know why it was significant, but she did what Nonna asked. She never asked for anything.

"I'm here," said Angela as she opened the door of her Nonna's tiny Chestnut Street house. A tail-wagging Lucky greeted her. Lucky demanded belly rubs, and Angela obliged.

"Hi, Angela. Thanks for taking me shopping. It's been too long since we have spent any time together."

"I'm glad I could take you today. What do you need at Kaufmann's?"

"I need a dress. It will be the dress I am buried in when I die."

"Nonna, don't talk like that; you aren't going to die. You'll be with us for a long time."

"Angela, please, this is important to me. I need to buy a pink dress. Pink was your Tatones favorite color on me. I know this sounds morbid, but I want to wear pink when I see him again. Please, humor an old lady."

"Well, I'll only take you shopping if you don't speak that way anymore."

Joan McGlone

They went to Kaufmann's, Steubenville's nicest department store in the Fort Steuben Mall. Nina enjoyed being with her granddaughter. She asked for Angela's help picking out the prettiest pink dress in the store.

The dress they chose was a very soft knit fabric in a pale shade of pink. It was simple and elegant. Nina wasn't concerned at all about the size; she just knew it was the right color.

After she purchased the dress, she and Angela had lunch at The Greenery, one of the finest restaurants in town. They chatted about life in general, and Nina enjoyed every minute of it.

Once they got back to Nina's house, she had one more favor to ask her granddaughter.

"Angela, I have one more favor to ask of you. It's a significant one."

"Of course, I'll do whatever you need. What is it?"

Nina pulled out a wrapped package from her dresser. She opened the tissue paper to reveal a simple white dress with lace trim. "This is the dress my Mama made me a very long time ago. It was my wedding dress when I married your Tatone Angelo. I want you to keep it safe for me, and when the time comes, I want you to make sure it is buried with me."

"I'm not sure Angelo will recognize me after all these years, so I'm not taking any chances. If he doesn't know me from the pink dress, he will surely know me if I have my wedding dress. I miss him and your mom so much."

"Nonna, I will do as you ask, but I know Tatone will know you by the love in your heart. Mom always talked about how much he loved you."

Two short months later, Nina passed away peacefully in her sleep. Angela kept the promise made to her Nonna. Nina wore the soft pink dress, and, folded neatly at the bottom of her casket, was the wedding dress her mother had made so long ago.

Angela prayed that somewhere, Tatone Angelo was waiting for Nonna to come home to his loving arms.

Made in the USA
Columbia, SC
24 August 2022